The Once And Forgotten Thing

Written By: J.J Sutherland
Illustrated by: Racheal Carl

Hope you
love it!

J Sutherland

TEMPEST & JAY

For Kristen, without whom there would be no stories.

And for Viggo, the main character of this book, to whom I feel I must formally apologize for (almost) everything.

Chapter 1

*E*VERYONE SWORE IT WAS *impossible. Camelot – the great fortress – was impenetrable, or so they all said. But as is often the case with the impossible, all it took was one person who refused to believe.*

In the end, no one would remember the story of the Saxon spy who very nearly destroyed the legend of King Arthur. It was an easy thing to forget, for only the spy himself ever knew the whole truth of it. Viggo might have returned to Saxony a hero – celebrated, congratulated, and doubtlessly rewarded. Single-handedly, he might have turned the tides of war. But the end of all that might have been began three nights after his escape from Camelot...

The terrain in this part of Britannia was among the easiest over which Viggo had ever traveled, and ironically – that was the problem. The low-lying fields and barren hillsides were wide and open, providing almost nothing in the way of sufficient cover. To make matters worse, the landscape glowed clear and bright beneath the full moon, easily betraying every shadow which flickered across it. No matter how cautious he made his movements, Viggo felt overwhelmingly conspicuous.

The slender stands of trees which occasionally dotted the countryside became his steppingstones. In each little grove he would linger, briefly, to catch his breath and strain his ears for shouts or footsteps, or anything else which might indicate he had been discovered. When he went, he went swiftly; clinging to the few precious shadows, side-stepping brambles, and crawling when necessary through bracken and gorse – all to try and hide his movements as he made his way ever westward.

It wasn't a matter of whether or not someone *might* be watching for him; it was only a matter of how long before he ran into more of them?

The gorse was a mixed blessing. The thick, unyielding shrubs were plentiful and provided by far the best camouflage; far better than the limp bracken, which was just as easy to trample flat while trying to hide among it. But the only way to get through the gorse was to lay on his stomach and shimmy along beneath the thorny branches, wincing each time one of the sharp spines tore at his face. He would just as soon have avoided the ordeal of it, had the reason for his journey not been so enormously worth the caution. This would all be a small price to pay when his mission was through.

And at least, in the meantime, there was his coat. He was especially glad of it every time he crawled through the gorse, for the thick leather held tighter to his body than a cloak would have done, and the thorns could not pierce it.

It proved its worth yet again when he crawled out from under a clump of gorse, only to dart back into the thorny bushes when a nearby shadow shifted toward him. A moment later he recognized the silhouette of a deer in the moonlight and frowned, irritated with himself for mistaking it as a person.

Had he the luxury of curiosity, he might have paused a while to question the abundance of unnatural nightlife in this part of the countryside. Ever since mountains had appeared on the horizon he had been jumping at shadows, which had all turned out, so far, to be deer grazing in the fields or rabbits darting to and from the gorse. More than once he had been taken aback by the chittering of squirrels, which should have been sleeping quietly in their holes rather than scampering through the treetops in the dead of night. He had even heard songbirds. Nowhere else in his life had he heard birds singing their chorus to the moon rather than the dawn.

In the back of his mind he knew this was peculiar, but since he had no ready explanation for it – nor the time to search one out – Viggo resisted his natural instinct to ponder the abnormality and kept focused on maintaining his stride.

Despite all obstacles he was making remarkable time, and his success thus far was enough to fill him with purpose, driving him onward without any thought of pausing for rest – much less curiosity.

It was only the sudden appearance of a cottage which finally stopped him short. The thing was small, unassuming, and so neatly hidden within a cluster of weeping willows that even the moonlight failed to reveal it until he nearly stumbled straight into its front door. Viggo turned to double back – meaning to go around the cottage – when the not-so-distant cry of some wild creature shocked him into stillness.

These plains were not so barren after all.

Almost immediately, a warm glow appeared in the nearby window, gleaming out from behind closed shutters. He should have made a run for it right then, but the fear of being heard rooted his feet to the earth. Perhaps if he just backed away slowly...

With his breath caught in his chest, Viggo took a couple of careful steps backward, his gaze completely transfixed by this sudden bit of unsteady light. It had appeared so swiftly at the sound of the cry, not as if someone had been woken from sleep, but as if someone had already been lying awake – waiting.

Waiting for him?

Upon second thought, that was unlikely. It was probably a woman. There would be many women lying awake and waiting; such was the nature of war.

By the time Viggo realized the amber glow had dimmed from the window, it was too late to take any more steps backward. The door

"Aeron?

swung open and a woman appeared, her pale face partially warmed by the candle she held out before her.

"Aeron?"

Wide eyes, full of fear and hope, picked him out of the darkness. In a moment of whimsical absurdity, Viggo found himself wishing he *was* this woman's sweetheart; if only to satisfy the yearning in her voice. He was sorry to have been right about the reason for her candlelight.

But there was no time for being sentimental; he had his own purpose to attend to.

He started to lift his hands in a gesture of denial, opening his mouth to offer an apology for not being the man she wanted. The candle fell to the dirt before he could utter a single syllable, flickering wildly as the woman rushed over it.

"Aeron! Aeron!"

With the candlelight behind her and the moonlight blocked out by the trees, it was too dark to see anything further of the woman's face. But he felt her frame – long and slender – as she thrust herself eagerly into his arms and clung tightly to him. Viggo's heart twisted with an unexpected stab of envy. Whoever Aeron was, he was a very lucky fellow.

Regretfully, Viggo pushed the woman away. He thought the sound of his voice – as he told her she had presumed wrongly upon him – would be enough to make her realize her mistake.

It was not.

No matter what he said or how he tried to say it, his words were no match for this woman's enthusiasm as she ignored his protests and bustled him into her home.

Immediately, Viggo saw the real reason for her haste.

Another candle came to life, illuminating a round table where two soldiers sat in the center of the little home. Upon second glance, Viggo noticed the crest one of them wore, identifying him as a Captain under King Arthur's command. Viggo pressed his lips together, grey eyes narrowing with disgust. He ought to have known this woman was up to something; she could not possibly have been daft enough to mistake him for someone else. It was ironic, really, to think he had escaped from Camelot with all its sentries and guards – with armies camped beyond its walls and patrols searching for him along every roadway – only to fall victim to a simple country woman.

Her grip on his arm tightened and Viggo swung his furious gaze into hers. Although the venom in his expression could have frightened any woman, her stare was unwavering as she spoke loudly to the soldiers.

"You were wrong!" she cried triumphantly, her tone carrying an unspoken but not so subtle *I-told-you-so*. "He is not missing – he has come home from the war! My Aeron is home."

There was a warm glow in her voice but her eyes, locked with his, were piercing and urgent. While the men looked on with suspicion, Viggo was struck with a realization so sudden, it was as though she'd cuffed him on the back of his head: she was lying. She was staring intently at him to keep from accidentally looking toward the soldiers, lest they see the truth in her eyes as easily as he could now. Viggo felt foolish not to have seen it sooner.

"*This* is your husband?" the Captain queried, deeply skeptical.

Gentle hands reached up to caress Viggo about the jaw, her fingertips delicately exploring every scrape and scratch inflicted upon him by the gorse. Silently, Viggo thanked those awful, prickly bushes. Not only had the thorns given this woman ample excuse to coddle him, but he imagined the damage done to his face probably lent credulity to her story. He slumped against her as though he were a man very much defeated by the rigors of battle, bowing his head into her hands to conceal his face. Hopefully his initial expressions of anger would be interpreted as fatigue.

"Yes," the woman was murmuring softly, "this is he. Changed and marked by the war, but still my husband."

Viggo heard chairs scrape back across the wooden floor, followed by approaching footsteps. He made a deliberate show of half-raising his eyes to stare wearily at the Captain and his soldier. They returned his look with one of undisguised contempt.

"See for yourself," the Captain began, seizing upon this opportunity to preach dutifully at his underling, "what kind of men these trouble-makers are. All of them, cowards! When the fighting becomes too much, they run home to hide in the arms of their *women*."

Viggo tensed even though these insults were hurled, not at him, but at whomever they supposed he was. The woman felt it and her grip upon him tightened, warning him to say nothing.

"Hurry now," she urged, "if you still wish to catch your man. If he is coming this way, as you say, he will surely see the light and turn away from here."

And he would have, Viggo thought – he would have done exactly that.

The Captain agreed with the woman's good sense, Viggo could see in his face that he did, but he seemed hesitant to show any open acknowledgment of a woman's intelligence. "Your husband must come with us."

"No, please!" she cried, and Viggo was only too happy to hide his face in her shoulder as she held him protectively. She smelled of sweet peas and rosemary, a distinct and pleasing change from the smell of ditches and dirt with which he was covered. "Can't you see my husband is ill? He hasn't the strength to go further. Besides, he has left the fighting. He is no longer your enemy! Allow me to tend him here."

The Captain did not seem particularly moved by her plea and so she changed tactics, playing subtly to his ego.

"He can report to you first thing in the morning but you must allow me to tend him this night, *I beg it of you!*"

While the Captain clearly did not think much of this woman or her opinions, he obviously enjoyed the sound of her begging. "First thing in the morning," he allowed, probably quite graciously, in his own mind. "I suppose after so long a time, a man is entitled to some things from his wife."

The Captain left with a leer upon his lips, his subordinate grinning on his heels.

For one long, breathless minute Viggo and the woman lingered in silence, listening to the fading tread of boots upon the dirt path. The soft arms left him, slipping away as the woman moved to the doorway and retrieved her candle, briefly holding it out into the night. When she was satisfied that both men had gone, she shut the door firmly behind her, pressing her back against it to block out further intrusion. The candle flickered beneath her face, illuminating her expression as it soured, her tongue seemingly distasteful in her mouth.

"I'm sorry," she said at last, her eyes shifting to him with new interest. "I didn't know how else to save you."

"Save me?" he asked, unable to think of a better question.

She nodded, crossing the room to slip wearily into one of the chairs abandoned by the soldiers. Her eyes were fixed upon the candle as she set it into a holder and spoke distantly. "They came earlier in the night, saying they needed my cottage; they expected a spy might pass this way. They said he had stolen something important. They even said he might come here, seeking shelter. I knew that if you did come, I would have to help you escape somehow."

Sensing that she had more to say, Viggo cast one last, hungry look toward the closed door and followed her. Seeing as how it would be foolish to attempt further travel until he understood what had just happened, he sat down across from the woman, ready to listen to whatever explanations she could possibly offer for her strange form of help. His first assumption, that she must be a fellow Saxon, seemed less likely when she raised her eyes and he noticed their unusual violet hue. She carried on, the words nearly pouring out of her like she was glad to be rid of them.

"A month ago, the soldiers came to tell me my husband was last seen in a battle along the northern front, where he had gone missing. They said I should presume him dead." She spoke with a lot less emotion than might have been expected from someone recently widowed, though Viggo guessed she may not have believed the men; either because she knew better, or because she simply did not want it to be true. "Neither of those men ever met my husband, and it seemed to me they probably hadn't seen this spy they were looking for, either. They told me to look outside first if we heard anything, to be sure it wasn't someone from the village. If I saw a man I didn't recognize, I was supposed to... lure him in."

That distasteful look was back in the tight set of her lips and the scrunch of her nose. Viggo had to hide his smile. "So you saw me and decided to lure me in by pretending I was your husband? That's an awful risky lie," he suggested gently, "for someone who doesn't like lying." In Viggo's experience, those prone to dishonesty did not carry their emotions about in their eyes like she did.

Pink flushed across her cheeks, and his smile became harder to hide.

"I suppose you knew right away?"

"Just about," he agreed, deciding not to admit how long it had taken him to figure it out. "But how did you know I was the man they were looking for?"

She shrugged easily. "Whether you were or weren't, I wouldn't have handed you over to those men. Besides, you haven't denied it."

That was true, he hadn't. She was quick. He took a closer look at those strangely coloured eyes and found them brimming with curiosity as she stared at him across the table. It seemed to him she must be exercising great self-control to keep from wheedling him with nosy questions.

Abruptly she rose, mumbling apologies for being a bad hostess. Though he tried to insist he needed nothing – that she had already done more than enough – she produced a small plate of food anyway. Unable to ignore his hunger with a chunk of real bread and some soft cheese sitting right in front of him, Viggo willingly ate every crumb.

"You'll stay here tonight," she decided aloud when he was finished. "In the morning, I'll go with you into town and we'll report to the Captain. I imagine there will be questions, questions for which you won't have answers. But I think we can convince him you're too ill...perhaps that you hurt your head in a fall and remember very little of the battle or how you made your way home. Once the Captain decides you are of no use, his soldiers will let you alone. And then, in a day or two when they have lost interest, you can be on your way."

Viggo raised an amused eyebrow, finding it funny how she ordered him about without any notion that he might have other plans. "Won't people think it's strange when your husband disappears so quickly after returning?" he suggested lightly, trying to point out the flaw in her logic.

Her grim smile was anything but amused. "My husband has never been faithful to me. No one will be surprised if he leaves. People talk. The Captain will no doubt have heard all about it."

No longer finding the woman funny, Viggo studied her in silence. She had honest eyes, he thought, and features that were soft when she smiled – even sadly. Locks of hair so fair they were ashen, almost silver, hung long and loose about a face far too young to match. If her husband – Aeron – was greeted even half as warmly into her arms as Viggo had been earlier, he would be a fool to ever seek the embrace of another.

When this war was over, when the fighting stopped and all the secrets were either disclosed or buried, Viggo would have nothing more than a dusty cabin to return to – if even that was still standing. Aeron would be coming home to these strange but lovely eyes. Viggo hoped he would stick around to appreciate them longer than the day or two this woman seemed to expect.

"I'm sorry," he finally offered, lost for better words. He apologized, not only for that which she had admitted to him, but more importantly for his own mistake in having assumed – even for a moment – that she was simple.

"Don't be." Her smile was genuine now. "If my husband's name can help you escape those men, it will have been his most useful contribution to this war. I just hope whatever you stole will help all of this to end more quickly."

"It will," he assured her, feeling the need to offer something, however inadequate, to repay her kindness. "And a small delay won't cost anything."

He did not admit to her that staying for a day or two as she had planned was entirely out of the question. In the morning, he would play along only to get a look at the land and see where the soldiers were stationed; then he would make a break for it. In the meantime, a chance to sleep under cover where it was both warm and dry was a welcome reprieve from his journey.

"You can sleep there," the woman said, rising and pointing to a soft woven rug which lay before the hearth. Although the fire had died out long ago, he could see there would still be warmth from the dim embers. "I'm sorry I can't offer you my bed in the other room but-"

"No, don't apologise. This'll do fine."

The woman's smile was relieved. Viggo rose to his feet and made his way to the fireplace, grabbing the iron rod which leaned against it so that he could stir the ashes back to faint life.

"The Captain and his man didn't seem too bright," he observed, wondering with bemusement just how far their little deception would have to go before he got his chance to run. "I'm sure it won't be hard to convince them we're married."

He glanced back over his shoulder to see the woman standing very still, twirling a lock of silvery hair vigorously around one finger. Though her smile was faintly amused, her eyes carried a look of sudden concern that suggested she might have finally come across a snag in her hastily contrived scheme.

"It will be much harder, I think, to convince the children."

Chapter 2

THE WOVEN RUG PROVED much more comfortable than the ditches where Viggo had been snatching brief handfuls of rest over the past three days. He slipped with surprising ease into a dreamless sleep and did not stir until he was brought suddenly to his senses by a jab to the ribs.

"Gywie, stop that! Let him alone."

Another jab.

"Gywie – oh never mind, he needs to wake up anyway."

A third jab struck him in the side, ever more enthusiastic for the veiled permission. Viggo opened his eyes. Above him stood a little girl, maybe four or five, with round blue eyes set into an even rounder face, all of it framed by a great mane of wild yellow curls. At the sight of him awake, her pink lips formed a wide smile.

"Hi!"

Not afraid of strangers, he deduced. "Hello there," he replied, returning her infectious smile. Stretching out his arms and back, Viggo sat upright to look her in the eye. "Gywie, is it? That's a pretty name."

"It means: gift."

Viggo looked up to see his hostess enrobed in a pale blue cloak, the clasp of which she fastened while staring fondly toward the little girl.

They looked nothing alike, he noted immediately, though it would have been far too impolite to voice this observation.

The girl was already wrapped up in a small, faded-yellow cloak, dressed for leaving, and Viggo glanced toward the window. There was no sign of daylight yet.

"What time is it?"

"I could only let you sleep for a few hours," the woman clarified, giving him the impression she might not have slept at all. "The sooner we go into town the better. You might fool the soldiers but you won't fool the townspeople who know my husband. The sun will be up soon. If we leave quickly, we can probably avoid being seen."

This addressed one question Viggo had tossed about in his mind before sleep had whisked it away. "I suppose I don't look anything like your husband, then?"

She chuckled mirthlessly and disappeared into the other room, leaving Viggo to stare after her with an odd assortment of mixed feelings. Gywie brought him back around to other thoughts.

"Come on!" she shouted, grabbing his hand and dragging him forward before he'd even gotten his feet under him. "I'll show you where to wash!"

She tossed aside the slender curtain next to the fireplace, revealing a little wardrobe-sized room. It had no latrine – there was likely an outhouse for that – but there was a pedestal and wash basin, along with a basket of clean rags and a bucket for the dirty water. The floor of the tiny room was slatted, so that whatever water spilled would drip through and soak into the dirt below. Viggo was impressed by the practicality of the set-up. There was even a large silver mirror hanging upon the wall, enhancing the effect of the single lantern which hung beside it.

Not a poor family, he decided.

Gywie stood watching him keenly. He stared back at her, expecting the gaze of a stranger to send her scampering away as it would have done with most children. Instead, she giggled loudly and waited for him to do something else that would entertain her.

"Gywie! Come finish your breakfast and let him be!"

The girl pouted but obeyed, allowing the curtain to fall back into place as she left. Viggo was pleasantly surprised to find the water in the basin had been warmed, though there wasn't enough of it to wash everything. He started by tending to the shallow scratches across his face, then scrubbed the worst of the grime from his hands and arms. When the water became too murky for getting clean with, he took a damp rag and swiped it down the lengths of his coat, washing away the dried mud and bits of bramble it had accumulated.

He was nearly done when he looked in the mirror and realized he had been seen, in Camelot, with all this scruffy growth upon his face. After a moment of indecision, during which he toyed briefly with the tiny pouch in his pocket, he realized he might not have another chance any time soon. Pulling it out, he removed the little iron blade and set to work. It might not be possible to get totally clean, but at least he could be clean-shaven, and hopefully this would help him blend in better with the townsfolk.

Feeling considerably improved, Viggo pushed aside the curtain and stepped back into the main room. The fire had been revived and new wood added to fill the room with comfortable warmth. Gywie was sitting at the table, her legs dangling from the chair in boredom.

The woman reappeared from the other room, a heavy green cloak slung over one arm. Her other arm was extended downward to push forward a second child, younger than the first, hardly visible beneath the drooping hood of his little brown cloak.

"This is my husband's cloak," she said, referring to what lay over her arm. "You can wear it instead of your coat in case anyone sees us pass."

Viggo hesitated, fingering the edge of his coat sleeve wistfully. He had been wearing it for as long as he could remember, and in that time the coat had become a sort of companion: its presence both familiar and dependable. It was a foolish sentiment, of course, yet he was loathe to part with it all the same.

She noted this hesitation and took a guess at its reason. "Unless...unless you've hidden what you stole in that coat?" she tried, failing in any meaningful way to conceal her curiosity.

"Yes," he agreed immediately, not exactly lying but not specifying any kind of truth either. So much the better if no one knew where his stolen secret hid. "But I'll wear the cloak overtop," he compromised, stepping forward to take it from her. "Thank you."

His gaze dropped down to the boy between them. He was a tiny waif of a child who seemed to be doing his very best to vanish amid the folds of his mother's grey skirts. Viggo knelt to his level, smiling in what he hoped was a reasonably non-threatening manner.

"Hello there," he tried.

Large brown eyes filled with suspicion, and the child shrank deeper into the heavy material. Despite the darker colouring of his eyes and hair, this child clearly looked like his mother; the soft, delicate contours of his face resembled hers precisely.

"True isn't fond of strangers," the woman explained, excusing his shyness. "You needn't worry though. I've explained to the children and they won't give you away. We should hurry." Her voice had become anxious. "We can talk on the way."

There was just enough light in the predawn for Viggo to get a clearer picture of the countryside. Only a few steps down the dirt path from the cottage and they emerged from the willow trees, walking out along a low ridge. Great fields of wild grasses, frozen with frost, stretched out as far as his eye could see, which he remembered well enough from his struggles to cross them in the moonlight. Thick clumps of gorse broke up the landscape and occasionally there were slender willows or a sturdy ash, all of them rigid beneath the hoarfrost. Nothing moved; nothing dared to. To Viggo, it seemed as if the whole world was holding its breath, waiting for the sun to chase away the icy hold of an autumn night.

His own breath, rising in glistening wisps about his face, made him grateful for the extra warmth of the cloak, even if he felt strange wearing something that belonged to another man.

The sound of rushing water caught his attention. A river was becoming visible at the end of the path. Glancing back, he could see now that it curved widely around the willows where the cottage lay concealed. Ahead, it followed the natural downturn of the land, and when they came up upon another rise he could see a small village cleverly situated in the river elbow. Viggo couldn't see where the river went from there, but he expected it likely cut a path west to the ocean. Had he not been interrupted last night, he probably would have followed it all the way to his destination; he probably still would – once he could get away.

The previous evening, Viggo had been roped into the woman's deception far too suddenly for questions to be asked, and afterward questions had seemed to be beside the point. Anyway, it had been too late for asking them. But today was a new day, and the sight of the village ahead – even if it was yet a ways off – brought his questions tumbling back.

"What place is this?"

"Dairefast."

Gywie whooped loudly and took off running down the hill. Her brother, True, stayed demurely behind, trailing them with a bit of his mother's blue cloak clutched firmly in his fist.

Viggo had never been this far west and he knew nothing of the towns here. If he remembered correctly, all the territories from here to the coast were controlled by Druids, who were now considered allies of King Arthur and the Britons. A frown of worry creased his brow as he wondered if this was a Druid town. If these people were Celts, then the soldiers Viggo had seen last night – no doubt sent from Camelot – were not their enemy as this woman suggested. His mind raced. It was possible the King's soldiers were so cruel that their own allies feared them, or perhaps the alliance between the Britons and Celt was still more uneasy than either side chose to let on. Of course another, more troubling possibility, was that this woman had deliberately mislead him.

Out of the corner of his eye, Viggo studied his hostess. Her soft voice with its distinctive lilt sounded Celtic enough, but she didn't for one moment look it. Then again, with her unusual colouring it would have been difficult to place her origins with any nation he knew of. It struck him with a touch of embarrassment that he did not even know her name.

"I feel silly realizing this just now," she blurted abruptly, having shared his thought, "but I didn't ask your name?"

"Aeron will do."

She laughed and glanced sideways at him. "But that can't be your name."

"Why can't it?" he asked with feigned innocence. "Your name, on the other hand," he added more seriously, "I will need." He was still unsure just how much of an act he would need to put on before he found a good chance to escape; the more he knew about her until then, the better.

"People call me Violet."

As far as names went, it was almost too appropriate. Something about the way she said it, however, worried him.

"Even your husband?" he challenged. He was not willing to go and hang his entire deception upon a nickname or something like it. But she smiled to herself and reassured him.

"Yes, even my husband."

"And your family name?"

Violet hesitated, and again, something about this was concerning to him. But he could not put his finger on why, and so said nothing.

"My husband's family name is Demeray."

Worry pulled once again at his brow. Demeray was a Celtic name.

"Are you Druids?" he asked. There was no sense in avoiding the question. If they were Druids, then there was no reason in the world for Violet to help him escape with information he had stolen from her King.

She was watching Gywie as she walked, wholly unaware of his rising suspicion as the little girl pushed through the reeds along the riverbank.

"My husband is. He is record keeper and scribe from here to the coast."

My husband is? Odd how she kept attributing these things to Aeron but never herself. Again, Viggo studied her profile out of the corner of his eye. She wasn't a Druid, he thought; she probably wasn't Celtic at all. Certainly, she wasn't Saxon. Where then did her loyalties lie?

Somehow, his worries faded as she scolded Gywie for throwing stones at a group of sleepy ducks. If she was scheming to deliver him into the hands of the soldiers, she could just as easily have done so the night before. For reasons unknown to him, she was no fonder of these soldiers than they were of her or of her husband. 'The enemy of my enemy is my friend' – that was one of the axioms taught by his Commander back home. If she chose not to share her reasons with him it was none of his business, so long as she remained willing to help.

Violet called the little girl back to her side as they neared the first buildings of Dairefast. Viggo could see no more than three dozen homes, most of these standing alongside the river. They were of sturdy wood construction, with thatched roofs and stone chimneys. This might not have been a wealthy city, but neither was it an especially impoverished village.

The well-travelled footpath broadened and became the main road through town. They passed a wide, squat building with an illegible sign groaning softly as it clung to a pair of frayed ropes dangling from the eaves. That was the tavern, Viggo decided, noting its sharp contrast to the larger, more prestigious homes across the street. Beyond them lay the town stables and workshops of craftsmen. As Violet had predicted, there was no one around yet to see them approach.

She pointed past the edge of town. "The soldiers' tents are just beyond the last house. I wish there was time to tell you more. But you are ill, after all." She cast a faint smile in his direction. "It's taken you a whole month to wander back from that battle where you disappeared. You might easily have lost some of your memories, so I think we'll get by. I'll try to do as much of the talking as we can get away with. I don't expect you'll need to know, but just in case you do, we've been married for five years; only a year after you lost your first wife."

She gestured with her gaze toward one of the more noteworthy houses, a respectable two-story affair of sturdy timber and finely hewn stones.

"That is the home you shared with her. If, for any reason, you need somewhere to go – go there. Nobody will think anything of it, so long as the children and I don't go with you. You never let us."

Viggo felt one of his eyebrows lifting of its own accord as he tried to make sense of this strange relationship she was describing. Oblivious to his confusion, she prattled on easily, taking Gywie's hand and leading the way ever onward through town.

"No matter what might be said or done to me or the children, you mustn't defend us. My husband would not and if anyone heard of it, you would certainly be found out."

The eyebrow which had gone up pulled down again, sinking into a frown. Viggo would have liked to ask what sorts of things she thought might be said or done? He did not relish the idea of impersonating the kind of man who would not even defend his own children. But Viggo didn't ask, because it was better not to get overly involved with this woman and her strange marriage. Besides, the bright red cloth of the soldiers' tents had come into view and he had more urgent questions.

"This is a Druid town?" he asked, just to confirm.

She nodded. "You're wondering why the soldiers treat me like an enemy, and speak of my husband as a troublemaker?"

He nodded. The first scarlet tent was taking shape; above it a pennant flapped in the breeze, bearing the dragon crest of King Arthur. Gywie no longer pulled wildly against her mother's grasp. She seemed subdued by the sight of the tents, walking closely alongside her mother in nervous silence. There did not seem to be much time left for explanations before they reached their destination, but between the slow pace of True's little legs and the quick pace of Violet's mouth, she still managed to convey a great deal.

"Not everyone took as well to King Arthur's peace treaties as he would have people believe. When it comes to past wrongs, some are not quick to forget. Most of the Druids have embraced peace with the Britons and encourage their people to do the same, but my husband is a stubborn man and there were others in this village who felt, as he did, that no peace could be had. When the war began, patrols from Camelot passed through here regularly. Certain men – including my husband – would harass them and chase them off. Eventually, someone decided the western front should not be left unguarded, no matter how unlikely an invasion from the coast might seem. These men came from Camelot about a year ago to watch over the town until there was no longer a Saxon threat. Rumors came ahead of them that the Captain had orders to arrest all the troublemakers, so my husband and maybe ten others fled in advance."

Viggo didn't know how Violet wasn't breathless with the speed of her words. She was even smiling to herself, though he couldn't see anything funny about her story.

"I think the Captain was angry to have lost them," she continued, "and he's treated the rest of us like the enemy ever since. My husband sends letters when he can, as do some of the other men. They will not fight for Arthur, nor for the Saxons, and so they follow the fighting and – as far as I can understand it – do little more than make a nuisance of themselves to both sides."

Suddenly, Viggo understood her smile. If the situation hadn't been so serious, he might have chuckled at the comical image her explanation conjured. He was about to ask why a garrison of soldiers had been posted in Dairefast when it was such a little town and not directly upon the coast, but the loud whinny of horses deterred him.

Viggo stopped short. Beside him, Violet did the same.

Three brightly coloured tents stood in a rough circle, a small number of horses tied up in the clearing between them. Soldiers were already milling about the largest of these tents, carrying water and firewood to start their day. In the middle of the clearing stood one man alone: the Captain from the previous night. He was staring off to the west and Viggo followed his gaze to see a small army approaching through the lifting darkness. Five men on horseback, with at least another twenty marching behind them on foot.

The man riding at the head of this new company dismounted and approached the local Captain. He was of equal if not greater rank, judging by his long red cape and the crest proudly displayed upon the shoulder of his uniform.

"Were you expecting visitors?" Viggo asked stiffly.

"No," Violet whispered, her voice touched with the first hints of real fear Viggo had heard. "If they'd come during the night from Camelot, we would have heard them pass on the road. They must have come west from the sea, from either Dionne or Lin Harbour."

"They're looking for me," Viggo deduced aloud.

Violet nodded, glancing nervously between him and the new arrivals. "This was a terrible idea," she murmured, the fear in her voice rising with anxious regret. "We should go back. Maybe-maybe the Captain will be so busy he'll forget. Maybe he'll forget about last night. Maybe we can…maybe we can get you across the fields before they have time to start looking. Maybe we should…"

Her breathless ramble was cut off by a shout that made them both jump. It was too late now for a hasty retreat; they'd been spotted.

Chapter 3

A s it turned out the shout had come, not from a soldier, but from a young woman of no more than twenty years. She came running out of the smallest tent to meet them, and though a couple of soldiers paused to glance after her, they were focused on the new arrivals and showed no further interest.

Violet embraced the woman, who outwardly looked to be her perfect contrast. Unlike the high buttoned grey dress and solitary demeanor of his hostess, this younger woman flaunted a dress of bright scarlet with a sweeping neckline that drew attention to the string of wooden beads about her throat. She was rather short in stature, and plain about the face, but her strawberry blonde hair had been braided back skillfully and there was great fire of personality in her hazel eyes. Whatever their apparent dissimilarities, it was clear she and Violet were fast friends.

"I'm so sorry I couldn't come last night!" the newcomer gushed. "When my uncle told me he meant to spend the night in your home I wanted to come too, but he wouldn't hear of it. And then when he came back and told me Aeron had returned..." The young woman trailed off, staring at the man behind her friend. "Oh." All the breathless excitement in her voice fizzled into flatness and she glared at Viggo as if his very presence were an offence to her. "I see he has."

Violet looked between them, her discomfort obvious. "Aeron, this is Helena, the Captain's niece. She's been a good friend to us while you were away."

Viggo scrambled for an appropriate response but Gywie, thankfully, spared him the trouble of finding one. Accustomed to being the centre of attention, she stamped her foot and reached for Helena with a demanding chorus of: "I want up! Up! Up! Up!"

Both women laughed and for a moment his presence was forgotten. Helena scooped Gywie into her arms and cuddled her close, both of them giggling with equally childish delight as they scrunched their noses and nuzzled them together.

His gaze slid back to the encampment, where the Captain and his friend were sitting down near an open fire, deep in conversation. Viggo wished there was a way to find out what they were saying.

"What is all this?" Violet was asking her friend.

"I don't know yet," Helena answered, shifting Gywie onto one hip to carry her more comfortably. "They've just arrived. Come on and we'll find out."

Helena started back toward the tents but Violet hesitated, her gaze flickering between him and the soldiers. "I told your uncle we'd come see him this morning," she called out finally, "but I don't want to stay any longer than need be. Aeron isn't very well."

"So? He can stay or leave, what do I care? Come on, let's go!"

"I'll be fine," Viggo whispered, and meant it; he didn't need Violet trying to protect him, he only needed her to maintain their deception long enough for him to escape.

Gywie shrieked with delight as she and Helena skipped down the slope, and after a moment of staring at him with a strand of hair pinched anxiously between two fingers, Violet followed.

Viggo held back, wondering if he should make a run for it now. What if he couldn't fool the soldiers? Every hour he lost was an extra hour the Britons spent searching for him. He should have been well away from here by now, he should have been-

A gentle tug on his fingers drew his gaze downward into the soft brown eyes of the boy. True stood beside him with an encouraging smile etched into his little face. For reasons Viggo couldn't quite explain, his anxieties evaporated like sunlight upon frost. Everything would be fine. Running now would only give all those soldiers something to chase. Lost time or not, it was best to stay the course and play along just a little longer.

Returning the boy's smile, Viggo set off after his 'wife', strangely pleased when True kept hold of his hand and walked along beside him.

Helena was being discreet about picking the right time to approach her uncle. She lingered near the open flap of the tent from which she had come, close enough to hear what was being discussed but not close enough to seem as though she were intruding. Violet stood uncomfortably at her side as Helena did her best to explain what she could in hushed tones. Viggo did his very best to listen in to both conversations at once.

"That's Captain Ellaway," Helena whispered, speaking of the newcomer. "He and his men are stationed in Dionne."

"I wonder what he and Donovan have to talk about?" Violet mused aloud. Viggo smiled to himself, appreciating the fact that she'd supplied the local Captain's name for his benefit. She was new to this game, but sharp witted and catching on quickly.

There was a noticeable contrast between the two Captains. In all the places Donovan was broad and stocky, Ellaway was narrow and oblong. The Captain from Dionne held himself seriously with an air of importance about him that Donovan simply did not possess. Ellaway was a nobleman, Viggo guessed, while Donovan was a war-time recruit. This probably explained the subtle under-current of rivalry between them.

"...it is still more likely he went east," Ellaway was saying, "but if he does try to reach the coast, he'll have no choice but to come through here. It's better for us to be here, watching for him, than just waiting in Dionne."

Donovan nodded with forced agreement. "Have you received any better description than I of the man we're looking for?"

The set of Ellaway's angular jaw told Viggo this was a matter of some frustration, likely for both men. "Hardly enough. That he stands average to other men with hair the colour of ready grain is not a lot to go on..."

"A typical flaxen-Saxon!" Donovan crowed, and then laughed at his rhyme, which he seemed to perceive as wit. Ellaway stared reproachfully until the other man composed himself with an awkward clearing of the throat. "I suppose they must not have gotten a very good look at him as he fled."

Viggo smothered a small, pleased smile as it jumped to his mouth. He knew for a fact that Arthur had seen him just as clearly as he'd seen the King. But giving too detailed a description would mean admitting the King had stood face-to-face with a Saxon spy and let him escape. If anything, this only confirmed the value of Viggo's stolen secret; the King could afford no loss of face.

"We know if he does come here, it will only be in passing as he heads for the coast." Ellaway was dismissive now. He'd thought this matter through and needed no further input from his counterpart. "And so, until we receive word that he has been caught elsewhere, nobody leaves Dairefast."

"This is a trade route! Merchants pass through here daily," Donovan protested in alarm.

"Let them come! Let as many come as they like. There is nothing suspicious about that. But anyone who tries to leave..."

The conversation turned to the more mundane matters of where Ellaway intended to set up temporary accommodations for his men. Viggo's gaze wandered. Through the open flap of the nearby tent, a large table caught his attention. A quick glance sideways assured him that Helena was still waiting for the right moment to approach her uncle. Checking to be sure no one else was paying attention, Viggo slipped inside the tent.

It was smaller than the other two and obviously reserved for the private use of the Captain and his niece. A portion of it had been curtained off for the girl, but Viggo was not interested in exploring how she or her uncle lived. He went straight to the table. Soldiers didn't travel with wooden furniture, he knew, and wondered if the table – along with the elegant chairs and the heavy wardrobe that stood in one corner – had been commandeered from the townspeople.

Atop the table lay the one item of real interest: a large map of the region, spread out and weighed down in the corners by four smooth river stones. This was Viggo's first comprehensive look at the area; back in Camelot, there had been no such opportunities. His decision to defy expectation and head west had been based upon a mere glance at a comparatively crude map sewn into a tapestry.

Without need for further explanation, he finally understood why both Dairefast and Dionne were considered important enough to warrant a garrison stationed in each.

Between the two towns, the landscape came to a natural bottle-neck. To the south, the Sinking Swamps covered the land all the way to the sea; even he knew tales of the many types of death which lurked within. To the north, there was a nameless mountain range that stretched like a wall across the landscape. For reasons unknown to him, symbols upon the map clearly forbid entry into these mountains or their foothills.

In the Captain's Tent

The only passage between these two natural obstacles was the river. It curved around Dairefast and cut a narrow valley between the swamps and the mountains until it reached Dionne, where it fanned into a delta and was swept away into the sea. To the south of Dionne lay Lin Harbour. He would need to reach the harbour if he hoped to catch a boat heading north into Anglo-Saxon held territories. From there his secret would buy him swift passage home and an easy audience with the Saxon Elders.

Viggo lifted his gaze over his shoulder to the open tent flap and the pale blue cloak he could see lingering near the edge of it. In perfect truth, he'd been harbouring some nagging irritation at her interference. She had taken it upon herself to decide what was best for him and in doing so had placed them both in a compromising position. But if she hadn't...

He looked back down at the map. If she hadn't come out to greet him, Donovan and his man surely would have. In the darkness, Viggo would have fled straight toward the river – probably very nearly fallen into it – and naturally would have followed it toward Dionne, running smack into Ellaway and his men as they traveled through the night. There was no avoiding it: he owed Violet and her quick thinking a debt of gratitude.

The wistful smile that crossed his face with this thought slipped away just as quickly. Things were always much simpler when he was accountable to – and responsible for – no one but himself. There would be no sticking around to protect her from whatever consequences came from aiding a foreign spy. Hopefully she'd had enough time, as she sat in the darkness waiting alongside those two soldiers, to realize as much.

"What are you doing in here?"

A soldier with a bucket of freshly drawn water in each hand paused in the mouth of the tent, the suspicion plain on his face.

"I'm sorry," Viggo said immediately, bowing his head and lowering his eyes with deference. He couldn't risk a scene, not with Ellaway and Donovan sitting just outside the tent plotting his capture. The only thing truly protecting him so far, he knew, was the prevailing assumption that he'd gone east. And yet, how to explain his presence here, in the Captain's tent?

To his surprise, True popped out from between his boots and glanced up at him. Unbeknownst to him, the boy must have followed him into the tent and been playing under the table this whole time. Viggo reached down at once and gathered the boy into his arms.

"I came to get my son."

It was a worthy excuse for any intrusion and Viggo was amazed by his good fortune. The boy could have given him away at any moment if he'd cried out or fought to be put down; but True merely wrapped his skinny arms around Viggo's neck and looked around, admiring the view from his newfound perch.

"No one is supposed to be in here," the soldier told him sternly. He didn't look ready to drop the issue, but Viggo doubted he was willing to drop those buckets of water on the Captain's woven carpet either. Smiling sheepishly, Viggo ducked past the man before there could be any further questions.

"There he is now!"

It took Viggo a moment to realize that Helena had finally spoken with her uncle and that she was now pointing him out to the two Captains.

He nodded to show he'd heard and allowed himself a slight hobble as he made his way to Violet's side. Hopefully he wasn't overplaying his part.

"Aeron Demeray?"

He nodded again, afraid to open his mouth lest they hear his heart pounding in his chest.

"This is one of the rebels who eluded you?" Ellaway asked curiously, studying him head to toe, lingering particularly on his left leg where sharp eyes had picked out the uneven gait.

Donovan's entire posture stiffened at this perceived slight against his abilities. "Yes, this is him."

With those four words, the Captain confirmed Viggo's identity not only to Ellaway, but to Helena and anyone else in Dairefast who might hear of it. And now that he had, Viggo suspected he would defend it to high heaven, for Donovan did not seem the sort to bear the burden of humiliation lightly.

Amusement mingled with adrenaline, producing in Viggo the sort of smug confidence upon which he thrived. He was glad he had not tried to make a break for it earlier. This was getting fun. In a satisfying way it was almost unsporting – when he thought of how much trouble these men were going to in order to catch him – that he should have the nerve to walk right into their camp and stand before them, letting them look him over in ignorance. It would all make for a great story to tell when he got home.

"Your wife," the Captain continued, "has just made a suggestion that could see you pardoned for your troublemaking."

"Oh?" he queried, not at all enthusiastic. Violet had said Aeron was not fond of Arthur or the soldiers, so Viggo could not be either.

"There is a Saxon spy who has escaped from Camelot. You may not be loyal to the King, but I know you've more reasons to hate the Saxons than most. Until this man is caught, no one will be leaving Dairefast. Your wife tells me your home across from the tavern sits all but empty. Any travellers who arrive will need a place to stay. If the rooms over the tavern fill too quickly, we shall send them along to your house. This would seem suitable payment for the trouble you caused. What say you?"

What was he supposed to say?

He leveled his gaze upon Violet, who returned it steadily with a hopeful look in her eyes, urging him to go along with her plan. Could that be what all this was really about, Viggo wondered? All of this scheming and subsequent risk, just to win a pardon for her wayward husband so that when he finally came home she would not have to see him arrested? Could her motives really be so simple, or her planning so unnecessarily overcomplicated?

"Fine," he said sharply, turning his attention back to the Captain. "I say it is fine. I'll go now and prepare the place myself." Unwrapping the little arms from around his neck, Viggo set True down next to his mother.

"You're still not well," Violet urged softly. "I'll come along and help you."

"No!" His rebuff was harsh; her face appropriately taken aback. He hoped she realized he was only doing what she'd told him to. If her husband did not allow her or their children into the house he had shared with his first wife, and if people talked as Violet said they did, then maybe they would hear about this and believe her story long after he'd gone.

Somewhere during the previous half hour the sun had risen, and the first curious onlookers had left their homes and wandered down to find out what had brought so many soldiers to their village. Lifting the hood of the borrowed cloak to hide his features from them, Viggo stormed off, looking for all the world like a man who had just been forced to strike a bargain that did not please him.

It was a relief to enter the quiet stillness of the house. For the first time since arriving in Dairefast, Viggo was truly alone. He was accustomed to solitude and for a whole minute he allowed himself to lean against the door and simply enjoy it.

He couldn't afford to linger though. Sooner or later, it was likely one of the Captains would send someone to check if the house had been put in order as promised, and he preferred to be long gone by then. Grey eyes wandered about the room, sizing up the situation.

The front door let into a large, open-concept living space that was not much to look at, though Viggo suspected it had once been quite comfortable. A quick jog of his memory told him Aeron lost his first wife six years ago, and nothing looked to have been disturbed since. Dust lay over everything from the neat stack of pots and pans abandoned near a cold stone fireplace, to dishes laid out upon the table for a meal that had never been served. Everything showed the touch of a woman skilled, artistic...and gone. The coating of dust had blurred the once-cheerful home into a single, uniform tone of decay, giving Viggo the odd impression that everything here had slowly but surely been fading out of existence.

By contrast, there was a single pathway scuffed through the dust, looking real and very much alive as it led across the room to an open doorway in the far corner. It was littered with dirt someone had tracked into the house and never bothered to clean up. Viggo followed this trail and peeked around the doorframe with interest.

The back room had no windows or shutters, and without a lantern it was nearly impossible to see anything. He could tell it was a bedroom only because daylight from behind him fell over one corner of a real bed – wooden frame and all. He approached and sat down to test it, relaxing as he sunk into the soft bedding and found it comfortable. It was dusty too, but not nearly as dusty as everything else.

This, he realized suddenly, made an awkward kind of sense. Violet had made no secret of the fact that her husband was unfaithful; likely this was where Aeron came to... Viggo shook his head, seeing no need to let his mind go any further in that direction.

Unexpectedly he tensed, his skin crawling with an eerie sense of danger. He had seen nothing, heard nothing, and yet all the same he knew that he was not alone. His gaze darted about anxiously for a candle or lantern, anything he could use to chase the shadows from the room.

It was no shadow, however, which slipped smooth, bare arms around his neck and pressed a warm body up against his back.

"Oh Aeron..." a voice like clear water burbled softly. "I've missed you."

Chapter 4

F OR JUST A MOMENT Viggo's mind went blank. The absurdity of
the situation was too much. It was only some instinct, straight
from the deepest and most deceptive parts of him, which kept him from
yelping aloud and leaping away.

What the hell was wrong with Aeron?

What sort of man came home from a year abroad and had a mistress
waiting, fully expecting him to arrive in her arms before he'd spent even
one day with his wife and children?

Knowing she would not be satisfied with silence for long, Viggo
reached up and ran his fingers tenderly along her arms, his mind racing to
one inevitable conclusion: he could never fool this woman. The darkness
may have tricked her, but it would not deceive her. Lovers could tell. Her
fingers would search out his features and find them different; they would
travel his body seeking out familiar marks or scars and stumble across
others where they should not have been. Even his voice and the use of
an endearment – or lack of an expected one – would all conspire against
him.

The moment she realized she had a strange man in her bed it would
all be over. He could almost hear her shrieks of fright now, bringing
help from passers-by. Not that he had any intention of letting it come

to that. He probably couldn't buy more than a couple of minutes, but they would be enough.

Viggo slid his fingers down to her wrists and gave them an affectionate squeeze, hoping against hope that if he spoke in only the lowest whispers, she would not be able to distinguish him from Aeron.

"I came as soon as I could. And I have a surprise."

She squealed with pleasure, tightening her arms around his neck. "For me?" she simpered, locks of hair tumbling past his face as she pressed her cheek to his head.

"Sit back and – and close your eyes," he instructed, annoyed with his breath for catching.

The arms pulled away obediently and he took a deep breath, steading himself as he turned around to face her. She had scootched forward into the light, and despite the danger she represented, Viggo found himself flushing at the sight of her. The shapeless linen chemise she wore was not so shapeless with her in it. Long, dark lashes nearly touched upon flawless cheeks as she followed his instructions, her full lips parted ever so slightly with anticipation. Hair like spun gold hung in playful curls all the way down to the small of her back.

Whatever might've been wrong with Aeron, it very clearly was not his eyesight.

Viggo reached into the pocket of his heavy coat and removed a long white handkerchief.

"Hold still."

Folding it over to make it long and slender enough, he wound the handkerchief over her eyes, securing it loosely behind her head. She gasped and reached out to lay perfectly smooth fingers against his cheek, checking that he was still there.

"Aeron!" she accused, and then giggled. "It must be true what they say...war *is* romantic."

Stupid girl.

It was fortunate neither one of them could see the expression on his face just then. Even way out here, it took a great deal of willful ignorance and self-absorption to say a thing like that. Viggo had not seen the front lines either, but he knew enough to make him lurch away from her touch.

"You'll like what comes next even better," he promised, forcing the words through grit teeth and stiff lips. The suggestion was enough to provoke further giggles of anticipation as he crawled around behind her. Fishing through his pockets, Viggo found the small coil of rope he vaguely remembered stealing somewhere along his journey. It was always smart to carry rope, even just a little...though admittedly, Viggo had not imagined using it this way.

He took her wrists, pulling them together and binding them at her back. Her breath caught. Almost there. He shushed her softly, making soothing little noises until he tied the final loop.

"There," he said at last, abandoning the undertones as he cinched down hard upon the knot. "That should do it."

She yelped and twisted against the rope, confused by his changed voice and the tightness of her binding. "Aeron, what are-"

Viggo slid the handkerchief down from her eyes to her mouth, cutting her off; with a bit of finagling he retied it so she would not be able to spit it out or writhe free – not for a long while, anyway.

She was still too stunned to have figured out what was happening, and Viggo took advantage of her daze to scramble off the bed and run back into the other room. There he found a small oil lamp on the mantle. Blowing off many layers of dust, he lit it and returned.

With light beneath his face, the woman on the bed finally understood that he was a stranger. She gasped at the revelation, her dark eyes drawing wide in that flawless face. Sizing her up, Viggo set his lamp aside and approached cautiously. To her credit she tried to kick him away, but he'd been expecting as much and easily caught hold of her, wrestling with the bed linens until he'd tied her legs together with a bundle of sheets. When he was satisfied that she could not escape, Viggo stood and retrieved his lamp.

"Stay here, I've got some housework to do."

In truth, he felt a little bad. She was confused and awfully frightened. But then he thought of those two children of Violet's. If he *had* been Aeron they would be waiting at home, right now, for their father to return and spend his first day back with them. And this woman, whoever she was, clearly wouldn't have cared. No, he didn't feel all that bad. Sooner or later, soldiers would come by to check on the place and they could set her free.

This thought gave him pause. When she was found, his pretence would be over.

It was immediately settled in his mind that he would have to make a run for it tonight, regardless of Ellaway and his blockade. There would be a way around them; there was always a way. He would rather have gone immediately, without any further waste of time, but even he was not foolish enough to attempt an open run across the countryside in broad daylight – not with so many men just waiting for someone to try and leave. It would have to be tonight, under cover of darkness.

But what if they found her before nightfall?

One problem at a time, he decided.

Returning to the front room, Viggo made quick work of a half-hearted job. It wasn't likely the soldiers would be expecting any better. He found rags to dust off table and chairs, cookware and dishes, and whatever else looked like it might be useful to travelers.

A wooden ladder took him up to a loft where he found large chests organized into neat rows. Upon inspection, each one was found to contain thousands of pages of carefully archived records: everything from births and deaths to yearly crop yields and contracts for the leasing of houses and fields. Whatever else he may have been, Aeron was a meticulous scribe. He also used expensive ink and Viggo was not above pocketing a bottle for himself.

The loft also revealed straw mats, which Viggo laid out for guests who would never come. There would no longer be a reason for forcing travelers to stay in Dairefast when the soldiers realized he'd already slipped through their grasp. All of this was just for show, to keep from raising alarm until nightfall. When he was satisfied with the state of the loft, he returned to the bedroom.

With the help of the oil lamp, a quick search of the room yielded the best discovery yet. In the far corner a trapdoor opened to reveal an empty root cellar, big enough to have housed two casks of wine or enough grain to last a large family through the winter. It would more than easily hold a grown woman.

She seemed to guess his intentions as he glanced between her and the open mouth of the cellar, judging them both for size. Ignoring her muffled cries, he jumped down to make sure the cellar had a proper shaft for ventilation. It had. The cellar would not keep her hidden forever, but if a soldier were to come by later in the day and make only a rudimentary inspection, she would not be found. It would buy him time until nightfall.

Viggo braced his palms against the wooden framework of the trapdoor and hoisted himself back out, kicking the fresh dirt from his boots as he stood and dusted himself off. The woman put up a reasonable protest which he did not begrudge her. By the time he'd lowered her into the cellar, all the muffled shouts and cries had given way to whimpering tears and he started feeling a little guilty about the whole thing again. He hesitated over the trapdoor, looking at her. It was cold in the cellar and a simple nightgown would not provide her with much warmth. Climbing back down to her, he pulled Aeron's green cloak off his shoulders and wrapped it around her. It hardly seemed to reassure her. Brushing some of the tears off her cheeks, he muttered a quiet apology.

She wouldn't be hurt, someone would find her soon, he really was sorry; words like these mumbled out from between his lips until the cellar hatch was finally lowered into place. He'd have liked it better if she were free to yell and curse at him so that he wouldn't feel the need to be apologetic at all.

Blowing out the lamp, Viggo returned it to its place. Now all he had to do was pass the time until nightfall.

It was almost mid-day when Viggo slipped back out into the street. He couldn't risk being seen without Aeron's cloak to disguise him, so he picked a clear moment when no one was about and made a dash for the river. It was still visible from the road, but far enough away that no one noticed him threading between the reeds toward the cluster of weeping willows.

Pushing through the curtain of hanging branches from the river side, Viggo stumbled unexpectedly into a garden. Tucked between the trunks of four great trees, neat rows of soil produced rosemary, sage, thyme, and a small plethora of other herbs he could not name off the top of his head. Pea vines climbed trellises woven from willow branches and blossomed with the promise of produce ahead. Other rows concealed vegetables beneath the ground, their leafy stems reaching out for the golden threads of sunlight streaming through the branches. He had no idea how all this was possible when they were well into the season of heavy frost, with snow soon to follow.

Skirting around the garden, careful to trample nothing underfoot, he soon found the same shuttered window he'd come upon the night before. The shutters were open to welcome the bright noon sun and a voice floated out through the window, singing cheerfully.

He tried the door. It gave to his touch and he slipped inside, shutting it softly behind him. What he saw was enough to bring a smile to his face, chasing off all thoughts of the golden-haired woman in the root cellar as he leaned against the doorframe to watch.

The singing came from Violet, who was twirling around with True in her arms, drawing thin shrieks of delight from his tiny frame. Gywie skipped along after them, throwing her arms about in time to the tune.

"When blossoms bloom upon the trees,
When the fields are full of flowers...
Lay yourself down next to me,
And pass the moonlit hours."

The boy was the first to notice but Viggo placed a cautionary finger over his smile, hoping True wouldn't give him away just yet. The boy said nothing, but his laughter stopped and he kept his eyes fixed on Viggo as his mother swirled him about the room.

"Summer grass is quite the tease,
But eventually the storm blows...
Stay by me in frosty breeze,
And hold me as the fire glows."

Violet's steps faltered as she noticed her son's silence. When she caught sight of Viggo in the doorway she stopped abruptly, her cheeks burning red. Gywie spun straight into the back of her legs.

"Hey!" the little girl protested, throwing her hands on her hips in annoyance. The pout on her lips morphed into a beaming smile when she saw what had caused the interruption. Skipping over, Gywie took his hand, dragging him toward the fireplace. Viggo obliged and followed where she wanted, never once taking his eyes – or his smile – off Violet. He enjoyed the flustered look on her face, like she desperately wished he would tell her how long he'd been standing there.

He wouldn't have, not even if she'd asked.

Gywie tugged repeatedly on his sleeve and he sat down near the hearth. She climbed into his lap to fiddle with his coat buttons, but Viggo wasn't paying any attention.

"Don't stop," he urged.

Violet set True down slowly, letting him scamper away the moment his feet hit the floor. "I...I don't sing."

"Yes, you do. And you should."

It sounded like she'd been making up the rhymes as she went. She had a gift, and Viggo wanted to hear it again. When she continued to hesitate, he pushed her with a gentle command, trying to sound persuasive rather than forceful.

"Do another."

Her gaze slipped away distantly, one hand reaching up to twist a bit of silver hair around her finger in embarrassment. But she indulged him, her voice greatly subdued as she stared through the open window and sang...

"If war should finally come our way,
If enemies surround me...
I'll travel to the salty spray,
Let ocean waters drown me."

He stared, taken aback by the morbid sentiment. He was further surprised to see a twinkle sparkling out at him from the depths of her eyes, echoed in her playful smile. She sang another verse, tripping over her own laughter as she walked toward him.

"The war came right up to my door,
And I dragged it in blindly...
Now look who's sitting on my floor!
Thank heaven he is kindly."

A laugh burst from his mouth as she dropped to the floor beside him, the stress and worry of their shared deception melting away. He had so many questions to ask her by the time they'd caught their breath, but she shooed Gywie away and urged him off the floor, suddenly intent on providing him a meal. A pot of soup had been simmering over the smoldering coals of her fire and she ladled some into a bowl for him. The smell of it steaming in his hands brought back the memory of that bit of bread and cheese, which had been greatly appreciated, but hardly filling.

The soup was the first hot meal he'd had in weeks and the first mouthful went down easy; it was the aftertaste which caught him off guard. Food took on a special flavour when it was left unattended too long: a burnt, gravelly kind of taste which could easily contaminate an entire meal. This meal was, undoubtedly, contaminated. He tried his best to hide any adverse reaction from his well-meaning hostess but she cringed and knew anyway.

"I bought this in town," she offered by way of apology, sheepishly supplying him with a large chunk of bread. He managed to choke down the rest of the soup using the bread to chase it. It was better than starving – though not necessarily by much.

Trying to distract himself from the bitter taste in his mouth, Viggo watched with interest as Gywie used an assortment of coloured inks to doodle her way around a patch of wooden floor.

"You let her draw on your floor?" he asked, surprised when Violet did nothing to stop her. He didn't think he'd ever met another woman who would consider letting her child near one pot of precious ink, much less several.

Violet grinned and pointed to the rug on which he'd slept. It was rolled up now and put aside. "I spread that overtop when people come so they don't ask silly questions. But I think it's pretty, don't you?"

He grinned also. In an odd sort of way it was rather pretty. He went and stood over Gywie, studying the drawings around her and eventually picking out some clumsy little birds that were pretty good for a five-year-old.

"These are pretty," he told her, meaning to praise her efforts. The little blonde stared at him like he was stupid and went back to scratching green ink as deeply into the wood as she could manage.

A blush crept slowly over Violet's features. "Those are...um...those are mine." She said it like she was apologizing for something. "I'm not very good at drawing, or...um..." Biting her lip, she trailed off with embarrassment.

"Or cooking?" he supplied helpfully, glad when she laughed instead of taking offence.

"That either."

"Then what are you good at?"

Her mirth evaporated and she stared at him, puzzled. Maybe no one had ever asked her that question before. "Dreaming, mostly."

It was an unexpected answer and yet Viggo found the sentiment strangely relatable.

"If you mean to ask what work I do, then for now I keep up as best I can with my husband's work. There isn't anyone else to do it who can both read and write. I wanted to teach some of the local children, but their mothers...well, let's just say I'm not much trusted here. I sometimes doubt anyone would have anything to do with me if I wasn't the only healer around for miles."

"You're a healer?" he queried, though he didn't know why that surprised him. Maybe it was because, looking around, he saw little in the way of potions or tonics – all the things one expected in the home of a healer. But then again, there had to be some secret to how her garden blossomed in the first breaths of winter.

"Not really, no."

She moved away, gathering the children to the table and setting bowls of soup before them, along with as much bread as they wanted. Viggo realized as he watched that he hadn't once seen her eat. He also noticed that both Gywie and True were clean and freshly dressed, and yet Gywie – and her mother – still wore their cloaks. True was the only one going about freely in a little tunic.

"But my mother was a healer," Violet continued, talking as she worked. "I learned enough from her to do some good. I think Aeron mostly married me because the village needed a healer..." Her mouth had a knack for getting away on her. She paused what she was doing and glanced at him over her shoulder. "I know what you must think of me."

His mind went back to the root cellar. He had thoughts, alright, none of which he particularly wanted to share with her. But as he mulled over the events of the last few hours, one important question came to mind.

"Why did you decide to help me? Was all this meant to clear your husband's name?"

He knew instantly by her blank stare that the idea had never even occurred to her.

"No...though I suppose that would have been noble of me, wouldn't it?"

She pulled a chair up to the table and sat down thoughtfully. He could tell she was about to start talking at length and so he sat down and crossed his arms upon the table, making himself comfortable to listen.

"Do you want to know the honest truth?" He nodded. "Do you believe we can know the future?"

The question took him aback. "No," he replied firmly, wondering what that had to do with anything. Knowing the future meant believing in fate, or destiny, or some such thing; but he refused to believe his actions could be decided for him.

She took no offence. "The Druids do. Sometimes, when they visit the Oak Trees, they claim to have visions of things to come. When the war began, the Druid priests declared King Arthur the inevitable victor. They call him the Once and Future King and say history will remember him well."

Viggo was confused. "What has that got to do with helping me? If your husband is a Druid, and you believe the Saxons are sure to lose this war, then why help a Saxon spy?" He wasn't sure why the answer was suddenly important to him, but it was.

She studied him a long time and Viggo would have traded almost anything to know what thoughts were running wild behind those violet eyes. At some point the children slipped away from their partially emptied bowls and scampered off, leaving them alone. Violet continued to stare at him like she was searching for something that had been lost a long time ago.

"I am not a Druid," she said at last. "I don't visit the Oak Trees to gain knowledge or see the future. But I do dream. And sometimes, when I dream, I see things. A few nights ago, I saw you."

She chewed her lip and watched him with an edge of caution, perhaps afraid to unnerve him. She most definitely *had* unnerved him but he tried hard not to show it.

"And what did you see of me?" he pressed.

"I saw that you would get away."

Viggo relaxed. "Then I hope your dream is prophetic." Of course, interesting as all this was, none of it really explained why she'd chosen to help him.

As if she'd read his thoughts, Violet shrugged in a helpless sort of gesture. "I didn't know what sort of person you were, whether you were a good man or not, but I know the soldiers here well enough to know what they would do if they caught you. I didn't want to be responsible for that."

"Tell me more about the soldiers."

She did so freely, telling him things about their arrival in Dairefast the previous year and her unexpected friendship with Donovan's niece. No spy could have found himself in more welcome company, for her tongue knew little caution. None of what she told him was of any real importance to his mission, but he listened with willing interest until she ran out of things to say.

"And have you decided yet?" he asked at last, when a silence had fallen between them.

"Decided?"

"You said you didn't know if I was a good man or not. Is everyone so clear-cut to you?"

He expected her to say yes. In his experience, war had a way of making people see good and bad, right and wrong, as entirely straightforward; anyone on their side was good, while anyone on the opposite side was – by default – bad. Violet's simple answer seemed, at first, to support this sentiment.

"Oh yes." But of course, as he'd already learned, she was anything but simple. "But I also believe good people can do bad things in weakness; just as bad people can do good things for those they love. It's only the very worst of situations that prove definitely if we are good or bad. I sometimes think maybe that's why bad things happen...to help us discover our truest selves." She tilted her head to one side. "What do you think?"

"Excuse me."

Viggo rose abruptly. In three long strides he was out of the cottage, leaving Violet to stare startled after him. He was surprised to see the sun already well on its way toward the horizon. How long had they been talking? Too long.

He rubbed a hand over his eyes as if this would help clear his head. Too much philosophy when he should have been planning his escape. There was something about the great emotion in that woman's eyes that drew him in and held him; but it was the passing thought that her eyes were every bit as deep and lovely as the words tumbling out of her mouth that had spooked him into running away from her. He had not meant to think it. He *shouldn't* have thought it. He should have been resting, readying himself to leave.

Frustrated with himself, Viggo pushed through the softly swaying branches of the willow trees to stand by the river. It rushed by happily, unbothered by his irritation.

Another hour, he thought, maybe two, and he would risk it. There was no use waiting any longer than that. The long shadows that lay over the land at twilight would help aid his escape. He remembered the map clearly. First, he would cross the river. Then he would go up into the foothills. That way he could bypass Ellaway and his men altogether and be in Dionne by morning.

He returned to the cottage. Violet emerged from the back room at the sound of him dropping coins onto her table. Her surprise was evident.

"What is that for?"

"For your trouble. And whatever supplies you can give me."

He intended to leave here owing her nothing.

"You're leaving *now?*"

Gywie heard her startled exclamation and came racing out of the other room, already protesting although she didn't yet know exactly what she was upset about. True came right on her heels. But for the first time that Viggo had seen, Violet was forceful with them. She grabbed Gywie's shoulders and turned the little girl firmly about, ordering her sternly back into the other room. Gywie pouted in his direction but finally stomped away. True was far better behaved and needed nothing more than a soft nudge from his mother to follow.

"Not yet," he answered when they were alone. "In a couple of hours."

"You'll never make it out of here! Ellaway-"

"Won't be a problem," he interrupted. "It has to be tonight. Something happened, at your husband's house. I can't stay any longer."

Should he tell her? He had no desire to cause her any pain but from the resigned expression on her face she had guessed anyway. He had better tell her, he thought regretfully, so that someone knew to look in the root cellar after he was gone. Of course, there would be trouble once the golden-haired woman got out and told everyone he was not Aeron; but perhaps Violet could pretend she'd had no choice, making it out as if he'd coerced her into the deception. Anyway, it was better to say something and be free from any further responsibility. Whether or not Violet chose to liberate her husband's mistress would be her own business.

"There was a woman waiting."

"I see." As expected, she wasn't surprised. Her eyes flickered over him, perhaps noticing the absence of her husband's cloak. If she wondered about it, she didn't ask; it was less important to her than this matter of a woman. "The one who looks like the sun fell in love with an hourglass?"

The description struck Viggo as being one of the oddest things he'd ever heard someone say out loud, yet strangely, it was also one of the most accurate. The fact that she had to clarify told him there was more than one woman whose involvement with her husband she had to keep track of.

"Something like that," he agreed vaguely. "You'll find her in the root cellar."

Was he mistaken, or was that twitch at the corner of her mouth a repressed smile?

"How do you plan to get past the soldiers?"

"The mountains."

It was a simple enough statement, yet it earned a surprisingly heated response.

"No! You can't. That would be even more dangerous!"

He raised one eyebrow. "More dangerous than being caught by Ellaway?"

"Yes," she insisted stubbornly. "You'll never make it going through the mountains, not even if you keep to the foothills. You'd be better off turning back the way you came than trying to go through there."

Back the way he'd came lay Camelot, where he could hardly dare to show his face again so soon. Beyond that were Arthur's soldiers, searching for and expecting him. It was on to Lin Harbour or nothing.

Her outright dismissal of his ability to get through the mountains irritated him. What did she know about him anyway? He did not believe in the impossible; he never had. The more people said a thing could not be done, the more he wanted to do it. It was this spark of rebellion which had gotten him into Camelot despite its rumored impenetrability, and he was not going to let his journey end here because Violet did not think he could handle a few hills.

"I'm going," he assured her.

She swept forward in a surge of anger, fired up with a frustration she would never get to express. The door blew open, startling them both out of their argument. A man filled the doorway, panting from some exertion. Viggo cursed aloud when he saw both Donovan and Ellaway behind him, peering into the cottage with eager, greedy expressions. He was instantly tense, ready to flee...but there was nowhere to go. The window was too small for a quick escape and he had seen no other door.

Viggo's gaze slipped beyond Donovan and Ellaway to their waiting men. There were too many of them out there. Any attempt to fight his way free would only amuse the soldiers and end in his humiliation.

So, that was it then. The woman in the root cellar had got out and told her story. Or they had discovered the truth by some other means. Either way, it was over. He glared restlessly at the man who stood blocking the door. Donovan and Ellaway, for all their zeal, seemed to be waiting on him, while he in turn stood like a statue and stared at Violet.

She was staring back at him with relief and horror in equal measure.

"Aeron?"

Chapter 5

Violet's startled cry ruined any chance Viggo might have had to go on impersonating Aeron Demeray. Not that the man in the doorway would have let him.

He was somehow not what Viggo expected. The meticulous records and the neat hand that wrote them had unconsciously left Viggo imagining a scholarly man, unsuited to physical labor. He should have known better than to make such assumptions. Though Aeron was not especially tall, he was lean and solid in the kind of way that Viggo would have thought twice before starting a fight with him. His face, probably once reasonably handsome, was gaunt with privation and bore heavy circles beneath furious eyes. It was the eyes that looked dangerous; they were dark and unreasoning – a watery brown like those of an animal – making the man behind them appear every bit as unpredictable.

Even as Viggo made these silent observations about the newcomer, his mind continued to race for some means of escape. Unable to come up with anything brilliant, he was almost relieved when Ellaway finally lost patience with the man in the doorway.

"Well Sir, is that your wife?"

The spell of silence lifted and Violet took a tentative step toward her husband. He made no move to welcome her.

"She was, when I left." His surly tone held open no room for explanation or forgiveness. Still in a partial daze, Violet eyed her husband top to bottom.

"You are well," she said finally, sounding genuinely gratified. Her honest satisfaction at his wellbeing was a far cry from the tender reception she had heaped upon her 'husband' only the night before. Viggo remembered suddenly that strange, inexplicable jab of envy he'd felt for the stranger whose homecoming was so desired and to be so warmly celebrated. There was nothing to envy here. Any fire which may have once burned between Violet and her husband had long since been snuffed out, leaving nothing more than cool familiarity.

"So are you," Aeron replied at length, and for the first time Viggo's presence in the room was acknowledged. "But a Saxon?" There was such overwhelming malice simmering in that watery gaze when it swung his way; Viggo braced himself, expecting Aeron's fist to swing next. The man went after Violet instead, catching her by the arms and shaking so hard Viggo could feel his own teeth rattling.

The moment Aeron stepped out of their way the two Captains burst into the cottage, circling around Viggo with their underlings pressing in for a closer look at the supposed spy.

"About average," Ellaway declared decisively, his grin hawkish as he took up a position on Viggo's right.

"Fairly flaxen," Donovan agreed, moving to Viggo's left. Both men looked him over as though he were the prized cabbage at a harvest festival.

"The timing is perfect," Ellaway concluded. "And to think he'd likely have slipped past you, if this gentleman had not reached us in time with his story!"

If the comment was meant as a barb, Donovan did not take it as such. The two Captains beamed at each other; all rivalry forgotten in their glee at a shared success. Let them enjoy it while it lasted, Viggo thought uncharitably. It would bring him a great deal of pleasure – when he was safely away on a boat heading north – to imagine the two men in a desperate race to blame one another for his escape.

The entire experience would have been more validating if they had at least been in a hurry to capture him. Instead, they carried on with self-congratulation; content to let his presence between them serve as the excuse to detail their every success. The more animated they became, the more Viggo fumed at having to simply stand between them, fighting the rising temptation to do something he would quickly regret. As much as he wanted to make a break for it, he knew he couldn't get away from them here. The sooner they hauled him off, the sooner he could start planning his escape.

"Didn't I say the woman couldn't be trusted?" Donovan demanded, still blathering on about himself and his role in the whole affair. When no answer was forthcoming, he paused to glance sternly at his men. Hasty mutters of agreement appeased him and he turned to clap Aeron on one sturdy shoulder, drawing the attentions of the quarreling couple.

"You should be happy, friend! I think it likely we have here, in your very home, the Saxon spy escaped from Camelot. There will be a reward for this! One you will share in, of course."

Had they caught up with him under any other circumstances, Viggo would have spoken up and vehemently denied the accusation, feigning innocence and twisting the matter around with clever lies. But even he couldn't imagine any plausible explanation for why he was here, masquerading as somebody's husband. Still, he wouldn't stoop to admitting they were right.

The best option was silence. Determined to say absolutely nothing to these men, Viggo looked past Donovan and tried to catch Violet's eye, hoping she would come to the same conclusion. As long as she said nothing in his defence, they might still believe she had been unwillingly coerced into playing his game – even if it had, in reality, been very much the other way around.

Unfortunately, her better nature overcame her good sense.

"Aeron, no," she muttered, grabbing his arm with the hand he was not crushing in his clenched fist. "It isn't like that at all. I can explain-"

Viggo flinched as Aeron's free hand cut off any explanations, sending Violet reeling into the bedroom doorway where she very nearly tripped over her own children. They clustered around and clung to her as she sank dazedly to her knees, pulling their small, frightened faces into her chest. When her gaze finally lifted, Viggo looked down at his boots, awash with guilt though it was not his doing. He wasn't sure which bothered him more: that her husband had hit her, or that she hadn't looked frightened when he did. How often did such a thing go on before one gave up on being afraid?

Guilt ignited into anger. He was angry at Violet for her misplaced valor. He was angry at himself too, for accepting her help in the first place. And he was angry, most of all, because he knew that even when he was safely away, he wouldn't be able to help worrying what would become of her on his account. What she had done was treason, a crime not easily pardoned in times of war.

"Deal with your woman later," Donovan urged, irritated that Aeron was wasting time upon his wayward wife when there was celebrating yet to be done.

"Go on then," Ellaway ordered, nodding Viggo toward the door. Nobody moved to force him, though perhaps they just assumed he would see their numbers and appreciate the swords hanging from their belts well enough not to attempt escape. They were wrong, but Viggo didn't want them to know it just yet. Swallowing his anger, he risked a final glance toward Violet and her children, wished he hadn't, and marched out the door with as much dignity as he could maintain.

After a brief discussion, two soldiers were ordered to stay behind and keep guard over the woman until the extent of her involvement could be discerned. This matter attended to, the remaining soldiers took up positions around the prisoner, marching him back into town with Aeron and the two Captains bringing up the rear.

Viggo matched the pace of his captors without prodding, his hands hanging visibly at his sides so as not to arouse suspicion while he took stock of the situation. Being that Dairefast was a small and presumably fairly quiet town – at least most of the time – it seemed unlikely to Viggo that the townsfolk possessed anything akin to a prison or dungeon where they could lock him up. Druids were not keen on such things anyway, so someone had told him once. It was possible they meant to take him to the Captain's tent, but the air of enthusiasm echoing in the voices of the three men behind him hinted otherwise. By tilting his head slightly to one side, Viggo managed to catch enough of the conversation to discern their intentions: they were headed for the tavern, where they meant to keep him overnight. Instinct told him that once they got him through the tavern door, his chances of escape would dwindle greatly.

He glanced about, considering his options. As a test, to see just how attentive and motivated the soldiers were, Viggo took a small, deliberate stumble toward one of them. The response was immediate and less than encouraging. The soldier he had encroached upon grabbed his arm, shoving him roughly back into his place. Commands were barked out from behind, and swords were drawn. The hand on his arm remained, a steady reminder that he was not to step out of line again.

Escape began to seem more distant.

As they entered the town proper, Viggo glanced sideways at Aeron's house, wondering if the golden-haired woman was still locked inside. Would anyone care if she was? He was not above using her as leverage if he needed to, though he wasn't at all sure if Aeron would care one wit about her whereabouts or safety.

They were approaching the tavern. Like most of the other buildings in town, it was already ablaze with cheery evening light. But unlike the other structures, which sat quiet and respectful, the tavern was alive and bustling with irreverence. Viggo could hear a cacophony of raucous voices making merry, as a man with a deep baritone belted out a lively tune. Feet pounded in dance. Even the washed-out sign hanging from the eaves seemed to be swaying in time to the music.

The hand on Viggo's arm pulled him to a sudden stop.

Donovan went on ahead, the boisterous clamour ceasing abruptly as he walked through the door. Viggo didn't know what was said but it must have been persuasive; less than a minute after the Captain went in, the townsfolk were coming out, suddenly having found it advisable to abandon their merrymaking in favour of turning in for an early night.

Watching them pour into the street, Viggo became aware of another sound, one so steady he had almost taken it for granted – the river. The river was rushing by just beyond the houses on the other side of the street. If he could jump into the river, they would lose him in the dawning twilight. He was certain he could swim across, get out somewhere on the other side, and make directly for the mountains. And how would they find him there, when he had seen on their official map that they were forbidden to follow?

There was no time for further consideration. Donovan was still inside and his men were distracted watching the townsfolk. This was his chance. Viggo lifted one leather boot and stomped down hard on the toes of the soldier closest to him, simultaneously jabbing his elbow into the gut of another. While their fellow soldiers turned in bewilderment to see what had made them howl, Viggo shoved his way between them and bolted into the midst of the departing crowd.

Trying his best to block out the shouts and screams that followed in his wake, Viggo focused on pouring speed into every pounding footfall as he ran between Aeron's house and the one beside it. His gaze fixed upon the swaying shadows of reeds dancing at the riverside. They were his goal; his finish line. Reach them, and he would be free.

Faster, he told himself. *Ignore the footsteps. They aren't gaining. Almost there. Faster!*

The moment he passed through the reeds Viggo launched himself wildly into the air, leaping for the water. He knew it would be cold, but he hadn't hesitated long enough to consider just how cold. River water filled his boots and cut through his clothes as though he weren't wearing any at all, shocking his mind as much as his body. It nearly enveloped him, chilling him right up to his neck...but somehow, no further than that.

Something was wrong. The water did not rush over his head or carry him away as he'd been expecting. One desperate thrash and Viggo realized someone had grabbed his coat from behind. That someone was kneeling on the bank, holding onto a fistful of brown leather to prevent the river from sweeping him to safety. In the dark, with water splashing into his eyes, Viggo couldn't see who he swung at, as he struggled to make whoever held him let go.

More footsteps caught up.

Out of the corner of his eye he saw the last rays of sunset glinting off drawn swords. The heart-hammering thrill of pending escape turned to outright panic. There was only one option left. Viggo began to squirm out of his coat.

Too late.

A hand caught him by the hair, eliciting an unintentional shout as strong fingers dug into his scalp. Another hand grabbed his arm, then his shoulder, and more until Viggo was hauled back out of the river; kicking and hitting and doing everything within his power to wound whoever came near him.

Damn whoever had caught his coat!

Catching his footing, Viggo spun about and came face to face with Aeron. The man no longer looked angry; he was grinning, wildly amused. Viggo tried to hit him too, but his arms were caught and pulled behind his back. The soldiers hustled him with greatest severity away from the river and into the tavern.

Empty tables were pushed up against dirty walls, a single chair left purposefully centered in the middle of the floor. Viggo was stripped down to his linen shirt and thrust into the chair, held in place by four eager soldiers while Ellaway gave instructions.

The Captain from Dionne was an intelligent man and this was obviously not the first time he'd dealt with a flighty prisoner. He avoided all the usual mistakes – such as ordering that his prisoner's hands be bound together, something all too easy to escape from – and instead directed that each of Viggo's arms be tied separately to either arm of the chair, wrist to elbow.

Effective, Viggo thought grimly, his anger ebbing as he realized it would no longer do him any good. He flexed his hands at the wrist and found them useless with his arms strapped down. When they moved on to binding his ankles, one to each front leg of the chair, he surrendered any lingering hope of escape.

They wouldn't kill him. Small comfort as that was, he knew they wouldn't risk losing out on a possible reward for his capture. His next chance at escape would come when they tried to return him to Camelot.

He surveyed the new surroundings. Only one civilian, other than Aeron, remained in the tavern. Viggo guessed he was the owner. Despite his being nearly twice Viggo's size in height and at least three times in width, he seemed flustered by the whole affair. Hands the size of bread loaves wrung together as he came forward with the hesitant suggestion that perhaps his furniture could be treated more gently. Looking around at the battered old tables and the many hundreds of scratches in the wooden floor – rivaled only by the many years' worth of grime – Viggo didn't think the big man need worry about anything the soldiers might do.

Donovan did not share the keeper's concerns either. "Get back behind your counter, sir."

Though the keeper physically dwarfed Donovan – and everyone else for that matter – he shrank back from the sharp tone of the command, scurrying away with mouse-like timidity behind the long wooden counter. He busied himself aimlessly with nervous, twittering movements and seemed greatly relieved when Ellaway gave him a job to do.

"Drinks, barkeep! Drinks for all my men! This is a night of celebration!"

A great cheer went up. Ellaway knew how to keep his men happy. For the next half an hour, Viggo was left to shiver ever more involuntarily as the men drank and celebrated his capture. It would serve them right, he thought miserably, if he caught a chill and died before they could return him to their King.

Aeron, he noticed offhandedly, indulged more than most. Just another one of his bad habits. Viggo was indulging in his own bad habit of snide thoughts when he noticed Ellaway making a careful search of his clothing.

"There's nothing here," the Captain announced abruptly.

Donovan, hearing him, shouted the men down into silence. "What do you mean there's nothing here?"

"I mean-"

Viggo grinned privately as Ellaway interrupted himself with a yelp. He yanked his snooping hand from the pocket of Viggo's coat like something inside of it had bitten him – which, in a way, it had. The culprit was a tiny shore crab, which they could all see dangling from a pinched finger when Ellaway held his hand up to look.

Viggo supposed he must have picked it up somewhere in his travels. He was surprised it was still alive, though not half as surprised as Ellaway.

The Captain shook the offending crustacean away, refusing to acknowledge the snickers his men were hiding behind their drinks. "I mean," he continued, trying again, "that there is nothing here. Nothing of *value*, anyway."

That last bit was added with a sneer toward the little crab, which had landed upon its back, tiny legs waving about with frantic, yet ultimately useless effort. The barkeep risked the ire of the Captain long enough to emerge from behind his counter and gather up the discarded crab, scurrying it to safety while muttering to himself that *it* had value.

"Have you searched everywhere?" Donovan demanded, choosing not to comment on Ellaway's odd debacle with the crab. Both he and Ellaway took turns searching and re-searching every pocket and seam of Viggo's coat and tunic. They lay his few possessions, one by one as they found them, upon a table, inspecting them also. Finding nothing, they ordered soldiers to search his person. Viggo's one attempt to protest the prying hands rummaging over his body earned him a sharp kick mid-shin which silenced him, albeit grudgingly.

"Where is it?" Ellaway demanded finally, taking up a stance before him with the brown coat clutched accusingly in his fist.

Viggo looked up into the nobleman's face innocently. "Where is what?"

"Don't play games!" Donovan shouted.

Ellaway was not so easily ruffled by an uncooperative prisoner as he was by a crab. Having regained control of himself and the situation, he stared Viggo down with confidence. Getting what he wanted was only a matter of time, and time was a luxury someone like Ellaway could well afford. Handing the coat back to Donovan, he leaned forward to bring his steely gaze even with Viggo's.

"Where is the thing you stole?"

Viggo no longer had to fake his innocence. "Whoever you may think I am, I've stolen nothing."

Ellaway's reply was not angry, only measured and practical. Still, it left Viggo wincing and licking the taste of blood off his lip.

"Where is it?"

His second denial was met with much the same response as the first and Viggo decided this might be a good time to retreat behind his original policy of silence. If they intended to use him for sport, they would do so, no matter what he said. And since he honestly had not stolen anything which he could produce to satisfy them, there was nothing more he could say which would not soon become pointless and repetitive.

Aeron came stumbling up from the table where he'd been communing with some cheap spirit and stood thoughtfully next to Ellaway. "Just what did he steal?"

Ellaway glanced over at Donovan and the look they shared could only be described as one of helpless embarrassment. Viggo nearly laughed. So, the King had not given a detailed description of him *or* his crime. This explained why they thought he had taken something; they did not understand he had stolen a secret, a simple yet valuable fact which they would never unearth by searching his person or possessions.

"The messenger wasn't clear," Donovan finally admitted, when Ell-away pursed thin lips and said nothing. "We were told something was taken directly from the King. There are whispers the King is planning a final push north that will reclaim the last of the stolen lands and end this thing for good. Perhaps those plans were stolen, or maybe a map with the positions of our troops…" His attention returned to the captive and he shrugged. "We need no longer guess; we'll soon find out."

"I don't think he'll be easy to persuade," Ellaway cautioned. Even though he stood wiping the smeared blood of a split lip off the back of his hand, his words heartened Viggo and rekindled his zeal for the game.

"You're not going to let them have all the fun, are you?" Viggo asked, leaning forward to look at Aeron. The man stiffened and glared, unable to grasp his meaning. "These two would never have caught on to me if not for you. Shouldn't this be your investigation? Why let them keep things from you?"

It wasn't easy getting through to a man whose sense was already swirling around the bottom of his mug, but Aeron got the gist of it. It didn't take much convincing for him to become suspicious of someone he already disliked. He glared at Donovan and snatched the brown coat, searching it for himself.

"You expect me to believe Camelot orders you to find something, without telling you what it is?"

Donovan stood straighter, squaring his shoulders with indignance. "If we knew what he stole," he replied hotly, "we would have told you."

Viggo leaned back cheerfully. The longer they argued among them-selves, the longer they went without beating him up.

Ellaway, seeing exactly what he was up to, spoiled his fun by intervening with a calm voice and sound logic. "You can see for yourself there is nothing on his person. Whatever it is, he's hidden it away somewhere. But not to worry, he'll tell us where eventually – they all do."

"Violet," Aeron spat, and Viggo stiffened, uncomfortable with this sudden change in direction. "He's left it with her."

To his relief, neither Ellaway nor Donovan looked especially persuaded by the suggestion, but the more cunning of the two men saw an excuse to be rid of the Druid nuisance for a time.

"You would be best suited to find out, my friend."

Aeron whirled for the door. Viggo didn't know why he shouted after him; he was in no position to protect himself, much less Violet. But Aeron was drunk. And though Viggo did not know how far his violence was prone to going, he knew from experience what could happen when drink fueled rage.

"I left nothing there! I came upon your home only by mistake!"

Aeron laughed deeply, nearly losing his balance as he teetered in the doorway. "You take me for a fool? She helped you," he slurred, pointing in accusation, "and she did it to spite me. You think I don't know my own wife?"

Viggo's anger flared, bellowed to life by Aeron's stupidity. It melted away the remaining chill from the river and he sat up straighter, eyes blazing. Violet's reasons may have been simple, but they'd been honest and well-intentioned, and he was outraged with Aeron for thinking otherwise. There was no way in hell he was going to let Aeron leave now, not when he would try drunkenly to get from his wife something she did not have.

"You don't even know her name!"

It was a guess, a gambit, based upon nothing more than a vague suspicion to which he'd been inclined when Violet first told him her name on the road. From the way Aeron straightened up and sobered instantly, Viggo knew the other man had – at some point – come to the same conclusion. Anger drained from puppy-dog eyes, leaving them lucid with genuine hurt.

"She told her name...to you?"

The depth of pain echoing in those words finally gave Viggo a better sense of the man. Aeron was not an angry man, he was an unhappy man, made miserable by a loss he could not cope with; and it was this inability to cope which compounded into anger. Unable to express this resentment as a scribe, he had run off to play soldier. But running from old wounds could not heal them. As so often happened with such people, Aeron had gone looking to take out his despair on others. Unsatisfied, he was lashing out at whomever was near enough to take the brunt of his failure.

Well, Viggo didn't intend to let him take it out any further on his wife and children, not so long as there was still something he could do about it. Pasting a wicked grin on his face, he shot Aeron the most insolent smirk he could manage. "You'd be amazed what you can learn about a woman just by sticking around for a couple of days."

Aeron flew into a rage. No one moved to stop him from raining down blind anger upon the captured spy in a series of poorly aimed blows.

Viggo pressed his lips together and kept his jaw clenched, withholding any satisfaction the other man might have gained from his grunts or groans. It did not stop the pain. He attempted to console himself with

"You don't even know her name!"

nobility: reasoning it was better him than her. Perhaps he couldn't be angry with her for trying to protect him after all, not when his better nature seemed to have the same devastating effect as hers did.

It was only when Donovan finally joined in, that Viggo's mouth betrayed him, releasing more yelps and other disconcerting noises than he was proud of. By the time Ellaway began making helpful suggestions, Viggo welcomed unconsciousness and was only too grateful when it came to collect him.

Chapter 6

T HE FIRST THING VIGGO became aware of when consciousness returned, was how much he wished it hadn't. He had no desire to try opening his eyes, and really, why should he? He could hear no voices, sense no movement; there was nothing to indicate any imminent threat.

He didn't know where he was or why he was alone and for a while it didn't matter, he was content simply to languish. It took some time of listening to the silence before he began to wonder what it meant. Had they left him unguarded? That didn't seem to make sense, and yet....all was still. Curiosity eventually won him over and he pried open swollen eyelids, noting with dismay that his vision on the left side was tinted a disturbing shade of auburn.

His first sight was of a lot of blood on the floor. For a moment, Viggo wondered where it had come from. Then he licked dry blood off his lips and remembered. Right. The movement of his tongue swirled heavy saliva around his dry mouth and he turned his head aside, spitting to rid himself of the foul taste. His stomach heaved with the sudden movement and he felt that soon there might be more than his blood and spit on the floor.

It took many minutes of sitting perfectly still with his eyes pressed shut for the nausea to subside. He never even heard the girl come in. It actually startled him, when he opened his eyes and saw her kneeling beside him. He recognized her as Donovan's niece but his bleary mind refused to produce her name. Viggo expected he would come across many such holes in his memory over the next few days.

The second thing that startled him was his inability to feel anything as she worked to cut his left arm free, not even the straining of ropes against his sleeve. After a moment of careful consideration, he realized he couldn't feel his other arm either. Were they just numb from being bound, or was something broken? Considering how the rest of him felt, it was probably just as well he couldn't feel it either way.

It wasn't until the girl finished cutting both arms free and had started on the ropes around his ankles, that he was startled yet again by a third and final revelation. The girl was helping him. He stared blankly at her, not knowing why.

"Come on, hurry lass," a deep voice behind him urged. "We don't have all bloody evenin'. Bring him over, get him warm."

"I don't think he can move. You'd better come get him."

The giant barkeep entered Viggo's field of vision. With one arm he scooped Viggo up like someone might a sack of flour, hefting him onto his shoulder and carrying him behind the bar. With his vision swaying, Viggo could barely make out the small doorway through which the keeper ducked to pass, bringing them into some kind of small living space beyond. Viggo was dumped into a chair near the hearth where the warmth of a crackling fire could reach him. He made no attempt at either protest or thanks – he was too busy trying to keep his stomach contents, meager though they were, from making an unwelcome appearance.

"Here lad, easy now! Take a wee smidge."

A wooden goblet was pressed to his lips and Viggo took a careful sip, gagging on the strong liquor and promptly vomiting. Though the act was unpleasant, he felt distinctly better when it was over.

He started to assess the damage, slowly rolling each shoulder as feeling began to return. The most important discovery was that his legs, although bruised in a couple places, were otherwise fine, which meant he'd be able to walk; and as long as he could walk, escape was still possible. Nothing else had fared quite so well. His stomach felt like it had been knocked over a few inches and the rest of his insides rearranged completely. As for his ribs... no, he refused to even think about his ribs right now. And he didn't need to see his face to know it wouldn't be a pretty sight for a while. But he could travel, and that was all that mattered.

The big man mopped up his mess. When he was done, he pulled over a chair and sat down across from Viggo, watching him intently. The Captain's niece came to his side, the top of her head barely even with his shoulder.

"Care to try again? When it don't make ye sick, it revives ye!"

The goblet was held out, this time as an offering. Figuring he had nothing left to lose, Viggo accepted it, gulping down the last of its contents before he could think too long on what they might be. The big man was right about it reviving him. His head began to clear, and immediately he began looking around for that which, so far, had been oddly absent.

The barkeep guessed at his thoughts.

"You'll be safe for a few minutes, lad."

A finger as thick around as a bread roll pointed across the room, guiding Viggo's eyes to the far corner where four soldiers lay heaped together, fast asleep. The giant grinned widely, startling Viggo with his lack of teeth.

"They was so busy drinkin' it down they didn't think about what I was given 'em!" He chuckled pleasantly to himself and held out a hand for Viggo to shake, mimicking the manners of the Britons. "Camlin, if ye please!"

Viggo stared dumbly at the hand larger than his head. It fell away without offense.

"Or even if ye don't," the barkeep added with a wink. He poured ruby liquid from a bottle into Viggo's empty goblet and Viggo couldn't help but notice there was nothing twittering or nervous about the man's movements now; all of that must have been a show, put on for the benefit of the two Captains. Again, he wondered what had become of Ellaway and Donovan.

Taking a cautious sip of this new offering, Viggo found to his relief that it was gentler than the last, slipping comfortably down his throat to pool warmly in his stomach. "O-others?" he coughed, trying to clear his throat.

"Aeron right passed out not long after ye did, and it took them fancy crests some time and effort before they could rouse him enough to go and interview the missus."

Viggo started. "She...s-she..." He couldn't formulate words for the anxious thoughts bouncing off the corners of his mind.

"Don't go gettin' excited, lad. Ye wore Aeron right out, ye did. I doubt he did any worse than goin' home and passin' flat out again. As to them fancy crests, ye can be sure Violet will keep 'em busy as long as she can."

This surprised him. He cleared his throat yet again and finally managed to utter a coherent sentence. "Violet knows you're helping me?" His voice was so thick and gritty it was almost unrecognisable to his ear.

The big man laughed. "Knows? It's not so much knowin', as it is expectin'. That lass is goin' through life on the notion that everyone will do as she's expectin' they ought to, and so I suppose in that way ye could be sayin' – she knows."

Viggo tried, and failed, to understand. "Why?" There was no possible way he could be worth the trouble – not to Violet, them, or anyone else.

Camlin laughed heartily and slapped a massive hand across his knee as though he'd just heard the most wonderful joke. "Don't flatter yerself, lad. Ye're just one more in a long line of 'em."

"What?"

"Birds, mostly. A cat or two... Oh yes, there was a rabbit once." When Viggo remained confused, Camlin made it as plain as he could. "Strays, lad! Strays! She can't help herself. Even that little lass of hers ain't her own. Just another lost soul in need of luv." He guffawed. "If ye asked me, she should have stewed the rabbit and I'd just as soon see ye hung by yer Saxon neck."

Viggo wasn't quite sure how to take that, but Helena elbowed the big man in his arm and he laughed good-naturedly.

The 'little lass' Camlin mentioned had to be Gywie, and if this was true, then Violet wasn't Gywie's mother – not originally, anyhow. Which certainly explained some things.

"Point is, she'd never be forgivin' us if we didna help ye, and so here we are. Come now lass, ye'd best start."

Viggo watched with half-hearted interest as the girl lifted a small cloth satchel onto the nearby table, feeling oddly that he should recognize it from somewhere. The longer she dug around inside, the more familiar it seemed, until eventually he realized he'd seen it in passing, resting near the front door of Violet's home. He was fairly certain it was still there when he left, making him wonder how Donovan's niece had come into possession of it. Somehow, Helena must have found a way to see Violet. Viggo wanted to ask if she and the children were alright. Instead, he frowned doubtfully as the girl set clean bandages on the table, twisting the lid off a small porcelain jar that looked to contain some sort of healer's potion. Without even explaining what it was, Helena wiped some of the creamy concoction from the jar onto a cloth and reached for his face.

Viggo recoiled before she could touch him.

The girl hesitated, glancing down at the cloth in puzzlement, trying to figure out why it had spooked him. "It's salve..." she explained uncertainly, then added, "...so there won't be infection."

He knew what salve was for, but instinct was a difficult thing to fight. He did not like sitting here feeling vulnerable while someone else tended to him. He would have preferred to be left alone to tend himself.

Helena and Camlin exchanged looks of concern, wondering what they would do if he refused their help. Viggo knew the sooner he relented, the sooner he would get out of here, so he took another fortifying swig of whatever the barkeep had poured him and nodded his consent.

"You know what you're doing?" he asked, making vague conversation as Helena began dabbing the salve carefully onto his temple. At least it was getting easier to speak.

"I have a pretty good idea. Violet's been teaching me."

Camlin did not seem capable of being left out of a conversation for long. "Is it true what ye said there, lad?"

"Is what true?" Viggo winced when the salve stung an open cut below his jaw, resisting the powerful urge to pull away once again.

"What ye said about her name?"

Viggo forced a cautious smile onto one corner of his mouth and shrugged the shoulder which hurt the least. "I have no idea. I just wanted to make him mad enough to stay."

Camlin roared with such unrestrained glee that Viggo was surprised the man did not fall out of his chair and go rolling across the floor. At least somebody was maintaining a good sense of humor about all this.

"That ye did, lad!" he gasped out finally. "That ye did!" And he continued to howl with mirth until Helena finished bandaging up some shoulder wound which Viggo preferred not to look at.

In an attempt to distract himself from Helena's work, Viggo threw out the first question he could think of to keep the big man talking. "The way Violet spoke, I didn't think she had friends here?"

"Oh, she hasn't," Camlin confirmed, wiping away a tear from underneath one eye. "Exceptin' for us. People here liked her well enough until she got sick with them babies."

Viggo yelped as Helena's hand slipped, bumping his shoulder where she'd just finished bandaging it. When he looked up to see why, her jaw was quivering.

"Don't," she hissed, her eyes flashing with fury.

Viggo shifted uncomfortably away. Whatever story Camlin was alluding to, he had no desire to hear it if Helena thought it was too private to tell. But there was no stemming the flood of words gathering in the giant's mouth.

"Leave it alone, lass. I'll not tell him any more than what everyone else already knows."

Helena threw the cloth down onto the table and turned away with a scowl. Viggo's coat and tunic had been hung from pegs over the fireplace and she began pulling them down, making a big deal out of a small chore just to keep herself busy. Camlin ignored her and leaned back in his chair, folding large hands over ample girth, greatly pleased to have acquired someone new to talk to.

"As I was sayin' before we was interrupted, she got terrible ill with them babies. The women who went to help her came back sayin' they'd seen somethin' unholy. There was a lot of talk and tales after that. Most of the women got to thinkin' she was some kind of fairy folk and that she was harborin' a changeling. Started keepin' their own children away." He shot Helena a toothless grin. "I thought it was all a great deal of tosh – still do. But most of the men went along with their wives. Thankfully I've not got one of those to persuade me to such foolishness. I find womenfolk far too prone to hysterics, don't you?"

Helena dumped the clothes on the floor and stormed out of the room.

Something about Camlin's story did not quite add up in Viggo's mind, but he hadn't the wherewithal to figure out why. Nor did it matter. He'd soon be gone, just one more rescued stray, never to see any of them again. Viggo finished the last of his drink and stood, pleased to find himself sore, but steady. It would be best if he didn't overstay his welcome.

His clothes were stiff from the impromptu soaking but at least they were dry and Viggo found some comfort in having them back on his body. Stuffing his hands into the pockets of his coat, he allowed himself a moment to appreciate having it; it had accompanied him on his travels for as long as he could remember and he was glad not to have lost it in the river. He was only sorry the rummaging Captains had emptied his pockets of all useful possessions.

The barkeep cleared his throat uncomfortably. "There's one more thing I think ye ought to know, lad."

"Yes?"

"It wasn't just for Violet's sake that I made up me mind to help ye. I like her well enough, but not enough to risk me own neck. It was a matter of conscience." He was subdued, and without his loud and cheery demeanor he seemed half the size. "Truth is, it's easy to talk about wringin' a Saxon's neck; another thing to see that man's blood on your floor. I suppose I just haven't got the stomach for it."

Viggo's brow furrowed in confusion. At no time could he remember the big man lifting a hand against him. "What are you talking about?"

"I'm not proud of it, ye hear? How was I to know?"

"Know?"

"That you wasn't Aeron!"

Confusion gave way to complete and utter bafflement, but Camlin was rambling on again and there was no stopping him long enough to ask any more questions.

"Aeron came in last night lookin' for his usual cask of ale and wantin' whatever news there was to be had. Of course, I had heard along with everyone else that he'd arrived earlier in the day. Being as he was always one of my steady regulars, I commented on how surprisin' it was he hadn't come sooner."

The man wrung his hands together, briefly uncomfortable.

"Soon as he started sayin' he'd only just arrived, I knew somethin' was amiss. I asked if he'd not been down with his family to visit the Captain that very mornin'? When he jumped up and blazed on out of here, I knew there must be some kind of trouble abrewin'."

"He ran right down to my uncle," Helena added quietly from where she stood in the doorway. Her arms were crossed guardedly and she eyed Viggo with quiet discomfort, refusing to look Camlin's way at all. "Nobody believed him, not at first, but as he told them about the fighting and how he was nearly killed in some fierce battle along the northern front, they realized he had to be who he said he was – which was when they knew you must be an imposter. I followed them to see what would happen, and hid until after you left."

Helena paused to chew her lip. She was looking him over like there was something about him she was trying desperately to understand, but could not.

"I wasn't able to talk with Violet," she continued, "because of the soldiers at the door. But I snuck up below the window and got her attention to see if she was alright. All she did was pass me her bag of medicines and wave me after you."

Viggo felt the inklings of a half-hearted smile rising onto his mouth but the look on Helena's face prevented it from taking shape. She blamed him for what had happened. Viggo pressed his lips together and nodded to show appreciation, though even this somehow seemed wrong.

"Here, lad, with my apologies." Camlin held out two small parcels of food and a flask of water. Viggo pocketed them with thanks. But the giant wasn't done. He also pulled Viggo's money bag from the pocket of his shirt, setting it on the table along with all the other possessions he'd rescued. Viggo stood and stuffed his things back in his pockets where they belonged. After a moment of consideration he pocketed the jar of salve also, feeling he might be needing it.

"Will you be wantin' yer little friend back?"

Camlin held up a clear jug. Inside, the tiny shore crab was snipping bits off a large chunk of some root vegetable, consuming each one in turn. Viggo's smile finally made a genuine appearance.

"I think he'll be happier with you."

Camlin nodded heartily and set the jug back on the table, beaming proudly at his new companion.

From the far corner of the room came a soft muttering as one of the soldiers tossed about in his sleep. Camlin rose, asserting that the men would not wake for a long while yet. All the same, he nudged Viggo towards the doorway.

"Don't you worry about a thing, lad. When them two fancy crests return, they'll find their men sleepin' sound, and me sittin' on the floor next to a cookin' pot, rubbing me head and mumblin' nonsense. It'll be quite the escape they'll be thinkin' ye pulled off!" His face was alight with such genuine glee at the scheme that Viggo gave a shallow chuckle, regretting it when every bone and muscle in his chest ached.

He liked Camlin.

"I'm sorry about all this," Viggo muttered, ducking through the doorway and skirting uncomfortably around the scarlet mess he'd left in the middle of the tavern floor.

"Don't be, lad. Gives me an excuse to clean me floors!" He grinned at his great joke and Viggo resisted the urge to chuckle again, settling instead for a wan smile.

Helena pulled open the front door and Viggo avoided making eye contact as he stepped up beside her, wincing when the cold night air stung the open cuts on his face. Though he was more than ready to leave, he found himself hesitating, unable to go beyond the threshold. His gaze slid up the empty street and lingered. Somewhere up there, Violet was keeping Donovan and Ellaway busy so he could escape. But what about later, when Aeron woke up and remembered?

"What will he do to her?" he asked softly.

A large hand settled gently upon his shoulder. "Nothin' worse than he's already done, ye can be sure of that."

It wasn't much of an encouragement.

Viggo looked back at Camlin and Helena; one with eyes full of shame, the other brimming with unvented anger. All at once, Viggo knew what was missing from Camlin's story. If Gywie didn't belong to Violet, then Violet had only one child of her own; yet Camlin had referred to her *babies*, as though there had been two...

"Tell me," he blurted, regretting the question as soon as it left his mouth.

Helena stared at him with disbelief, completely exasperated. "You can go, isn't that enough for you?"

But Camlin understood. "Ye wasn't here lass, ye didna see. He brought the rage of Aeron Demeray down upon his self for the sake of a woman he barely knows. I'd say he's entitled to knowin' why."

"Oh, alright, fine. You want to know?" the girl demanded. This time it was Camlin who tried to calm her, and she who would not be stopped. "I'll tell you. Why shouldn't you know? Everyone else does, and they couldn't wait to tell me when I arrived. You want to know why I hate him? Because he's a greedy, selfish pig. Because Violet was hardly five months along with his babies when he...when he..." The words stuck in her throat and choked out her breath, leaving her lips quivering over empty space.

Camlin pulled Helena close as tears spilled down her cheeks, wrapping her up in an embrace so large she almost vanished. "There, there lass." His face was uncharacteristically somber as he glanced back at Viggo.

"What she be tryin' to say is that Aeron had his wee indulgences. After his first wife died...well, a man has to cope, ye understand. But he couldn't quite be rid of them, even after he bought Violet from them traders and married her." The giant was far away now, talking his way through a memory. "It was the night of the solstice. Aeron came back right cheerful from his visit to the Oaks, sayin' we was all set to have a profitable year. He drank a round with everyone here and went stumblin' off with a mangey bit of skirt. Then he made the fool choice of goin' home to his wife for more. Next day she be terribly ill and them babies came early. That little girl of hers didn't make it. The boy...well, he was just about the frailest thing you ever did see – still is – but he pulled through alright."

Viggo paled, regretting having asked the question far more than he possibly could have imagined.

"Now don't go way thinkin' I mean ill against him; I've known Aeron Demeray since he was a wee lad, and a mighty fine one at that. But it was a terrible thing he done, an unforgivable thing, and he's never forgiven himself either. He lost Violet the moment that babe drew her last breath. Never tried to win her back – knows he never could."

Helena clawed free of the giant's grasp, pushing him away as though his touch had become venomous. Her voice returned in force. "Don't you dare talk about what *he* lost! Not one person in this horrid little village stood by her after that. You Celts and your damn superstitions!"

Camlin raised one reproachful brow. "Now what would yer uncle be sayin' to language like that?"

"Damn my uncle!"

He chuckled. "That's a good lass."

Viggo saw no humor in their exchange. He wanted to leave, to run away from this tavern and this town and forget he'd ever heard such a sickening story. Instead he stood with his feet rooted to the floor, his eyes fixed on the dark road which led up toward a cluster of willow trees and a small cottage where there ought to have been three children...

Helena's gentle touch upon his wrist made him jump.

"I'll go straight there and make sure they're okay. You need to go. Violet had enough problems without you coming along and making everything worse. You've caused nothing but trouble here so just...just go, and take your stupid stolen whatever-it-is with you."

He nodded, trying to swallow the lump in his throat though he may as well have been trying to swallow rocks. "Don't tell her what happened here," he pleaded.

Helena frowned. "That's the first thing she'll want to know. What am I supposed to tell her?"

Nothing seemed appropriate. Viggo could hardly think. Nothing he could possibly say seemed as though it would matter, except perhaps...

"Viggo," he said, before he could change his mind. Violet had asked for his name, and he'd told her teasingly to go on calling him Aeron. Now he couldn't stand to leave her thinking of him in that way. "Tell her my name is Viggo."

"Excuse me?"

But again, Camlin understood. "We'll tell her. Off you go now, lad. Safe journey to ye! And I hope ye never make it to wherever it is ye're goin'!"

Viggo scoffed but couldn't quite bring himself to match the giant's smile as he stepped out into the street, retracing the same path he'd taken earlier. This time he didn't rush, or even bother to hurry, as he plodded wearily toward the river; there was no one to stop him. No one to grab his coat and hold his head above water when he jumped into the river and the current swept him downstream. No one to help, either, when the cold water proved even more paralyzing than he remembered, and his injuries more severe than he'd realized. It took several tries before he finally caught hold of some tall grass and pulled himself gasping and shivering onto the far bank.

Sitting up and looking back, Viggo could see Dairefast reduced to a demure glow in the curve of the river. Closer was Ellaway's temporary camp. Watchmen kept lookout and fires burned brightly, but it all seemed so distant with the river between them. Viggo didn't even bother trying to conceal his movements as he climbed to his feet and began trudging alongside the river, moving as fast as he was able to try and regain a little warmth.

He wrung out his clothes as he went, slapping at his arms whenever they began to go numb again. His mind was made up to keep going until he reached the first upward slope of the land. Then he would seek out the nearest bit of shelter, whether it be trees or a boulder or anything else that would break the wind and provide some defence against the coming frost, which was already crystalizing in the air he breathed. If he thought he could do so without being seen, he'd build a fire.

It felt good to have a plan again, and even better being free to execute it.

Thanks to the warming effect of Camlin's brew, he didn't feel the cold quite so badly as before. If anything, the swim had given his aching body new motivation and offered his mind something productive to focus on; by concentrating on his need to be warm and dry he could block out everything else.

It worked – almost.

There was still a voice lingering softly around the edges of every thought, refusing to be silenced. The harder he tried to block out her song, the clearer her violet eyes became. Those stupid, unforgettable eyes. They had been so distant and sad when she sang, like maybe she'd glimpsed all of this already.

"If war should finally come our way,

If enemies surround me...
I'll travel to the salty spray,
Let ocean waters drown me."

The song repeated over and over until Viggo wanted to shout at her to get out of his head and leave him alone. Why couldn't he just let this go? Violet had said she dreamt of him getting away, and she'd been right. He was free of her now, and of her wretched little town. Soon he would be free of Britannia and its King altogether. All he had to do was reach Lin Harbour, and from there set sail upon the wide, open ocean.

Ocean waters...

He hoped Violet's poetry would not turn out to be as prophetic as her dreams.

Chapter 7

MORNING BROUGHT NEW STIFFNESS and a whole other kind of cold. The first sprinklings of winter had fallen and Viggo woke to find himself blanketed in snow. He groaned aloud at the sight of it, sparkling white and indifferent all around him, then sat up to brush it away. The movement made him aware of other things, like how tender his ribs felt. His stomach hurt too, though whether that was from abuse or hunger he couldn't yet be sure.

Upon further consideration, Viggo wished he had not brushed the snow away so thoughtlessly. His clothes were knitted with ice crystals where they had not fully dried, and without the insulating layer of snow, the wind sent the chill of them shivering across his skin. He began to move each bruised limb in turn, stretching against the aches and trying to find in himself the motivation to get moving again so that he might get warm.

Simultaneous to this physical taking of inventory, he also took a mental inventory of the previous night, as a means of making sure no further holes had formed in his memory. Everything seemed clear enough, right up until he had chosen his hiding place and dropped off for an hour or two of fitful sleep.

The foothills were not what Viggo had imagined. They were nothing like the gentle green hills he had seen laying demurely at the feet of other mountains. These 'hills' were more like cliffs. They jutted abruptly out of the ground, tapered off here and there to form narrow shelves of rock, then rose sharply once again. His brief attempt to traverse them the night before had been as treacherous as it was nerve-wracking. Every footstep loosened silt and pebbles which fell away in a shower of sound; each one sounding to his nervous ear like an avalanche that would, at any moment, alert the soldiers camped in the valley below.

Forced to accept that he would not make good progress in the dark, he retreated to the riverside where he soon located a clump of gorse. There was a stand of boulders within the mess of tangled thorns which he thought might provide added shelter. At the risk of a few extra scrapes – which seemed entirely negligible under the circumstances – he had crawled carefully beneath the brush and found a small, clear area where he could curl up next to the stones without fear of being seen across the river. Lighting a fire had still been a big risk, but since he doubted anyone was out searching for him yet, it was a risk he'd been willing to take. Now, with the chill of morning cutting through him, he was glad he had, if only to have warmed up and dried off a little before the snow started.

Not that everything about the cold was bad. It had brought down the swelling around his face and his eyesight was clear once again. These observations brightened him and brought him to task. By now, of course, the soldiers had discovered his escape and must be searching for him. It was time to get moving.

Viggo leaned his back to the rock and peered cautiously around it, seeking out the river through the twisted thorns. He saw no one. Lowering himself onto his stomach, he wiggled under the stiff vines, crawling out of the clump the same way he'd come in. When he was head and shoulders free of the gorse, he paused once more to look around.

A soldier stood directly across from him on the other bank.

Viggo had no idea how he'd missed him and the how didn't matter – it mattered only that he had. He didn't dare breathe lest the soldier see the steam rising upward. Keeping perfectly still, Viggo lowered his gaze to avoid the risk of making accidental eye-contact. The temptation to watch the hunter was the greatest weakness of the hidden. The eye was drawn to movement and it could easily overlook things, even obvious things, so long as they remained motionless; but eye-contact was impossible to miss and always a dead give-away.

Viggo waited for what seemed like forever. When he finally dared to risk an upward glance, the soldier had moved on. He walked slowly along the riverbank, staring across the water toward the sloping cliffs. It was a relief to know they weren't yet crossing the river to search for him, but Viggo didn't fool himself for a moment into thinking they wouldn't if he was spotted. He stayed exactly where he was until the soldier was called back to his encampment.

Beneath the snapping red pennants, Ellaway's camp was animated. Even from this distance, Viggo could hear the shouting and general ruckus. He imagined much the same commotion going on in Donovan's tents and the thought of it made him smile. He'd told himself he would enjoy the thought of the two men desperately trying to place blame for his escape – and he did. They would be racing now, separately of course, to see which one of them could track him down first.

Well, they were doomed to disappointment, both of them. Possibly also demotion, he thought, cheering himself with the idea.

Viggo wriggled free of the gorse and sprang to his feet. His ribs ached anew but he was beginning to feel that nothing was broken, only bruised. Spurred on by this positive development – and the worry that soldiers might soon return to search across the river – he skirted around the gorse, ready to get moving. The sight of paw prints brought him to a swift halt, momentarily overshadowing any threat posed by the Britons.

The prints were large, each one the size of his own hand. Viggo's gaze followed the tracks as they meandered along the river and went directly up to the gorse, where the wolf had stopped and stood for some time. Viggo shivered, not from cold, but from the realization that the wolf had known he was there. It had carried on eventually, continuing to follow the water. The snow was too fresh for the tracks to be very old.

To have continued along the river with a wolf about would have been foolish, and there was only one other alternative. Viggo took the cliff face with a running start, deciding not to worry this time about the dirt and stones giving way under his boots and hands. The moment the sharp incline tapered off, he dropped flat in the snow, shuffling around to face the river again. From here he could see down into Ellaway's camp and he waited with bated breath to see if his mad scramble had drawn notice.

Seconds gave way to minutes and no alarm was raised. It seemed the camp had finally come to some kind of order, with soldiers in full armor lined up just outside the tents. Viggo recognized Ellaway by his long red cape as the Captain strutted back and forth before his men, no doubt growling orders. Viggo strained his eyes for any sign of Donovan, or anyone else he might recognize, but saw neither.

Ellaway finished with his men and the long double line of them set off up the valley. Viggo watched for some time as they progressed, noting that every so often they left one man behind. It was a dragnet, he realized, laid out to catch him. Again, he was impressed by the Captain's cleverness. They might even have stood some chance of catching him that way, if he wasn't already across the river.

An erroneous thought struck him. How many soldiers remained in the camp? Would it be possible, he wondered, to sneak back over the river and steal some helpful provisions – such as a sword? His departure from Camelot had been too abrupt for procuring one. But with a wolf not far off – and wolves rarely travelled alone – it no longer seemed wise to be without a weapon of some sort.

A more sensible voice in his head told him the wolf was the very reason not to chance it. He picked out the tracks again and followed them as far as he could with his eyes. Though he saw nothing, he didn't let himself pretend it was gone. Even with a heavy sword he felt certain he could swim across the river again if he had to, but he didn't fancy the idea of getting to the riverbank and looking up to find the creature waiting for him. Nor did he have the desire to linger here any longer. The wolf could just as easily climb the cliff and double back to find him.

The first soldier in Ellaway's net was far enough away that Viggo didn't worry overmuch about being seen as he got back to his feet and continued straight up, surmounting another sharp incline, then a third. The air got colder as he went.

He had not forgotten Violet's warning about the mountains, even though there had never been a chance to hear the explanation. Whether she had been referring to the difficult terrain and wolves, or to some other threat he was not yet aware of, he didn't know. But either way it seemed prudent to heed her warning, at least to some extent. He decided to climb only as high as he could go without losing sight of the river. It would be his guide when he began moving westward again, to keep him from accidentally getting turned around or lost. Hopefully he could achieve just enough elevation to feel safe from the wolves and any watchful eyes.

By the time the uneven terrain became more solid beneath him, Viggo was beginning to think that maybe Violet had been over-eager in her warning. He smiled to himself, remembering what Camlin had said about women being prone to hysterics. Violet hadn't struck him as that sort of woman. But there was nothing here on the mountainside to raise such alarm. Wolves could be dangerous, that was true, and the going wasn't easy. But eventually the silt began to even out and cliff-like hills gave way to sturdy mountain slopes. They were grey and barren, and with the snow upon them they admittedly looked inhospitable. But they weren't frightening enough to think he'd be better off heading back to Camelot.

It was hard not to let himself think about those two children as he finally turned westward, and began trudging over hard stone where the wind had whipped the snow off into drifts. Though he didn't want to even consider it, death wasn't out of the realm of possibility where treason was concerned. Gywie and True didn't deserve to be without their mother.

He told himself firmly that it wouldn't come to that. Violet's consequences for helping him might be unpleasant, but Aeron wasn't likely – whatever Viggo might personally think of him – to allow Donovan or anyone else to kill the mother of his son. Anyway, they had him to chase, and since he'd never told Violet exactly where he was headed there was nothing left to be gained from her. Hopefully she would be forgotten in the mad scramble to figure out how he'd escaped and where he'd gone. At least they couldn't blame her for that.

When fatigue began to outweigh the desire for progress, Viggo stopped. It had begun to snow again but there was nowhere to take shelter. He cleared snow off a rock and sat down to admire the falling flakes. Although tempted to build a fire he dismissed the idea out of hand. He would need to go a great deal further before he took the time for any serious rest. His laborious upward climb had warmed him and shaken the ice from his clothes. As long as he maintained a steady pace, he would be alright until daylight began to fade.

It surprised him to see how far he'd come already. The river was a broad ribbon of blue below and the soldiers that stood periodically alongside were little vague figures of silver and red. Had he really gone so high? He'd have to be more attentive moving forward.

Viggo silently thanked the apologetic barkeep as he pulled one of the food pouches from his pocket and unwrapped a bit of cured meat and bread. It made for a satisfying breakfast. He didn't touch the flask of water; that was to be saved for an emergency. Instead he gathered up a handful of snow which he rubbed over his face. Not only did it make him feel cleaner, but it invigorated him and he was soon back on track, carefully checking his position along the river every few minutes. He scooped up small handfuls of snow as he went, popping them into his mouth. Despite the cold and his unfortunate delay, he was beginning to feel optimistic again. Another day, maybe two, and he would be back in Anglo-Saxon held lands. In less than a week he could be home.

The sun was long past the half-way mark in the sky before Viggo stopped to rest again. The many hours of exercise had tired him out but done him good. He'd stretched away all the stiffness from his muscles and though they still ached, they were not failing him. All the same it was a relief to sit down against a tree trunk and close his eyes for a minute.

These were the first trees he'd seen, he thought idly, and they were barren and bleached by the sun. How odd to have a mountain with hardly any trees. And now that he was thinking about it, there were other things missing too.

Viggo's eyes opened. He listened intently but heard only silence. For some reason he found himself remembering the night he darted across the open countryside toward Dairefast, thinking of how odd it had been to see animals grazing and hear songbirds singing out in the darkness. Now, in the daylight, the mountains were filled with eerie silence. Where had everything gone?

Viggo looked around slowly. Some animals might already have gone to ground for the winter, but not all. There should be squirrels in these trees, or mountain hares with their thick white coats coming in, or little birds flitting about for the last available berries. At very least, he should have heard their chirps and seen the occasional scratches or tracks in the snow. But he hadn't. The only sign of animal life he'd seen since waking were those wolf tracks. He wasn't sure what that meant, but it was beginning to unsettle him.

The hair on the back of Viggo's neck bristled and he scrambled to his feet, bracing one hand against the tree as he looked around. Something was watching him. Spinning about, Viggo peered wildly through the falling snow, looking for anything that stood out against the whiteness.

There was nothing. And yet he couldn't shake the sinister feeling crawling up and down his spine.

Something was definitely watching – something close.

Hooting from directly above nearly stopped Viggo's heart. He jumped and leapt backward a good many paces before he realized what had sent him scrambling. A snowy owl sat in the highest branches of the dead tree. Viggo would have laughed at himself if his heart hadn't been pounding so violently. At least he wasn't crazy.

The bird was magnificent, maybe only two feet in height with yellow eyes set in a mask of purest white; tiny black feathers mottling the breast and wings. Large, round eyes watched him closely. Another hoot echoed softly over the snow. As his heart slowed, Viggo managed a smile. There were animals here after all.

His smile turned to a frown. Owls were predators. But where was their prey? Why had all the prey been out at night, when owls and other predators preferred to hunt, rather than during the day when it was safer?

Unless it wasn't safer.

"Pretty bird!"

Viggo nearly jumped out of his skin. He whipped around to see large blue eyes beaming upward through the drifting snow, fixated on the owl. He blinked rapidly, sure he was seeing things. An apparition had appeared only a few feet away, an apparition that looked startlingly like little Gywie standing in the snow wearing only her faded pink dress and boots.

He moved slowly towards her. "Gywie?" he tried, expecting the illusion to vanish at any moment. A trick of the snow, perhaps? Or maybe this was just another side effect of Aeron's rage.

He froze when her gaze left the owl and met his. For a moment they just stood, staring at each other through the snowflakes. Surely, she wasn't a...a... but no, Viggo didn't believe in ghosts. He knelt cautiously and reached out to her, touching her sleeve. She was real enough.

"It's okay," he soothed, when her eyes widened and she backed away from him. His mind raced, wondering how she'd gotten here; wondering further how he was going to get her home. "Everything's okay. Just...just come here and we can look at the bird together." He felt that if he could just get her safely into his arms, they could sort the rest out somehow.

But her blue eyes were no longer focused on him. They stared upward, filled with sudden awe. Her little hand lifted and pointed at something over his head. *"Big bird!"*

"Big Bird."

Viggo heard the swooshing sound of air being displaced as something large landed behind him, sending a tremor through the ground. The owl's hooting trailed off into the distance. Much as he didn't want to, Viggo turned around.

He found himself staring into a pair of golden eyes. They hovered like twin moons above a great curved beak, hooked like an eagle's but exceptionally larger. Tiny blue feathers covered the bird-like face and extended down the length of the muscular body. Viggo had never seen a griffin before. Wings, each longer than a grown man, were suspended over the creature, ready for flight. His heart pounded in his ears again. Warm breath curled over his face; a blue tail flicked. Golden eyes slipped past him.

"Run," he whispered, drawing the creature's attention back to himself. It cocked its head curiously and continued to study him.

"Viggy?" The small voice was less awed now.

"Gywie, run!" he screamed, and turned to run after her.

He heard the sound of the wings again right before something slammed powerfully into his shoulders and sent him sprawling into the snow, the wind completely knocked out of him. Gywie squealed and tripped over her own heels, landing on her backside where she hollered even louder. Viggo wanted to shout at her to get up and go but couldn't find the breath. Great paws settled over his shoulders with talons extending, wrapping carefully around his arms.

Then they were airborne. The swiftness of their ascent caused Viggo to gasp in a lungful of frigid mountain air. He tried to watch Gywie as long as he could, but her cries were soon lost to the howling wind and eventually her pink dress vanished amid the snow.

Viggo didn't dare try to get free. The griffin flew him higher than he ever would have ventured, carrying him in minutes to the very top of the mountains. If he fell from this height, there would be little left of him other than a body, broken upon the rocks. There wasn't anything he could do except reach up with trembling hands to grab hold of the talons, hoping desperately that splitting him open upon the rocks wasn't exactly what the griffin had in mind.

Chapter 8

THE FIERCE COLDNESS OF the wind forced Viggo's eyes closed. He didn't see the cave until he was suddenly thrown free, rolling limb-over-limb across cold hard stone. By the time he came to a stop he was too weary with fear and adrenaline to bother moving. He lay where he'd landed, staring at the jagged ceiling of the cave. He might have been just as happy to stay there and let the griffin eat him except that somewhere, alone on the snowy mountain, there was a little girl barely dressed for the cold.

Driven by the memory of her frightened voice and wide eyes, Viggo summoned his remaining strength and sat up. The griffin filled the mouth of the cave, golden eyes watching him intently. Fear quivered through every nerve in his body as he braced for the inevitable attack, but the griffin merely stood there, staring. Eventually, trembling gave way to uncertainty. What was it waiting for? It was clearly positioned to prevent his escape, yet it made no move to hurt him.

His gaze strayed to take in his surroundings. He sucked in a breath, pressing his palms firmly against the cold stone to steady himself. There were bones. A *lot* of bones. They had been picked clean, gnawed extensively, and organized into neat piles, relative to size, around the edges of the cavern. If only he could have found some comfort in knowing he was destined to be dinner for a tidy predator.

Panic seized him and he scrambled to his feet in a burst of reckless energy, grabbing the nearest bone and brandishing it like a club. The griffin watched curiously as he waved it toward the bird-like face.

"You had better let me go!"

He could have sworn the creature looked amused. If it had possessed eyebrows, one of them would surely have been raised in a comical expression of indifference. Standing at least ten feet to his less-than-six, the creature saw nothing in him to fear. Viggo looked down from the pitying eyes to his improvised weapon. "Yeah..." he admitted slowly, "...that was kind of stupid." He tossed the bone aside, back onto the pile from where it had come.

"Are you going to eat me?" he asked, growing impatient with the suspense though he was by no means in a hurry to rush his demise.

He did not really expect the creature to answer, and so her nod surprised him. He took a second, more careful look at the blue-feathered face. This was no animal. There was thought behind those eyes, an intelligence far beyond any beast he had ever encountered.

"You can't." He wasn't sure it would listen to him, or even that it could understand, but he was willing to try talking his way out of this, if it were possible. Did it have a sense of humor? He tried smiling. "I wouldn't taste very good."

If it was possible for a beak to smile, it did. The griffin bowed its head in acknowledgment of his words and finally stepped towards him. Long, blue feathers swept the floor as it extended one curved wing around him, exerting surprisingly gentle force to steer him deeper into the cave. Viggo went along with it, both because he was curious and because he had no other choice.

Twenty yards later, the griffin stopped. Very little light from the cave mouth penetrated as deep as they'd come, and though Viggo was sure this posed no problem for the cat-eyed griffin, it left him in near blindness. Unexpectedly, the griffin opened its beak and let out a roar that shattered his nerves along with the silence. He fell to his knees, trembling not only from the sound but also from the immense heat of the flames blasting from the griffin's mouth. Never, in all the stories he'd heard, had Viggo been told of griffins breathing fire. Then again, he was beginning to suspect anyone who had actually met a griffin probably wasn't alive enough to tell the tale.

Fiery breath blew over hanging stalactites until the rock absorbed enough heat to glow with orange light, dim but sufficient. The griffin had produced lanterns. Viggo stared at her, struck with newfound admiration.

A soft purring sound came from her throat as Viggo climbed back to his feet. She was answered immediately by eager mewling. The lusty whimpers drew his attention to a nest of woven twigs beneath the glowing rocks, where tiny reflective eyes had appeared. He took a step closer and made out three kits, each of them big as a full-grown barn cat with wings tucked loosely at their sides.

"You're a mom," he whispered, and she beamed with the common pride of all mothers. Viggo tried to step closer but her wing curled tightly around him, warning that he should not. She did not trust him near her kits, he realized, and frowned. "Why did you show me?"

She tilted her head aside and brought her face right up to his, staring at him intently. Understanding dawned and made him nervous all over again. "You want me to know why you have to eat me?" he guessed, swallowing hard when she purred with pleasure at his kind suggestion. While Viggo appreciated the thoughtful gesture, he was going to have to disappoint her this time. "You can't," he repeated, earning her amusement once more. She turned heavily around in the confined space and began pushing him more forcefully back into the outer cavern.

"You don't understand," he explained, speaking rapidly before she decided their cozy little heart-to-heart was over. "I know you have to feed your kits; I understand that. They need you to survive, but right now I have a kit who needs *me* to survive." He pointed toward the cave mouth and the billowing snow beyond it. "Did you see the little one with me? I have to go back and take her home. Do you understand?"

The griffin stopped and sat back on her haunches to rest, slowly lowering herself to the floor. With one wing she kept him near and blocked him from the exit. Out of the corner of his eye, Viggo watched the snow fall and thought wistfully how great a distance so few feet could seem.

The griffin lowered her beak and looked apologetically into his eyes. She seemed to be saying: *I understand what you mean...but you understand I still have to eat you, right?*

Viggo shook his head, frustrated, wondering what else he could say or do. His hands came up automatically in a soothing gesture that he did not expect would do any good. Time was running out. Had this been a wild horse, he would easily have known what to do. But as it was, he did not know if he should be treating the griffin more like a dangerous animal or a dangerous person.

The griffin had no time for his patronizing gestures. Lifting a paw to his chest, she pushed him down onto his back with minimal effort. His hand landed in something sooty.

With a slight lifting of her paw, the griffin extended her talons, making plain to him what she intended to do. Then, ever so slowly, she closed her eyes. Viggo was confused. When she opened them and stared expectantly, he gave a helpless shake of his head.

"I don't understand."

The griffin gently touched the tips of her talons to his chest. Viggo sucked in his breath. This he understood. Again, the griffin gave an exaggerated blink, checking afterward to see if he got her meaning. All at once, he did. She wanted him to close his eyes.

His fist closed around ash instead. "I uh...I'm not sure I understand. Show me again?"

She was gracious enough to oblige. The moment her eyes opened Viggo flung a ready handful of old cinders into them. She screeched and he rolled aside, escaping out from under her paw a second before he would have been crushed by it. It took mere seconds to get on his feet and dart out of the cave, slipping and tumbling through the snow as he took off down the mountainside. His frantic haste knew no caution; the threat of a twisted ankle or broken arm paled in comparison to the threat of being eaten.

He risked one glance back over his shoulder and spied the griffin's blue form pressing her face desperately through the snowdrifts. Viggo knew it wouldn't take her long to clear her eyes and begin pursuit. Looking forward once more, he gasped and leaned backward, digging his fingers into the snow for purchase as he struggled to a frantic halt right before the edge of a steep embankment. Too steep, he thought, gazing down in a panic. Too steep to *climb* down, anyway. But with the snow to cushion him...

He threw himself down the embankment before he could think on it further, and went hurtling down the slippery slope far faster than he was comfortable with. His leg caught on something hard and he was sent tumbling, his sense of direction momentarily abandoning him as ground and sky switched places with alarming frequency. And then he was falling, dropping through dead air, the world still spinning dizzily around him.

The snow broke his fall and engulfed him. Fighting his first instinct to sit up and brush it away, Viggo held his breath and waited, listening for some noise to indicate the griffin's presence. Maybe it had lost sight of him. Maybe it wouldn't find him buried beneath the snow...

But Viggo knew that was a foolish hope. The snow wouldn't hide him. He'd seen foxes scent their prey beneath the snow long before they were near enough to pounce. The griffin would likely track him the same way. Reaching up, he brushed the snow from his face, instantly sorry to have been right.

The griffin was not pleased. Her eyes, still framed with soot, were bloodshot rather than golden. Breath curled like angry steam from slits in her beak. Her paw pressed down on his chest, crushing him deeper into the snow until he could feel solid rock at his back. There was no getting away this time. Every one of his ribs screamed in protest as she continued to lean her weight upon him, forcing the breath from his body until he could no longer draw air in.

"Don't hurt Viggy!"

THE ONCE AND FORGOTTEN THING

Fear gripped him tighter than the griffin ever could have.

The creature glanced up, looking off to his right for the owner of the bossy little voice. Viggo's mouth gaped as he struggled to gasp out a warning. He couldn't see Gywie, but a rock, flying over his head and bouncing harmlessly off the griffin's beak, told him she wasn't far off. The griffin hissed with annoyance and Viggo squirmed, doing everything within his power to claw his way out from under her giant paw. Talons extended in response, curling through his clothing and nicking into his chest. He couldn't even scream.

"I said, leave him 'lone!"

Another rock flew overhead. The desperation was nearly unbearable. Viggo wanted to yell at Gywie to stop, to let him go; he wanted to tell her everything would be okay if she just walked away and forgot everything that had happened here. Above him, the griffin snarled, hot orange flames gathering in her beak. All at once he was sorry to have escaped. If he'd just stayed in the cave and let the creature eat him, he would not have led it back to Gywie.

The arrow appeared like a Valkyrie – unexpected and miraculous. It pierced the griffin's cheek like a slap, knocking her aim away from Gywie. The griffin roared in pain and Viggo felt a blast of warm air as flames billowed overhead, striking harmlessly off to his left somewhere.

Alert now to some danger more threatening than the pebble-throwing girl, the griffin crouched low over her prey, her wings instinctively rising into a ready position. They made an easy target for the second arrow, which lodged neatly between blue feathers and elicited another fiery bellow toward the sky. The griffin took a wary step back, releasing him.

:ized the opportunity to scramble backward, pushing away with hands and heels until he came up against something solid. He didn't dare try to get up and run with the griffin watching. She spared him a warning glance – to be sure he hadn't escaped completely – and narrowed her eyes, searching out the source of the attack.

Viggo searched too. He soon spotted her above them on a snow-covered crag, an imposing cloaked figure holding a bow two-thirds her own height, another arrow already nocked and ready. Her hood might have hidden her face, but Viggo knew who she was – he'd have recognized that pale blue cloak anywhere.

"Leave them!" she called out, her voice muffled to softness by the snow.

A wailing cry of protest cut through the air as the griffin gazed longingly in his direction. She pawed the ground three times and looked upward, demanding an answer. In response, Violet drew back her bowstring, the gleaming silver arrowhead nearly touching the polished wooden bow. There was no way for her to miss.

The griffin snorted. Viggo tensed when she turned back to him with fury burning in her eyes as well as her growl. He had no doubt she would have killed him instantly out of spite if she thought she could get away without further injury. Still, he almost felt sorry for her as she lowered her face to his feet, pressing one paw down over the arrow protruding from her cheek in an attempt to pull it free. It snapped in half instead. The griffin snarled again, gnashing her beak over the half that remained lodged in her face.

It was clear she blamed the archer for this. The griffin lifted her massive head with deliberate slowness, hissing a low warning. Rather than try to fly with the other arrow still stuck in her wing, she turned to the sheer cliff from which Viggo had fallen. Her talons found easy purchase despite the snow and just like that, she was gone.

Viggo was filled with the strange surrealism that came of being alive when he had not expected to be.

"Gywie!"

He rolled over, climbing slowly to his knees so he could look around for that little voice from behind. Viggo spotted the blonde girl standing not far away with tiny fists full of pebbles. She threw them happily into the air with the departure of the griffin and clapped, unaware of how close a call it had been and how perilous their situation still was.

Violet slid down through the wet snow, her hood flying back from her face as she scrambled to reach Gywie. Falling to her knees, she tossed the bow and arrow aside, wrapping Gywie up first in a little faded-yellow cloak, and then in a smothering hug. Seeing them safe in one another's arms, Viggo began to relax.

True was here too, he realized, spotting the little boy on Violet's back. His skinny arms were fastened around her neck with steadfast determination, his dark eyes wide with obvious alarm. It wasn't the griffin which seemed to have frightened him so much as the snow. He kept pulling his feet away from it, desperately shaking off every flake that landed upon him. Later, when he wasn't overcoming a near-death encounter, Viggo would look back on the boy's aversion and be amused.

Violet was not amused; she was angry. She didn't snap or shout but the tightness of her lips and the flashing expression of her eyes were enough. She was glancing between him and the girl, and Viggo could not tell for sure which one of them she was mad at. "Did you...did you take her?" she asked finally, her voice barely a stiff whisper.

"No!" He was shocked by the question. "I didn't... no! I have no idea how she got here, I just turned around and – and there she was." He hardly knew how to explain it when he still didn't understand it himself.

Her furious violet gaze shifted back to Gywie. "You ran away? Gywie, you *know* better!"

Blue eyes flashed with equal vexation and one tiny boot stamped down in the snow. "I wanted an adventure too!"

Violet's pale face slowly drained of its remaining colour. "You wanted an adventure..." she breathed, repeating the words of Gywie's childish ignorance. Anger subsided, softening into confusion. "How did you find Viggo?"

"The whisper voices told me."

Gywie's response was so matter-of-fact that Viggo felt stupid for not knowing what she was talking about.

"You can hear them?" Violet asked, astounded.

"Uh-huh. Come on, True!" the girl screamed, already over her scare and imagining they were over theirs. Grabbing her brother by his pant leg, she did her best to drag him down beside her. "Let's have an adventure!"

True took one look at all the snow she was pulling him toward and wailed in fright, clutching tighter to the blue cloak and yanking his mother's hair in the process.

"Not here," Violet shushed, glancing about nervously as she stood and gathered up her bow and remaining arrow. She had no quiver, Viggo noted regretfully, and one arrow wasn't likely to be of much use if they encountered the griffin again. Her eyes lifted skyward, deepening her concern. "It'll be dark soon. The griffins don't hunt after dark, but we'll still need shelter. Follow me."

"Griffins?" he asked, picking his way carefully after her, no longer minding how she ordered him about. "You mean there are more?"

She glanced back over her shoulder. "The locals call this mountain range the Great Nyth. It means 'nest'. There are *a lot* more."

Viggo was humbled into silence. He followed in Violet's footprints as accurately as he could, afraid to step on something that would slip out from under his feet and injure him further. Gywie was not nearly so careful. They'd hardly been walking more than a minute when her feet flew out from under her and she tumbled into a snowdrift, bursting instantly into tears. Violet stopped and looked back. She didn't make the sound out loud, but he could hear the groan echoing in her expression. Since her arms were busy behind her back, supporting True's weight, Viggo knelt down beside Gywie.

"Come on," he invited, holding out his hand.

She rubbed a fist over her cheek and sniffled. "What?"

"Climb on my back, just like that." He tilted his head, indicating the way Violet carried True. Gywie brightened instantly and scrambled to her feet, nearly choking him as she wrapped surprisingly strong arms around his neck. Violet didn't say anything as he stood and adjusted the girl's weight, but there was relief hung upon the corners of her tense smile.

The extra weight didn't slow him down or aggravate his injuries as much as he expected. Or maybe, at this point, he was getting used to hurting everywhere and simply couldn't tell the difference anymore.

When the ground eventually flattened out and there was room enough, he pulled even with Violet, his mind swirling with all the questions he wanted to ask her. He wanted to know how on earth someone half his size had tracked him so accurately; and how Gywie had managed, furthermore, to catch up with him. He wanted to know what the whisper voices were, and why they knew where he was. He wanted to know too, as a minor matter of curiosity, why Violet seemed to know her way around forbidden mountains. But when he saw her wet cheeks, all the questions died upon his tongue.

This wasn't the time. He tried to imagine how she must have felt when she realized Gywie was missing. She wouldn't have wasted time on fear; instinct would have taken over and kept her level-headed enough to find her daughter. But that adrenaline was gone now, and all the fear she hadn't made time for earlier was weeping silently from her eyes.

"I told you not to come here," she said briskly. He couldn't tell any longer if she was mad or not; her voice was too muddled with emotion.

"You never told me why," he argued, attempting, childishly, to defend his actions.

"I never got the chance!" Large eyes, glistening with tears, swung sideways and caught his gaze with accusation. "Do you realize what you've done?"

"I'm guessing you'll probably tell me," he muttered.

"There is a Druid pact protecting the people who live along the Nyth. The griffins are bound not to leave their home, and humans are sworn not to enter. Each time the pact is broken, the other is allowed to retaliate to an equal degree. The moment you set foot on these mountains you gave one of them permission to leave."

"And now you've given it permission to hurt someone?" he guessed, following this logic. The way she bit her lip and looked away was all the confirmation he needed. He was sorry to see the unhappiness on her face and know she had not wanted to do what she'd done, but had done it anyway – because of him. Though this did not seem the right moment, he felt he should thank her for saving his life. It wasn't lost on him that she could have grabbed her daughter and fled, leaving his fate to the hungry griffin.

"There." She brought him back from his thoughts, lifting her hand to point out a small patch of darkness among the rocks. "We can spend the night there."

The dark spot turned out to be a cave much smaller than the griffin's cavern. The ceiling was low, too low for standing, forcing them to crawl in: first the children, then Violet, and finally him. At least it was a dry and felt safe, even if it was dark and uncomfortable.

Violet was doing her best to turn the whole thing into a game for the children. They cuddled against her, hanging onto her words as she regaled them with a pretend story about a troll cave full of gold and gemstones. Gywie's eyes roamed the cave walls, greedily searching for signs of treasure. Was this all part of having an adventure, she kept asking? Violet assured her repeatedly that it was.

From somewhere beneath her cloak, Violet produced food for the children. When they both had mouthfuls of bread, Viggo decided to venture one of the questions nagging at the back of his mind.

"What did she mean by saying she wanted an adventure *too*?"

Violet caught a strand of her hair and spun it tersely around her finger. "I think that might have been my fault," she admitted sheepishly.

"Helena came and announced to everyone that you'd escaped. After the soldiers ran off, she gave us your message."

With his eyes adjusted to the dim light, Viggo could just make out her grateful smile across the gloom. He could also see the bruise that had formed high on her cheek from Aeron's earlier rebuke and it caused him to look away, hiding his scowl from her.

"But Gywie...she heard what Helena said and kept asking where you'd gone. I didn't want to say I thought you'd be going into the mountains, because she knows that's dangerous. So I just told her you were going on an adventure. I guess I should have known better, but then Aeron woke up, and he was so angry that-"

"Mommy says the barley makes Aeron mad!" Gywie supplied helpfully, interrupting Violet's ramble before it could gain momentum.

Violet shushed the girl and handed her another piece of bread to keep her mouth busy. Viggo set his jaw and said nothing. He'd seen what the barley – once it was fermented into ale – did to Aeron.

"I sent the children away with Helena while I tried to calm him down," Violet continued, trying in a roundabout way to finish answering his question. "He told me to get out."

Out of the corner of his eye, Viggo saw her shrug.

"So I took him at his word and left. It was a good thing he told me to go, actually, since I knew I was going to have to look for you, and try to find you before a griffin did. But by the time I caught up to Helena, she'd lost track of Gywie. We found her cloak laying by the riverside, where Helena said you'd gone, and that was why I wondered..."

To Viggo's relief she did not repeat the accusation, though he could no longer blame her for wondering if he'd taken the child. He felt he should have something to say to all of that, but nothing came readily to mind.

"We should try to make a fire," Violet advised finally, alleviating the strained silence. "In the mouth of the cave it'll provide warmth and keep predators away."

"I'll go," he said immediately, and crawled out into the darkness. With the failing light, and very little vegetation upon the rocky mountainside to begin with, it took him some time to scrounge together enough bits and pieces that he thought might burn. He was cautious at first, watching for the griffin or one of its kind to return. Violet had said they didn't hunt at night, but he wasn't at all convinced until a rabbit darted across his path, startling him. He stood for a minute, staring after it, and noticed the first chirps of little birds flitting out of their hiding places. And suddenly he understood why the animals preferred to come out at night. Around here, nights were safer.

By the time he'd struck a fire and coaxed it to life he was too exhausted to do anything more than lean back against the cave wall and close his eyes. Violet sang softly to help the children fall asleep and though Viggo couldn't understand the language in which her songs were sung, he still found them soothing. For a while he tried not to think about anything, but eventually the stinging ache in his chest drove him closer to the fire, knowing he needed to examine the new injuries the griffin had left him with.

He was just undoing the leather ties of his tunic to see how deeply those talons had pierced him when Violet crawled quietly to his side. She had left her cloak over the sleeping children and he was surprised to realize it was the first time he'd seen her without it. There was something oddly misshapen about her beneath the heavy grey fabric of her dress, though he did not waste time lingering on the observation.

"Are you hurt?" she asked anxiously, and then answered her own question as she looked him over in the firelight. "You *are* hurt!" He wished she wouldn't look so guilty. Why should she care? It wasn't him she cared about, he reminded himself. She cared about every stray that passed her way; Camlin had said so. He was just one of many.

"I never wanted this to happen..." she was mumbling, as if somehow all of this was her doing. Biting her lip, she reached out carefully toward one of the cuts high on his cheek. He leaned away to avoid her touch.

"I'm fine."

The blunt lie came out with a sharper undertone than he'd intended. For a moment she hesitated, uncertain, and then her gaze dropped to his open tunic. "The griffin," she tried, reaching for his shirt to see the damage for herself. "You should at least let me take a look."

"I don't need your help!" he snapped, swatting her hand away. He was as surprised to have said the words as she looked to hear them. But there they were, hanging uncomfortably out in the open, and there was no taking them back.

He averted his gaze from the hurt in her eyes and stared stubbornly into the fire. He hadn't meant to snap at her. But he excused himself on the grounds that he was tired, hungry, and more shaken from his encounter with the griffin than he wanted to admit. And anyway, being angry at her was easier – and quite possibly safer – than whatever else he might feel if he gave in to the small, annoying part of himself that actually liked the idea of accepting her help. Accepting her help had caused nothing but trouble for both of them.

"You should just go," he muttered.

Viggo knew full well how foolish he sounded. Violet knew these mountains, and he wouldn't have made it this far without her. But he hated her pity. Besides, he had spent a lifetime doing exactly this; driving people away because it was easier than letting them in. Everyone had their limits. Good deeds, in his experience, were rarely good deeds for the sake of themselves; goodness was a flower that withered without sufficient praise and appreciation. She would soon give up and go, just as everyone eventually did.

Only, she didn't. He could feel her violet eyes lingering upon him as she sat in silence, watching him for a long while. "I know you don't need my help," she said at last, making him flinch with the understanding in her voice. "But if you change your mind – if you *want* my help – I won't be far away."

She left him to his thoughts, crawling to the back of the cave where he could hear her settling in with the children to sleep.

Viggo closed his eyes, letting out a sigh of frustration. So much for that. She wasn't going anywhere, and for tonight at least, neither was he. He lay down next to the fire, wishing the cold stone floor of the cave would open up and swallow him whole.

The stupid thing was he did need her help, and they both knew it. But he wasn't used to accepting help. More to the point, he wasn't used to anyone caring enough to offer help so persistently. It would have been easier to accept her help if the concern that came with it didn't sound so genuine, or look so warm and attractive whenever he made the mistake of looking too deeply into her eyes. To make it all worse, she was right about everything. Who knew where griffin claws had been?

Fishing around in his coat pocket, he found the salve she'd made, rubbing a little dab into each of the five holes in his chest. Fortunately, the talons had not punctured very deeply and the little marks the griffin had dug into his skin were likely to heal without causing him any real trouble. He was careful to keep his back to Violet as he worked, so she wouldn't know he was, even now, accepting her help. Her help seemed strangely impossible to avoid.

He breathed deeply, letting out a softer, more regretful sigh as he returned the jar of salve to one pocket and propped his head on his elbow. It wasn't her fault she had such captivating eyes; that was his problem to deal with, and he wouldn't take it out on her again. Tomorrow he would apologize, he decided, and would find a way to make it right. And maybe, once things were settled between them, he could ask all the other questions lingering in his mind. They tumbled about inside his head until at last he began to doze. He was very nearly asleep when the feel of something shifting beneath his coat startled him. Lifting the brown fabric in alarm, he sighed with relief when he saw it was only Gywie slithering over his hip. She froze when she realized she'd been caught, grinned, and continued merrily on her way, plopping down in front of him and stretching out comfortably. She obviously intended to stay.

Viggo raised himself onto his elbow and glanced over his shoulder, uncertain Violet would like her daughter sleeping so near a strange man. But she looked to be asleep with True nestled in her arms, entirely unaware that Gywie had escaped her. Viggo lay slowly back down and found Gywie's head tilted back, her wide blue eyes watching him curiously.

"Why are the whisper voices so mad?"

He didn't know exactly what these whisper voices were, but he could guess they had something to do with the griffins. "Probably because I did something I wasn't supposed to," he admitted honestly, watching to see what she'd think of him.

She nodded thoughtfully and reached over to pat the back of his hand with her much smaller one. "I'll keep you saved."

It was all he could do to resist a laugh as he grinned and ruffled a bit of her blonde hair. "I know you will."

She beamed at the validation and yawned. Viggo pulled her close so he could wrap his coat securely around the both of them. As she began to doze, Viggo's mind wandered back to the griffin and those little rocks Gywie had thrown. Those rocks had delayed his impalement long enough for Violet to find them. Though Gywie looked too far gone with sleep to hear, he leaned forward anyway and whispered a quiet *"thank you"* into her ear. A sleepy smile touched her mouth.

She was warm and he found her presence unexpectedly reassuring. This, along with the exhaustion of the day, combined to pull Viggo quickly into a dreamless sleep where he was content to stay for the remainder of the night.

Chapter 9

WHEN VIGGO FIRST WOKE, he didn't know where he was. He was sore and uncomfortable from sleeping on hard stone and bright light shone in his eyes, making him wince. It wasn't until he stirred and felt the little body against his legs that he remembered. The girl was still asleep. He glanced drowsily over his shoulder to see if Violet and True were sleeping also. The little boy was there alright, snoring softly, but Violet was nowhere in sight.

All Viggo could think of was how hungry he felt. No, that was an understatement; he wasn't hungry, he was *starving*. It had been a whole day since he'd eaten anything and until he silenced the gnawing growl in his stomach, he wouldn't be able to focus on much else. Ever so carefully, so as not to wake Gywie, he slipped a hand into his coat pocket and removed Camlin's second satchel of food. As an after thought he also grabbed the salve, setting both aside while he wriggled out of his coat, leaving the garment tucked over the sleeping girl.

It didn't feel nearly as cold as it had the night before. Viggo crawled carefully over the remains of their fire and peeked out into the sunshine, scarfing provisions as he went. The first snowfall had come and gone. Melt water skipped down the mountainside, forming an endless supply of tiny waterfalls as it pranced and weaved among the rocks. There was something inherently intelligent about water. It seemed to always know where it was headed and seek out the fastest way of getting there. Viggo wasn't even sure he knew where he was headed anymore.

Seeing no sign of any griffins, he emerged fully and stood, stretching himself out where he was stiff from the cave. Violet sat on a dry rock some ways above him, wrapped up again in her blue cloak. Her eyes were closed, her face to the sun, but she was not unaware of her surroundings. Viggo saw the bow laying within easy reach by her feet, while the one remaining arrow dangled from her fingertips.

"Is it safe to be out in the open?" he called softly, climbing up to where she sat.

She opened one eye to watch him as he sat down beside her. "Possibly not, but I couldn't stay in that cave any longer." She twisted the arrow between her fingers. Viggo found himself intrigued by the silver feathers it had been fletched with. "I don't do well in small spaces. Besides, my presence here doesn't break the pact."

Viggo mulled this over and finally frowned, confused. "I thought you said humans aren't allowed to enter the Nyth?"

Her other eye opened and she smiled. "I did, didn't I?"

He waited but she offered no further explanation. Instead she sat quietly and watched him as patiently as he was watching her. Viggo remembered what she had told him last night – that she wouldn't be far when he wanted her help. Hoping to break the silence, he held out the little jar of salve like a peace offering.

"I wanted to thank you for this." He enjoyed the look of surprise that flickered across her face when she saw he had kept it. It made a smile come sideways to his mouth. "And I wanted to ask... there was something Helena bandaged, on my shoulder..."

It was hard to ask her for help, harder than he knew it should be.

"I never did get a good look," he fumbled, searching for words, "but it should probably be checked. It would be hard for me to reach by myself..."

A complete lie and they both knew it. He could easily have reached it himself, but he hoped she would realize he was trying to say sorry; that making peace with her was more important than whatever wounded pride was making this so difficult.

Violet reached down and scooped up a handful of melt water as it trickled past her cloak, washing it over her hands before she snatched the salve from him. He turned partly away, undoing the ties of his tunic to give her access to his shoulder. Her fingers were cold and so was the salve, but she was deft at her craft and not once did he feel either pain or pressure as she unwrapped the bandage and tended the wound beneath. He almost didn't realize she was finished until she declared her completion with the strangest announcement.

"Sunrise."

He swiveled back to her as she twisted the lid onto the jar of salve, her expression satisfied.

"Excuse me?"

Her gaze jumped to his. "Fair is fair. You told me your name – now you know mine."

"Sunrise? That's...your name is Sunrise?"

Colour crept slowly over her cheeks like morning light tinting the clouds at dawn. "I know it's unusual," she apologized. "You can see why

I don't usually tell people. There would be too many questions, and people would think I'm strange, well, stranger than they already do, and it's always just been easier not to bother with-"

Smiling, he reached over to touch the back of her hand, putting a halt to her unnecessary explanations. "It's a beautiful name."

For a while they were content simply to sit and smile at one another, a comfortable silence settling between them. Any lingering fury she might have felt toward him was gone, along with all his irritation from the night before. What remained was something new and unspoken but strangely pleasant and, almost in an unexpected sort of way, rather comforting. To Viggo it felt an awful lot like trust. She trusted him, though he couldn't for a moment imagine why. She shouldn't. And yet, he trusted her too.

Realizing suddenly that his hand was still upon hers he pulled it away, hiding his embarrassment with a question. "I know you're not a Druid, and that doesn't sound like a Celtic name..."

"No," she agreed.

"I'm guessing you're not a Briton either?"

"Not exactly, no."

He waited for her to supply the answer he so obviously wanted, but she merely stared at him passively until at last he pressed her.

"Well?"

"Well?" she echoed innocently. Viggo was startled to realize she was *laughing* at him! Not out loud she wasn't, but he could see the barely suppressed mirth gleaming out of her eyes, like she was daring him to come right out and ask the question. So he did.

"Where are you from then?"

She laughed softly and looked away, her gaze sweeping above and side-to-side, checking for danger. Viggo automatically did the same, all at once remembering their vulnerable position. But he saw nothing to indicate danger, and Violet – Sunrise, he reminded himself, turning this new name over in his mind – Sunrise didn't seem worried.

"I don't think they know where we are yet," she offered eventually. "I think Gywie would have woken if they did."

"The whisper voices?" he guessed.

She nodded. "The griffins don't talk like you or I do. They talk in their thoughts, each one hearing all the others at once. Like honeybees. Or so I've been told. I can't hear it myself..."

"But Gywie can?"

Sunrise nodded again and fiddled distractedly with the arrow. "I suppose she can. I had no idea until yesterday. We used to come here a lot, her and I, before True. It was always sort of fun going somewhere no one else could follow. Maybe she learned to hear them then."

Not for the first time, Viggo found himself puzzled, struggling to make sense of what she was telling him. The trouble was that it didn't make sense. How was it she and Gywie could come here without breaking the pact, but he and True could not? Nothing she said about herself ever seemed to add up quite right. He decided to switch tactics and try asking the question he most wanted answered.

"How did Gywie follow me in the first place?" He couldn't imagine her walking that far, much less managing to overtake him; not even if the griffins had somehow told her where to find him. It was unnerving to think the creatures might have known where he was and been watching long before he'd become aware of their existence.

Sunrise's grip upon the arrow tightened and she twisted it more deliberately between her fingers, suddenly preoccupied with staring at its slender shaft.

"You have a lot of questions" she acknowledged. "And I'll answer them, but I have a question I want you to answer first."

He briefly chewed his lip, wondering why she suddenly seemed nervous. It was making him nervous too. "Alright."

"When we first met you said you had stolen something, something you said would help the war end more quickly."

Viggo stiffened, concerned with where this was heading. He remembered the conversation in question and she was only half-right. It had been her, not him, who suggested that he'd stolen something; he simply hadn't disagreed with her. But if he recalled correctly, he *had* agreed that the war would end quicker on account of what he'd done. His mind flickered back to what he'd seen in Camelot – the secret that had all of Britannia trying to find him. If she meant to ask him about that, he would have no choice but to refuse, most importantly because he could not justify endangering her in that way, not even to satisfy her curiosity.

"If what you stole does what you say it will, if Saxons win the war and eventually take this land, what will they do about the griffins?"

The question took Viggo aback, confused by its relevance. He wasn't an Elder. Such concerns were far beyond his realm of interest or influence. But she was watching him closely now, waiting in anxious silence as though his answer meant a great deal to her. He supposed she was worried about the broken pact and whomever the griffins might choose to attack on account of it. Perhaps she hoped his people could offer some protection from the griffins when they came.

"If it makes you feel better," he tried, "my people don't believe in sharing their lands with other kinds – the Elders preach strongly against it. They're furious about King Arthur's peace treaty with the dragons. You said the griffins have a pact with the Druids?"

She nodded and he shrugged offhandedly, seeing only one possible answer to her question.

"The Elders wouldn't tolerate such a thing. My best guess is soldiers would eventually be sent to drive the griffins out."

Rather than looking relieved, Sunrise sucked in a tremulous breath and shut her eyes. She turned away from him, hugging her arms protectively around herself, her shoulders quivering as if she were fighting back tears. He stared, stunned and dismayed to have upset her so terribly without even knowing how he'd done it.

"I-I'm sorry," he stammered, though he had absolutely no idea what he was apologizing for. His hands itched to reach out for her, to touch her again and somehow fix whatever he'd just broken. But he didn't know if such a touch would be appropriate and instead tried to think of something more to say. She interrupted his efforts, tossing a soft question over her shoulder without looking back.

"Do all your people feel as your Elders do, that every kind except your own should be driven out?"

"I don't, uh..." He trailed off as soon as he'd begun, realizing he was attempting to answer a question he did not understand. "Are we still talking about the griffins?"

With a deep sigh of composition, Sunrise turned back to him. He tried to gauge the emotion in her face, but her expression was purposefully blank and she would not look at him. In her hand she held a small map which she spread out on the rock between them like a chasm. It seemed there would be no further answers after all. Her finger indicated a spot along the mountains, not all that far from the coast.

"This is where we are – close to Dionne. But I don't think going there is a good idea. When I followed you, I saw soldiers spreading out through the valley. They'll be waiting for you in the city. Besides, there aren't any boats in Dionne, and that's what you're after isn't it? A boat?"

A hint of a smile touched Viggo's mouth. For someone who seemed to be guarding a great many secrets of her own, she was awfully hard to keep things from. There was nothing he could do but nod and agree.

"Then I think we should forget about Dionne and go directly to Lin Harbour. It's just southwest and not far. You'll find your boat there."

"We? You still plan on helping me get away?"

He was greatly relieved to see her smile return, even if it was faint and she still did not look at him. "I told you I would, didn't I? I made a promise to you the moment I dragged you through my door. Maybe not in so many words, but a promise just the same. I keep my promises."

Viggo respected that and said nothing to dissuade her. He could finally admit, at least to himself, that he wanted her help, and her company, for as long as she was willing to offer them.

"How do we go directly?" A careful study of the map brought a furrow to his brow as he realized a direct route from their current location to Lin Harbour would take them through the one place he had absolutely no desire to go. "You can't mean through the Sinking Swamps?" There was no way he was brave enough to try that. If she was, well, he would admire her courage... but from a considerable distance.

"Not through," she mumbled quietly, and he wished she would not continue to avert her eyes the way she did. "Over."

"Over?" Now he was truly baffled. "How do we go over?"

"We can't go down into the valley and we can't stay here much longer. Over is the only way."

She stood. Leaving her arrow behind on the rock, she stepped over a couple paces to a place that was both flat and dry. Before Viggo could ask again what she meant, Sunrise undid the clasp of her cloak, shrugging it off so that it fell into a semi-circle at her feet.

"What are you doing?" he asked, watching uncertainly as she began unbuttoning the neck of her grey dress.

"Shhh," she hushed, continuing downward.

Unexpected warmth rose into Viggo's cheeks. Realizing it brought the heat rushing all the way to his ears, he half-turned away, not sure he should be watching whatever it was she was doing. Even so, his curiosity got the better of him and he glanced at her again out of the corner of his eye.

He would have been lying if he said the sight of her dress slipping off her bare shoulders didn't quicken his heartrate, just a little. She maintained reasonable modesty in a sleeveless petticoat, held in place by a tightly laced bodice. But it was not her clothes that caused him to stare with his mouth agape. It was her wings. They rose from between her shoulders, lifting high over her head as she stretched them with obvious relief.

Wings!

No wonder something about her looked odd beneath all those heavy fabrics she wore. Somewhere, in the swirling, awe-struck fog of his mind,

Wings!

a great many things finally began to add up, amounting to one simple truth that explained all the rest of it: she had wings.

Almost reluctantly, she lifted her gaze to his, a smile stealing onto her lips when she saw his open-mouthed expression. "Well?" she asked him shyly, tugging hopefully on a bit of silver hair. "What do you think?"

But he was too stunned to think.

She had wings!

They were hawk-like in shape, wide and sweeping, at least ten feet from one wingtip to the next if he had to guess. Slender silver feathers caught the early morning light like polished mirrors. It would have taken a poet to find appropriate words for what he thought.

The anticipation in her eyes turned to disappointment and Sunrise bent down, gathering her discarded garments into her arms. It impressed him that she was not already shivering without them.

"Well, now you have your answers," she murmured quietly, wrapping her dress and cloak up into a bundle and hugging them to her chest as she stood and stared off in the other direction. "I'm a fairy. One of those *other kinds*. And if you think you can tolerate my presence a little longer, I'll fly you past the soldiers. They'll be searching for you on the ground – not in the skies."

Viggo recoiled, physically struck by how ugly his own words sounded coming off her tongue. Now he understood all those questions. She wasn't worried about the griffins; she had been trying to judge what his reaction might be when she revealed the truth of what she was. A hollow spot formed in his stomach as if someone had punched him, leaving him winded and breathless, desperate for air yet nearly unable to draw it. No wonder she could not look at him. By his own words, she must think him repulsed by her – though nothing could be further from the truth.

The urge to touch her returned with shocking fierceness, propelling him to his feet. More than anything he wanted to reach out and pull her into a hug, to physically reassure her that her presence was *desired* rather than tolerated, but that felt too near a line he was not allowed to cross. So instead he stood there, running his hands through his hair to keep them occupied as he searched desperately for the right words. He wished he could tell her that her wings were beautiful; that he was sorry she had to hide them; that he would love to know what they felt like. Those were all the things he should have said when she'd asked him what he thought. Instead he'd given her dumb silence, which she had grossly misinterpreted.

"Sunrise?" When she didn't respond he finally gave in and reached out to her, catching her arm to pull her around to face him. She turned but carefully avoided his gaze, staring purposefully at the ground as if this could stop him from noticing the faint shine of tears in her eyes.

Determination caught fire in his stomach, setting him ablaze with resolve. Unwilling to let her go on with her wrong idea, Viggo cupped her chin gently and forced it upward until Sunrise finally, hesitantly, lifted her eyes to his. He still did not know how to tell her what he felt, but for the first time in a very long time he made absolutely no effort to mask his feelings. He threw himself unwaveringly into the great depths of violet before him and hoped desperately that Sunrise would find in his unrestrained features that for which he did not have the words.

Her breath caught. Understanding lit in her eyes like sunlight dappled on water and she flung her arms around him, holding him as tightly as she had on the first night they'd met. He hugged her back with equal fervor, his relief marred by a familiar jab of envy. The sharpness of it didn't surprise him this time, only made him uncomfortable. To distract himself from it, Viggo kept focused on her wings; studying the silver feathers up close. He didn't dare to touch them though they looked incredibly soft.

To his disappointment, Sunrise let out a soft sigh and pulled away, leaving him cold where she'd been. At least she was looking at him now and her smile was warm. "Let's go find your boat."

They woke the children. Gywie needed only a glance at her mother's visible wings to shout with joy and throw off her cloak, revealing tiny pink wings of her own. True was happy too, though his joy was quieter and seemed to be rooted in the discovery that the snow had vanished overnight.

"This is incredible," Viggo said honestly, finally finding some appropriate words as he watched Gywie skip and prance around the rocks, fluttering up into the air whenever she felt like it. It was hard to believe he hadn't noticed her brightly coloured wings before, when she'd appeared on the mountainside without her cloak; but considering the circumstances, he forgave himself for missing them. "I only ever heard of fairies in stories, back when I was a child. I never imagined...I mean, I never thought...well, the stories always made faeries sound tiny."

"Pixies," Sunrise grumbled with good-natured annoyance. "Pixies are tiny, not fairies."

He smiled sheepishly. "I'll remember that."

The last of the provisions Sunrise brought were split between the children. True got the decidedly larger portion only because he sat and ate properly, while Sunrise had to chase Gywie about in an attempt to slow her down long enough to eat anything at all. The girl was full of enthusiasm for a new day and food was little more than a hinderance to the exuberant outpouring of all that youthful energy.

Viggo kept watch. The longer they stayed, the more nervous he felt, sure that the griffin would eventually return to exact some kind of revenge. He wasn't at all sure how the griffins would go about handling the breaking of their pact and he had no desire to stick around and find out. Despite this rising unease, he was reluctant to suggest they hurry; he enjoyed the happy antics of the little fairy girl. He kept waiting for True to join in, but the boy just sat quietly and watched. It wasn't odd to Viggo that a child of this age was too shy to speak around strangers, but it did seem odd that True wouldn't play.

"Does he miss his father?" he asked finally, when Sunrise was kneeling next to him to slide her bow and arrow into the bundle with her clothes.

Sunrise glanced curiously toward True. "No, I don't think so. Aeron left about a year ago. I don't think True really remembers his father, and even if he does, he didn't seem to mind leaving."

Leaving. Viggo couldn't tell if she said that word with finality or not. "Will you go back?" he asked, hurriedly adding – "To Dairefast?" – even though that wasn't what he meant at all. It was a personal question, perhaps too personal, and yet he felt compelled to ask it, knowing he would not be happy to part ways with her until he knew the answer.

Unsurprisingly, she saw right through his words and knew exactly what he was asking. "Yes," she said, straightening up to look him in the eye. "As I said, I keep my promises."

"Even when other people haven't kept theirs?"

Her smile was guarded and resolved, yet it failed to hide the sadness. "I made a vow, of my own choosing. It's mine to keep, regardless of what anyone else does."

Gywie ran up to them, interrupting loudly with wide, wet eyes. "Mommy, why are there so many voices?"

"They're holding council," Sunrise guessed aloud, waving one hand to gesture True urgently to her side. "It's time to go, before they make any decisions."

Viggo quickly retrieved his coat, shrugging himself into the garment and stuffing the jar of salve back into his pocket. Sunrise knelt and True scrambled onto her back, snuggling down between her wings with his face turned skyward. Flying was obviously nothing new to him, even though he had no wings of his own. Gywie spread her pink wings and soared off without waiting. Viggo stared after her in awe.

"Are you ready?" Sunrise asked, holding out her hand.

Viggo stared at her slender palm as though it were a portal to another world, which in a way, it was. She was inviting him to partake of something he had never dared to imagine, something he had gone his entire life without knowing was possible. And just like that, he was supposed to be ready for it?

"Not really," he admitted, taking her hand anyway. He felt a warm, ticklish sensation at the touch, like tiny pinpricks of light dancing between their fingers. The sensation tingled up his arm and swept through his entire body, thrilling and unnerving him simultaneously. He was so absorbed in the feel of it that he did not immediately notice his feet had left the ground.

"I'm flying," he breathed, when he saw his boots hovering over the ground he'd been standing on moments earlier.

Sunrise grinned coyly at him, basking in his uncertainty and excitement. "Not yet, you're not."

What Viggo felt when she spread her wings and swept upward, pulling him along with her, was not completely dissimilar to what he had felt when the griffin caught him up into the sky. The sharpness of their ascent made him gasp, his stomach leaping into his throat as the ground vanished away from under him with nothing to catch him if he fell. But this was Sunrise, he told himself firmly, and not a griffin. He trusted her. He *trusted* her.

Thoughts of trust echoed in his mind like a mantra until he became accustomed to the height – or at least, until he could force himself to ignore the unease of it. As he relaxed, he become aware of things, like how beautiful the mountainside looked from this angle. The sheer immensity of it amazed him. On the ground it was just ground. But from here he could see snow-white peaks towering far above them while so much vastness sloped away below. When he looked up toward the horizon, he saw the sun suspended like a jewel over the glistening ocean.

"This is amazing!" he cried, and found suddenly that he was laughing with the sheer wonder of being in the air; of soaring above danger as though it were a trivial, mortal concern. The griffins, Ellaway, Donovan, their soldiers...all of it felt so far behind him, already relegated to distant memory. He never would have imagined when he first set off for Camelot, leaving behind the laughter and disbelief of his Commander and fellow soldiers, that he would find himself somewhere like this. It was like an impossible dream from which he might wake at any moment if he focused on it too closely.

When Viggo finally mustered the courage to look down, he saw the valley slowly sliding past beneath them. Even from this height he could see the soldiers dotted along the riverside, their tunics showing them up like blots of scarlet upon the browning grass. They must have been out all night watching for him; probably each one with a proper fire and a full skin of wine. Lucky devils.

"Viggy!"

Gywie squealed his name to be sure he was looking as she spiraled into his field of vision with a vibrant swirl of pink wings. She was showing off for his benefit, darting back and forth in front of him to keep his attention, which he gave her willingly. Her little wings enthralled him with their quick, powerful movements, each one facilitating a bit of her play. His smile pulled wider still as he changed his mind about those devils below. He was the lucky one. Those poor soldiers were stuck down there, in one place, following orders; while he was up here, freer than he had ever been, doing something most people could only dream off – something that, back in Saxony, he never would have been *allowed* to dream of.

Back in Saxony, children were taught fearful stories of fairy kind who stole children, leaving nightmarish changelings in their place. As he got older, he heard similar stories repeated with gruesome detail around campfires and tavern tables. When war broke out with the Britons, the Elders frequently alluded to such stories in their decrees, reminding people that any alliance with other kinds could not be tolerated by the civil or sane. Viggo supposed some part of him had always assumed these stories were true because everyone else believed them and he hadn't known not to. But now, watching Gywie summersault through the air, he could see it had all been lies.

He stole a glance up toward Sunrise's wings. They were full of the air, soaring rather than flapping, with only the occasional, subtle shift of guiding feathers to keep them going in the right direction. He wondered how anything so magnificent could be viewed with such suspicion? It made him wonder what other things the Elders lied about.

With the threat of detection slipping out of sight and mind behind them, Sunrise shifted them into a gentle descent. The landscape beneath changed abruptly from the open fields beyond the river to the famously ill-fated Sinking Swamps. From above, they did not look as ominous as the rumors made them out to be, though Viggo knew that was hardly a fair assessment when he could not see into the swamp proper. Thick, gnarled branches snaked out in all directions, supporting a heavy canopy of sunburnt leaves that blocked his view of whatever lurked beneath. He was glad to be getting this rare glimpse of the place from above rather than within.

It was hard to guess just how fast they were going, but even at what felt like a leisurely pace, Viggo was astounded at the speed with which the land slipped away beneath them. Thinking of how long it would take him to walk the same distance, he found it easier to understand how Gywie had caught up to him; she clearly hadn't been following him on foot.

"Come on, True," the little girl shouted, flying near to reach for her brother. "Let's have an *adventure*!"

Though the boy feared strangers, and snow, and was strangely reserved when it came to play, he seemed to have no reservations when it came to heights. He took his sister's hands when she reached for him, pushing off Sunrise's back without any fear of falling. The two children giggled in mirrored delight as they spiraled off through the air together.

Viggo felt a tug upon his hand as Sunrise pulled him closer, drawing him up alongside her. He glanced over to see the wind sweeping her silver hair back from her face, her eyes glowing with utter delight as she watched his wild smile. He felt like a child in her presence; she had opened his eyes to seeing everything as it really was, and not as he had been told to see it.

"Well?" she called loudly, giving him a second chance to answer her question from earlier. "What do you think?"

For once, the right word came easy. "Beautiful."

Sunrise bit her lip with pleasure and released him. The loss of her touch was so unexpected that Viggo's heart leapt into his throat with the expectation that he would fall! But he didn't. Despite the surge of fear that pounded through his chest and reverberated in his ears, he sailed forward at a steady pace, unsure if his continued flight was his doing or hers. Another laugh built in his throat as fear ebbed into renewed wonder.

He was flying!

Those strange pinpricks of light which still coursed through his body emboldened him to throw his arms outward, embracing the gift he had somehow harnessed.

Viggo felt the griffin more than saw it, and he would realize too late that he'd heard it before that. At first, the distant sound meant nothing, lost as it was amid the rushing wind. It wasn't until Gywie cried out that he noticed the faint whistling and realized it was growing into a steady rush.

"Go 'way, birdy!"

Viggo saw a flash of blue out of the corner of his eye, and just like that Sunrise was gone as though she'd never been. In the griffin's wake a rush of wind hit him sideways, sending him spiralling out of control. The tingling sensation which kept him aloft evaporated, plunging him headlong toward the trees below, his arms flailing for purchase that did not exist.

The dizzying swirl of ground and sky reminded Viggo of his fall on the mountainside. Only, this time there was no way to lose his sense of direction: Gywie's frightened shouts followed him from above while Sunrise's agonizing screams ascended from below.

Chapter 10

C ONSCIOUSNESS FELT OPTIONAL. VIGGO teetered at the edge
of it; neither hurt enough to be urged completely into the void,
nor well enough not to be tempted. It was Sunrise's screams that told
him he needed to come back – not because they continued, but because
they had stopped, and he had to know why. Fighting his way though the
darkness that threatened to encompass him, Viggo became aware of one
all-consuming sensation: his legs were on fire.

His eyes flew open in a panic, checking immediately to be sure this
wasn't literal. It wasn't. In fact, he was in much the opposite predicament
– he was half submerged.

As best he could figure it, once he'd broken through the canopy he
must have hit the swamp like a utensil dropped into thick pudding.
There had been enough momentum to drive him in up to his hips where
he had stopped...and stayed...and was stuck. He tried to stretch his legs
and could not. The goo into which he'd fallen was thick and unyielding
unlike anything else he'd ever encountered.

And it was hot!

As Viggo looked around he saw evidence of this heat in the bubbles
that rose slowly to the surface of the green slag and popped open with
sulfuric steam. The whole surface of the swamp – all that he could see of

it anyway – bubbled and steamed like a cauldron coming ready to boil. Viggo knew if he didn't find a way to get out of here soon, that thought would quickly become more than a clever analogy.

The Sinking Swamps were not entirely swampy. Nearby and almost within reach was solid ground. Viggo stared at the place where dirt and leaves dropped away into broiling slime and realized, had he landed only three feet to the left, he might have hit the ground and broken his legs – or worse. The heat suddenly seemed preferable, even if it was beginning to make him sweat.

Motion caught his eye and drew his gaze upward. In this place of steam and shadows, sunlight seemed oddly out of place. And yet there it was, streaming down upon the griffin from the hole she had punched in the canopy. She was shaking out her feathers, tucking her wings comfortably against her sides as she settled down over subdued prey. Viggo knew from the blue of her feathers that this was the same one who had carried him off – the one Sunrise had shot with her arrows.

Sunrise was motionless but alive. Their eyes met and he saw desperate fear quivering across her face. She didn't dare fight. The griffin had caught her from behind, piercing long talons through both of her wings. Any move, any attempt at escape, would only tear them further. The creature stood over the fairy deliberately, delighted to hold her face-down in the dirt and know there was nothing she could do. Around the griffin's claws, silver wings were slowly staining scarlet. Little whimpers of pain crossed Sunrise's trembling lips with every breath but she no longer screamed; she knew it was pointless.

"Hey! Hey, over here!"

Viggo waved his arms and began shouting. When his initial attempt to draw the griffin's attention away from Sunrise failed, he got louder, demanding she look at him; insisting she remember who had broken the pact in the first place. He even threw out the temerarious suggestion that the creature come and eat him instead, though this offer was not strictly self-sacrificing. Unable to so much as wiggle his feet – much less wriggle himself free – Viggo had come to the unfortunate conclusion it would take someone far stronger than himself, someone about the size and strength of the griffin, to pull him from the swamp. If he could just get her to come for him, he could worry about not actually getting eaten afterward.

But all his efforts were ignored. The griffin's only acknowledgement of his steady outburst was one feather-tipped ear, which turned briefly in his direction.

Sunrise spied her one remaining arrow at the same moment he did, laying almost directly between them, taunting them both by being just out of reach. In terms of actual distance it was not so far away, but with both of them stuck in place it may as well have been miles.

The griffin had enjoyed taking time to admire her catch, but she was ready to move on with her revenge. With clear forethought and poetic justice in mind, she raised one paw and set it deliberately over Sunrise's left wing. Though she no longer had an arrow lodged in her wing, nor in her cheek, the griffin obviously had not forgotten where they had been or how they had come to be there. The fairy's renewed screams, as the griffin ripped slowly through silver feathers with her talons, made the beast purr.

Viggo tried for the arrow. Straining with all his might, he managed to get his fingers into the nearby dirt, clawing frantically through the moist earth to reach just a little further.

Inches, he thought angrily, *he was inches away!*

It didn't really matter that he had no idea how much good a single arrow would do, even if he managed to get it. He just needed to do something. His only reward was feeling his left hip sink downward as he listed in that direction. All the same, his hand was a little closer. He leaned harder, felt the wetness oozing up to his waist, and finally closed his fingers around the arrow.

It was too little, too late.

The griffin was through with revenge. She opened her beak wide and Viggo saw the hot flames gathered in her mouth, aimed directly between the fairy's torn wings. Panic overtook him and he shouted again, his fist clenched around a useless arrow. All the griffin needed to do was shoot that fire and Sunrise was gone...and there was absolutely nothing he could do about it.

Viggo couldn't explain what happened next. He looked on in frightened amazement as the swamp itself turned on the griffin. Vines dropped from the trees of their own volition, reaching out as living things to wind themselves around her beak like a bridle. A bellow of flame – meant for the fairy – blew harmlessly into the canopy as the vines snapped taut and yanked the griffin's head skyward. Angered, she reared up, releasing her prey as she thrashed wildly to break free.

The vines continued coming from all directions, encircling blue wings, pulling the griffin ever further away. Viggo watched real fear appear in her eyes, and heard it as thunderous roars turned to plaintive shrieks. She pawed the dirt, violently ripping through the vegetation with her beak to keep from being overrun. For every vine she broke, another appeared to take its place. Even so, vines were no match for brute strength and talons. Just when Viggo thought she might be getting the upper hand over the hostile foliage, a tree root rose from the ground and snagged one of her back paws, wrapping it up and cinching down tight. The griffin was caught.

Viggo let out the breath he'd been holding, only to have it catch in his throat. From his ever-sinking vantage point, he could see boots approaching the griffin from behind. He saw the glint of polished iron a split-second before she did; right before the sword plunged into the creature's side. Her wail was deafening. The razor-sharp beak whipped around with greater speed than the newcomer was prepared for and sank into the man's chest, dragging him to the ground.

Viggo recognized the dark hair and verdant cloak and knew it was Aeron. Sunrise had realized it too. She made a heartbreaking attempt to stand that ended with her collapsed upon her knees and Viggo seething at the helplessness of his own predicament.

Aeron scarcely managed to roll aside as the griffin released him, only to try and spear him again with her beak. He was slow getting up onto his knees, much too slow. Viggo sucked in his breath when he saw how the other man held his chest, blood trickling out from between his fingers. The griffin must have bit deeply. Though he saw it coming, Aeron wasn't nearly fast enough to escape the swipe of long talons as they ripped through his side and knocked him back down.

For a few moments the Druid lay perfectly still, panting as he gazed up into the feathered face above him. Golden eyes stared calmly back. They were talking. Though Viggo couldn't actually hear the words passing between them – if there were any – he could see the battle of wills being fought in their expressions. It was a battle the griffin meant to win. She opened her beak with a hiss, poised to strike again.

Viggo did the only thing he could. "Here!" he shouted, as he threw the arrow.

A vine uncoiled from above, snatching the shaft mid-air and delivering it into Aeron's waiting palm. Without hesitation he thrust it upward, driving the arrowhead deeply into the soft flesh of the griffin's neck. A strangled cry echoed through the trees. Already sagging from the sword lodged in her side, it did not take long for the griffin to collapse to the ground, her gurgling gasps for breath soon stilling into silence.

"Aeron!"

Though she could not stand, Sunrise mustered the strength to drag herself to her husband's side. Viggo felt this might be the wrong time to announce that his waist had vanished completely into the mire, or that the heat was so intense he could no longer feel anything below the knee. He looked around again for something he could grab hold of to pull himself free. But since there wasn't anything within reach, it was impossible to keep from watching the tragic scene playing out before him.

"What are you doing here?"

Aeron was hurt badly. Viggo didn't have to see him up close to know that much. When Aeron answered his wife's question his voice gurgled and wheezed much as the griffin's final breaths had done. Viggo had never seen someone die before, not like this.

"I was afraid you wouldn't come back this time." Sunrise managed to maneuver his head into her lap as he spoke, and he tilted his eyes up to look at her. "I came to the Oak Trees to ask where you'd gone."

She began to cry. "I've always come back."

He smiled weakly and reached up to touch a bit of her disheveled hair. "That's what the Oak Trees told me too."

Sunrise swiped the tears from her face and reached for his tunic, fumbling desperately with shaking hands to get it open. "It's going to be fine, everything's going to be fine. I can fix this - we can fix this. We..."

Aeron hushed her tiredly and grabbed her hands to stop her work. She pleaded with him to let go but he refused, tightening his hold to keep her close.

"I was angry because it didn't work."

She only sobbed harder. "I tried, I tried to do everything you asked. I wanted to be enough-"

"You heal people, fix them...make them better," he continued, no longer seeming to hear her. "I thought having you would fix me too. But it didn't. You didn't..." Words wavered unintelligibly on his lips as his voice petered off into a croak. Whatever his last words, Viggo did not hear them.

Sunrise shouted his name and begged him back.

Viggo looked away, blinking tears from his own eyes. Anger rose like bile into his mouth, so intense he could taste it. He was angry at the swamp; angry at the griffin; angry at himself for ever taking his Commander up on the dare. He was even angry at the woman he'd seen, the woman with hair like fire whose existence had sent him gallivanting west, bright and eager and full of the secret to which he'd laid claim.

Panic clawed at his thoughts, trying to take the place of anger. He pushed both aside. If he didn't get out of here soon, whatever was left of his legs wouldn't be worth saving. The steaming slime was nearing his ribcage and the pungent smell of tar oozing up from below was almost enough to make him gag. The harder he pulled, the more the verdant muck clung to him and sucked him in deeper.

Finally, when it was halfway up his chest, Viggo stopped trying. There wasn't any point. He couldn't get out, not without something substantial to grab hold of. And there was no one to bring such a sturdy thing within reach, no one but . . . *the children!*

Where were the children?

He was shocked to realize he'd forgotten all about them. Grey eyes darted madly about, searching for any sign of blonde curls or the little brown mop that usually followed. He saw neither.

"They're up there."

The pained whisper startled him into noticing Sunrise. She had crawled up to the edge of the swamp, dragging her limp wings through the dirt to reach him. With one arm she clutched her ribcage as if she might fall apart otherwise; with her other hand she pointed, and Viggo followed her raised finger toward the gaping hole in the canopy where both children were stuck.

At some point Gywie must have tried to follow them through the trees, but in doing so she'd become hopelessly snagged upon the branches. The harder she fought to free herself, the more tangled her wings became with the gnarled stems. True had fallen into a knot of branches below her. He was frozen with fear, too terrified to move as the slender limbs sagged precariously beneath his weight, threatening to drop him.

"Can you still feel your legs?"

Viggo glanced back at Sunrise. Her face was pale and numb, her eyes glazed over with a complete lack of emotion. She was in shock, he reasoned, and did not bother asking about Aeron. Had there been any chance the other man was still alive, Viggo had no doubt she would still have been at her husband's side.

"Not below the knee," he replied at last.

"Alright," she mumbled distantly. "That's still alright."

It didn't feel alright, not to him. "How do I get out?" He didn't mean to sound anxious, and he hated to press her – especially now – but he was running out of time. The swamp had reached his armpits.

"You can't," she replied wearily.

"Can't as in...not at all?"

"Not unless you could fly out."

Viggo stared. She could fly. More importantly, she could make him fly. "Can you...?" It somehow didn't seem right to ask. If she could have helped him, she would have done it already.

"My wings," she told him flatly. She glanced once more toward the children and he could see in her eyes that she was thinking deeply on some matter; weighing out a decision that needed making. "I need my wings to fly. I also need them to heal. I can't share my flight with you while they're like this, not without..."

As she trailed off, her eyes brightened with certainty. Whatever thought she had been grappling with was settled and the determination with which she looked at him made him uneasy.

"You get them out of here."

She reached out across the bubbling slime and grabbed his hand. He nearly wrenched it away. He was afraid of that sentence she hadn't finished; afraid of why she was suddenly entrusting her children to him. But when he felt those soft pinpricks of light tingling through his fingers, he knew he could not have pulled away even if he'd wanted to. They were cold this time, and they did not sweep through his body like before, but crept sluggishly up his arm, spilling into him like a thousand glimmering specks of dust. He wasn't sure if it was a good sign or bad when Sunrise's eyes fluttered shut.

"Get them out of here," she repeated, her breathlessness betraying what this was costing her.

Viggo wanted to argue that he wasn't going anywhere without her, that *she* could get her children out of here and he would help. But he knew it wasn't going to happen like that, and he couldn't bring himself to lie to her.

Dull though they were, those little pinpricks of light finally got where they were going, tinging all the way down to his toes. The effect was instant. The swamp released him, sliding woefully away as if it had been commanded to do so. He began to float, Sunrise's hand dropping away as he rose out of the hot slag. It squelched and burped in his wake and finally closed over the place where he'd been, leaving no evidence of his presence.

He could hear the children as he continued his ascent toward the tree-tops. They were shouting, crying, calling desperately for help. Though he had by no means mastered the art of flying, with diligent thought Viggo found he was able to will himself in their direction, maneuvering just enough so that he was within reach of True when he came upon the first branches. The pinpricks were already fading as he latched onto the first sturdy limb, probably just in time.

"Viggo!"

True called his name and reached out frantically in his direction. Viggo was both surprised by the sound of the boy's voice – which he had not heard before – and by the clarity with which the young child pronounced his name. But there was no time for surprise. The branches beneath True sagged with his movement, creaking ominously.

Viggo braced himself against the bough and leaned out as far as he could, cursing under his breath when he could not quite get hold of the boy.

"Can you reach?" he called, straining further to close the gap between them.

True did better than reach. With a frightened squeak he launched himself through the air and into Viggo's arms, clinging like he might never let go. The branches he'd been caught on snapped upward without his weight, sending a shower of broken twigs and leaves fluttering to the ground.

Viggo clutched the boy with one arm, holding him close for comfort as he looked around for his sister. Gywie's face was red and streaked with tears as she thrashed in a desperate effort to free her wings from the branches. She had a lot of fight in her, he'd give her that; but she was too far away to reach. There was only one thing to do, and none of them were going to like it.

"I'm going to take True down," he called, drawing Gywie's attention. She wailed and threw her little hands out wide in his direction, her puffy eyes so wild with desperation that his heart tripped over a pang of guilt. He didn't want to leave her. But there wasn't any other choice. "I'm going to take True down and come right back for you. Gywie, I'm coming back for you – do you understand?"

She tried so hard to be brave, sniffling and rubbing her eyes as she nodded. The courageous calm lasted for less than a minute and then she was flailing wildly again, frightening Viggo with the thought that she might successfully wrench herself free, only to fall and hurt herself below.

True's slender brown eyes were enormous. Viggo looked down into them and wondered how much the children had seen. "You're going to have to get on my back," he decided aloud, knowing as soon as he said it that True was not going to listen.

"No," the boy replied flatly, and clung tighter to his neck.

"You don't have to let go," Viggo assured him hastily, attempting to pry the boy's legs from around his waist. "Just slide over a little, onto my back...there you go." True's grip didn't relax for an instant but he did, eventually, allow himself to be shifted around.

The next trick was going to be getting down the gnarled tree without falling. His legs still stung from the knee down and Viggo shook out each foot in turn, trying to overcome the discomfort. The misshapen branches turned out to be a blessing. There were no shortage of hand or foot holds and Viggo reached the forest floor quicker than he'd anticipated. But when he stepped aside into the clearing and tried to lower True to the ground, the boy wouldn't budge.

"I have to go back for your sister," he explained urgently, though he wasn't thrilled about the idea of leaving the boy down here alone. He was afraid True would wonder off and see what had become of his father and the griffin. But he couldn't bring himself to take the boy over to his mother, not without knowing whether or not she was. . . not without knowing her condition.

"No," the boy repeated, and like most children, Viggo supposed this was his first and favourite word.

"True..." he warned, but the boy repeated himself anyway.

"No, look!"

Viggo looked. He reached up just in time to catch Gywie in his arms, her unexpected arrival dragging all three of them into a heap. It took Viggo a minute to overcome his surprise and by the time he had his wits about him, Gywie had already crawled out of his arms and scooted away. She sat in the dirt nearby and began plucking twigs out from between her feathers, irritably mumbling words Viggo was fairly certain she wasn't supposed to know. True, on the other hand, continued to cling to his back in silence. Viggo sighed. At least they were both safely out of the tree. All that remained was to see if there was anything he could do for Sunrise.

"True, I need you to stay with Gywie for a minute."

He was expecting another stubborn refusal but the boy released him and trotted meekly off to his sister's side, sitting down as he'd been told. Viggo smiled with relief and reached out with one crooked finger to tap Gywie beneath her chin, gaining her attention.

"And I need your help," he told her, forcing his smile to be real. She brightened at once. "Can you keep True here? Don't let him go, not even for a second, okay? I'll be right back."

The small fairy nodded eagerly and put her arms around her brother, pleased to be in charge. Viggo brushed his finger gratefully over her cheek and climbed to his feet, steadying himself for what he would see as he walked back toward the edge of the swamp.

It wasn't what he expected. The griffin was gone. So was Aeron. Viggo's wide eyes picked out the disturbed place among the carpet of decomposing leaves where the two of them had fought and fallen. There were two paths that had not been there before, one wide and one narrow, where someone – or something – had dragged their dead bodies across the forest floor and into the swamp. The surface slime swelled as he stared at it, belching out a soft mouthful of steam. The hairs on the back of Viggo's neck stiffened. Whatever the someone or something had been, he knew with sudden certainty that they were still nearby, watching. It was time to go.

He darted over to Sunrise and knelt beside her, touching her arm to roll her from her side onto her back. Her face was devoid of colour and her breaths were strained, but she was alive and for now that was enough. He gathered her awkwardly into his arms, afraid of doing further damage to her tattered wings, but more afraid of letting her – or any of them – spend another second next to the swamp. It felt like the ooze itself was watching them.

The children brightened and scrambled to their feet when he returned, questions rising to their mouths when they saw how he carried their mother. He interrupted before they could ask.

"She's fine. She's just...sleeping." It wasn't a total lie. "Gywie, I need your help again. Hold your brother's hand and keep him close. We have to go."

The children obeyed without protest, following where he led them. He urged them along as fast as their tiny feet could go over uneven terrain; but no matter how far they went or how urgently Viggo pressed them, that eerie sense of being watched and followed did not diminish.

Chapter 11

V IGGO WAS BEGINNING TO think the Sinking Swamps went on forever. Whichever way he went he eventually came across it, bubbling and lurking in wait for him. When he turned away to try another route, he inevitably reached the same impasse. He had a reliable sense of direction and until now there had never been any reason to doubt it. Even without sunlight to guide him, he was relatively sure they had maintained a steady course toward the river valley, never once doubling back onto their own path. But no matter how long they walked, or how sore his feet became, or how tired the children began to tell him they were...he still could not get them away from the swamp. If he hadn't known better, he might have begun to suspect it was following them about, always just a couple of paces ahead.

That was a ludicrous idea, and Viggo knew the moment it came into his head that he was no longer thinking straight. The swamp wasn't following him and it obviously ended somewhere. He knew it did, for if Aeron could make it in on foot, then it stood to reason they could make it out. But as to where, exactly, they might find their way out...on that point Viggo was well and truly lost. Perhaps he had lost his sense of direction after all. Maybe it was this damn mist steaming off the surface of the swamp that was messing with his mind.

All he knew for sure was he could not go on like this much longer.

"Viggy?"

"*What?*"

The harshness of his own voice startled Viggo out of his reverie and brought him to a stop. He turned back to see Gywie watching him with wide eyes. Beside her, True stared up at him with more concern in his little face than any boy his age ought to have been capable of. Viggo sighed.

"What is it?" he asked, purposefully softening his tone.

Gywie fidgeted back and forth, digging the toe of her boot into the dirt. "I gotsta pee."

Viggo stared. The request wasn't unreasonable. But with so much else weighing upon his mind, the simplicity of it was nearly beyond him. Forcing himself to look around, he sought out some solution. There were trees everywhere.

"Okay, go ahead."

"*Here?*" she demanded in utter disbelief.

"There isn't anywhere else, at least not for a while. Here is as good a place as any."

There was something very grown-up and snobbish about the way Gywie looked around with her nose in the air, her lip curling with disgust. Releasing her brother, she ran up to grab Viggo's legs, her blue eyes stretched wide with phony innocence to get what she wanted.

"I'm scared!"

The only thing Gywie looked scared of was not getting her way, though she had already won, for Viggo did not have the strength to stand there and argue with her.

"Okay," he relinquished, beginning to realize just how badly he needed to rest and catch his thoughts. This was as good a time as any. "Hold on."

Viggo took another, more critical look around and finally picked his way toward an ancient oak tree with massive roots exposed above-ground. The roots were thick with moss and Viggo lay Sunrise down in a sheltered hollow between them, wishing all the while that there was someplace better to put her. She was still breathing – still alive – but she was also drenched with sweat, and when he brushed her hair back from her face he found she was hot to the touch.

They could not go any further until he did something about her wings. Whatever thing he felt watching them was not going away, and there seemed no sense in running from something they obviously could not escape. They would stay here, he decided, until he could come up with some better plan than trudging aimlessly through the Sinking Swamps. Besides, the children probably needed the rest as much, if not more, than he did.

Gesturing True over, Viggo gently put his arm around the boy. "Can you stay with her?" he asked, nodding towards Sunrise. "Just for a minute?"

The boy bobbed his head with dire seriousness and squirmed away, cuddling up against his mother's side and stroking his hand gently upon her cheek as if this could make everything alright again. Viggo smiled wistfully at the innocence of the gesture. Taking a deep breath, he stood and turned back to Gywie.

"Alright, let's go."

"You can't come!"

Viggo hesitated, wondering if he'd misunderstood what the girl want-ed from him. "I'll just come long enough to help you...erm, find a place."

She considered this, nodded agreeably, and took his hand; looking around expectantly as though she hoped he might divine an outhouse. Viggo wished that he could have. Instead, he pulled the little girl along to another tree, one wide enough around to provide her with some privacy.

"Will this do?"

She inspected the rotting leaves dappled around the base of the trunk and the many small, prickly plants growing up between them. Her nose scrunched tight in her face again.

"It's all icky!"

"Just go ahead behind the tree and be quick," he urged.

She latched onto his leg again. "But then I won't be able to see you!"

"Do you want me to come around the tree with you?"

The little girl released him with a wail. *"But then you'll be able to see me!"*

Viggo drew in a deep breath and held it, biting his tongue, wondering if it was shameful to plead with a child – for that was what he wanted to do. He wanted to plead with her to understand how hard this already was and beg her not to make it any harder. But losing his patience would not help stymie hers.

"How about this?" he tried, when at last he had mustered the compo-sure to speak without sounding entirely desperate. "I'll come around the tree with you, and then I'll turn around."

She pursed her lips and eyed him with deep suspicion.

Come on Gywie, please...

"Okay."

Thank heaven.

They walked to the other side of the tree and Viggo turned around.

"Further 'way!"

Obligingly, Viggo took a couple of steps forward.

"Further!"

By the time Gywie finally decided she was comfortable, she had *'furthered'* him right back around the tree to where they'd started. Viggo did not bother to wonder why she could not have just gone on her own in the first place – somethings were better left unquestioned. He merely stood with folded arms and stared at the tree until she finally reappeared, her blonde head poking carefully around the trunk as if to make absolutely sure he had not been peeking.

"You all done?"

"Uh-huh!" She skipped out over the knobby roots and smiled brightly at him, rewarding him with her outstretched hand. He took it, returning her infectious smile with one of his own.

It fell as they started back toward the massive oak tree.

He stopped short, tightening his hold on Gywie's hand to pull her a step behind him. Sunrise and True were exactly where he'd left them, but they were no longer alone. True sat up to watch the shadows gathering nearby, though he didn't look nearly so alarmed by their presence as Viggo felt.

In truth, Viggo did not know what they were, except that they looked like shadows. There had to be at least ten of them, all half his height, all vague in form and shape. They were inky black and possessed no discernable features at all, except for the silver eyes which gleamed waveringly out of their shadowy faces like coins dropped in a pool. Whatever they were, they had clustered around the unconscious fairy and seemed to be awaiting his return.

"Is this him?"

"It is."

"The pact."

"He broke it."

"Pact-breaker."

"Trouble-maker."

"Much damage."

Soft, murky voices all murmured in agreement. Their simple, straight-forward accusations gave Viggo the unsettling impression he had come up before a convening of Elders; one which had already judged him guilty.

"Who are you?" he demanded, and as an afterthought added: "*What* are you?"

"Ignorant," one suggested.

"Human," another corrected.

"Not one of ours."

"Another breed."

"A *distant* breed!"

"Should we tell him?"

"Should he know?"

"He should not."

Again, there were deep mutters of agreement. Viggo's natural instinct to argue was tempered only because he did not know which part of all that he should be arguing with. Not that they would have listened even if he tried. They were wholly wrapped up in their own discussion now, their arguments bouncing so quickly between them it was impossible to tell, at any given moment, which one of them was speaking.

"She broke the pact also."

"She did."

"She did!"

At first, Viggo assumed they must be referring to Sunrise, but as he struggled to keep up with their rapid, clipped sentences, he soon realized they were talking about the griffin.

"The council ruled."

"Save retaliation."

"Until winter."

"When food is scarce."

"Wise choice."

"She ignored."

"The ruling."

"She ignored it."

"Sought revenge."

"Unwise."

"Excuse me," he interrupted, attempting to wedge his way back into the conversation. He was tired of being ignored and no longer as frightened of the strange creatures as he probably ought to have been. "What is going on here?"

They paid his little interruption no mind. As their conversation continued, Gywie twisted her hand out of Viggo's grasp and scrambled away to be near her brother. Though he was sorry for the loss of her small hand in his and the comfort it provided, he made no attempt to call her back.

The sprites – or whatever they were – seemed oblivious to her presence anyway.

"Retaliation was excessive."

"Death."

"One of ours."

"Unfortunate."

"One of ours," they began to repeat, their voices resonating grief. *"Ours! Ours! Ours!"*

One voice spoke out of tune with the chorus.

"Why?"

For one long, agonizing moment, the swamp descended into silence, with everything hanging upon the answer to that question. The voices returned in a flurry, rising swiftly in pitch and excitement.

"To save his mate."

"Who angered the griffin."

"To save him."

"Yes, him!"

"Because he broke it!"

"The pact!"

"He broke the pact!"

"His fault!"

"All his fault!" came the final, unanimous agreement.

Viggo felt choked as he followed the broken logic and realized he could not disagree with where it had taken them. Though much had been omitted from their little dialogue, they had boiled events down to their essence and they were not wrong. All of this was his fault.

"What do you want from me?" he asked finally, wearily, tired of surprises; tired suddenly of this whole journey.

"Fix it!"

Shrill shouts of agreement filled the air.

"Yes, fix it!"

"Make it right."

"Yes, you."

"*You* make it right."

"How do I make it right?" he asked, his gaze straying from the shadow sprites to Sunrise and her little ones. Gywie was calling into her mother's ear, shaking her arm and looking perplexed when she stirred feverishly but did not wake. It would not be long before the children figured out this was more than sleep.

One of the diminutive creatures came forward and Viggo was surprised to hear it speak fluently, in a voice that sounded like it was echoing up a stone well.

"We are the inhabitants of the Oak Trees. You may call us Dryad. The griffin was within her rights to leave the Nyth and harm the fairy, but there had been no deaths among her kind. She overstepped herself. In her haste to kill the fairy she took a Druid from us instead. Both are now dead and the pact is mended, but our justice is not satisfied. A life lost demands a life given. You broke the pact. It is from you we demand our justice. You must stay with the fairy until the shadow of death has passed her by."

Viggo stared, too exasperated for words. All of this...just so they could tell him to do what he planned on doing anyway?

"Will you take her with you and protect her young?" the Dryad pressed.

"Of course I will!" he snapped. The frustration swelling in his chest burst like a dam, releasing a flood of impatience. Every minute they stood around talking nonsense was a minute he could have been tending to Sunrise's wings or looking for a way out of this swamp. They were wasting his time. "If you were the ones following me, then you already know that's what I've been trying to do."

Silver eyes narrowed into silver slits.

"He is another breed."

"No respect."

"Cannot be trusted."

"Not trusted."

The last murmur echoed excitedly from one little creature to the next. *"Not trusted, not trusted!"*

"Do you promise?" the lead one interrupted finally, silencing its fellows. "Will you swear us an oath to take her from here and keep her until she is well?"

"No!" Viggo exploded. He didn't care that his fury startled the children. In that moment, he would not have cared if he startled the whole bloody swamp. Something had cracked inside of him; all those walls he built to hold back emotions were gone and he could no longer stem their surge. They washed over him like a tidal wave – exhaustion, uncertainty, fear, guilt – dropping him to his knees. The Dryad wanted more than he could give.

"I can't promise that! I can't. I'm going to try but I can't *promise* because I can't find a way out of this bloody swamp! And even if we do get out there are soldiers looking for me. I can't promise that I'll be able to avoid them all. I don't know where to go, I don't know what to do, I don't know anything about fairy wings or why she won't wake up or how to make her better..."

Viggo was surprised to feel warm tears sliding down his cheeks and taste the salt of them upon his lips. "But I will try," he finished softly. "I can promise I'll try."

For a while the Dryad looked on in silence as Viggo stared helplessly down at his hands, spent for words. And then True got up. He left his mother's side and trundled over, wrapping his little arms around Viggo's neck and hugging gently. Viggo hugged him back, burying his wet face in the boy's brown hair with more gratitude than he would have known how to express.

"The boy," one of the Dryad muttered with new interest.

"One of ours."

"He knows."

Viggo glanced up to see the shadow before him smiling. He wasn't sure how he could tell, exactly, since it had no mouth or cheeks or eyebrows; but something in the way the eyes squinted looked happy and pleased.

"You speak truth. We will help you on your way."

Viggo heard a murky gurgle and looked over to see swamp water slurping over the ground toward them, heaving and rolling like there was a living thing prowling just below the surface. It slowed as it neared, lingering for a moment to let off a belch of hot steam before reversing into slimy retreat. In its wake it left behind two items: Sunrise's blue cloak and Aeron's sword and scabbard, both clean and dry. Viggo stared incredulously at the gifts, beginning to understand that the animate vines and tree roots had nothing to do with Aeron or the Druids – it was the Dryad who controlled the swamp. He turned to thank them.

They were gone.

He was fortunate to already be on his knees or he might have sunk to them again from sheer relief. For once he did not care to try and sort out the how or the why. He simply hugged the little boy in his arms, heartened to see one of True's rarely bestowed smiles.

"Okay," Viggo said, taking a deep breath to gather his thoughts. The stop had not proved very restful, but it had certainly cleared his head. "Let's take care of your mother and get out of here."

Little heads bobbed in eager agreement.

Producing the flask of water he'd saved, along with a cloth out of

Aeron's sword and Sunrise's Cloak

his pocket, Viggo began the careful task of cleaning the long tears gouged into Sunrise's wings. Her feathers were as soft as they looked, though it was difficult to appreciate their beauty while they were matted with blood and dirt. There wasn't enough water in the flask to clean all her broken feathers as he would have liked; he used up every drop cleaning out the cuts and punctures the griffin had left her with. With this accomplished to the best of his ability, Viggo switched to using the salve, smearing all that was left into the freshly cleaned wounds.

There was no longer any way to hide from the children that their mother had been hurt. They sat nearby, holding one another's hands, watching closely. He was relieved they didn't cry or ask questions, for he wouldn't have known how to comfort or answer them. He talked as he worked, explaining to them what he was doing, hoping the sound of his voice might reassure them and inspire some confidence that their mother was going to be okay. The only thing he did not voice aloud were his concerns to the contrary.

Sunrise had begun to tremble, almost imperceptibly, but he could feel it whenever he touched her. Resting the back of his hand against her forehead, Viggo frowned.

"Are you two ready to go?"

"I'm hungry!" Gywie protested.

"Then let's go find some lunch," he agreed, his forced cheeriness startling her into silence. She bounced to her feet, hauling True up beside her, watching eagerly to see how he would bring about this happy turn of events.

Viggo attached Aeron's sheathed sword to his belt and lay Sunrise's cloak overtop of her, covering her as best he could before gathering her back into his arms. Both would be useful in case they ran into any soldiers; without the latter, he might have had a hard time explaining to them – or anyone else for that matter – why he was carrying around an unconscious woman in her under-dress.

As he stood and tried to decide which direction to take, a nearby tree bowed aside. The trees beyond it also pulled apart from one another, opening a clear path for them to take. He grinned. The Dryad were as good as their word.

He set off with renewed purpose, instructing the children to run ahead where he could keep an eye on them. The murky swamp water no longer blocked them at every turn and that omnipresent feeling of being watched finally evaporated. With the Dryad on their side it seemed there was nothing left to fear from the Sinking Swamps.

The gnarled swamp trees soon became a forest of sturdy oaks, the putrid mess of decaying vegetation beneath their boots subtly shifting into a carpet of golden leaves and sharp twigs, dotted occasionally with acorns the squirrels had yet to find and stash away for winter. This change of scenery cheered the children and Gywie began inventing games with the acorns, tossing them at her brother or kicking them to see how much distance she could get.

Viggo enjoyed the sound of her laughter and was content to let her play as he listened for the sound of the river in the distance. He would have to call her back and quiet her when he heard it, before her noise could draw the attention of soldiers waiting in the valley.

But Gywie heard the river before he did.

With a whoop of joy, she took off running through the trees and was gone before he could stop her. Though Viggo called after her to keep quiet and come back, she either didn't hear or didn't care, for she did neither.

His heart sank. He'd hoped to leave the Sinking Swamps without drawing attention; maybe even continue west just inside the tree line until they reached Dionne, which he believed was closer at this point than Dairefast. Gywie had shattered that hope. There was no way the soldiers could have missed the little girl running out of the forest. And just in case they had, her joyful shouting would get their attention quickly enough.

There wasn't anything to do except follow Gywie out into the sunshine and be grateful that True was still walking obediently at his side. His mind raced with possible scenarios. The sword did him no good; he couldn't fight off soldiers with Sunrise in his arms, and putting her down to fight would only leave her vulnerable. Somehow, he was going to have to talk his way out of this one. But there was no explanation which sounded good, not even to him.

It was hard to say if anyone would believe the truth about Aeron. They already thought of Sunrise as a traitor. When the soldiers saw the two of them emerging from the woods together – without her husband – they would draw their own conclusions. What if they thought he had killed Aeron? What if they thought she had?

All his dizzying worries soon came to naught. When Viggo stepped into the open there was no one around but Gywie. She clutched her cloak in one tiny fist and dragged it through the grass behind her as she skipped towards the river, her pink wings catching the sunlight.

Viggo followed as far as the road that paralleled the river and stopped to stare in both directions. There were no soldiers; no soldiers anywhere.

He couldn't explain it. Their fires were still there, stamped out and abandoned along the roadside. It was doubtful the Dryad had frightened them off, nor could he blame their absence upon the griffins, since the pact was mended and the creatures were confined once again to the mountain range. The soldiers must have been called away by something urgent. Maybe, when they got to Dionne, Viggo would find out what could possibly be more urgent than catching him.

Chapter 12

SUNRISE'S CONDITION HAD WORSENED by the time they reached Dionne. Though it defied discretion, Viggo entered the town by the main road and sought out the nearest inn. It turned out to be a respectable-looking establishment where the innkeeper took a ready interest in his plight, leading him straightaway to a furnished room upstairs.

"Here," the tall man urged, holding open the door and looking on with anxious concern in his pale face. "Put her in here."

Sunrise still wouldn't wake, but what troubled Viggo was how wild and desperate her breathing had become. He was in such a hurry to cross the room and lay her down upon the bed that he did not notice the innkeeper following him. Nor did he notice, at first, when part of Sunrise's cloak slid aside, revealing silver feathers.

"Wait," the innkeeper muttered, his narrow face darkening as his brows drew together. "What is that? You can't stay here with *that!*"

Following the keeper's gaze, Viggo realized his mistake. There was no way to hide Sunrise's wings now. He held his tongue, struggling to remind himself that only a day ago – or at any other point in his life, for that matter – the innkeeper's response might not have seemed so unreasonable to him. He too had been raised to fear the other kinds. And though the Celts were not as wholly intolerant of them as his own people were, they certainly put a great deal more stock in their own myths and superstitions.

Even so, there was no excuse for referring to any person as a *that* – no matter what kind they were.

"*She,*" he clarified finally, drawing a deep breath to keep his voice calm, "is hurt and we are staying."

"Where her kind go," the innkeeper replied with a point of his finger, "changelings always appear. There are a lot of children in this town! I'm afraid I simply can't-"

"*We're staying.*"

The innkeeper recoiled, taken aback by the sharpness of Viggo's interruption and offended by the finality. Viggo carried on with a clipped promise to pay whatever it took to secure the room, provided the innkeeper left them in peace for as long as they needed.

"And send help!" Viggo shouted after him as the keeper retreated, pulling the door closed behind him with a curt thud.

"And lunch!" Gywie squealed anxiously.

Viggo's first request upon arriving at the inn was that someone send for a healer or physician. At Gywie's insistence, he'd also asked for enough food to satisfy both children. It seemed unlikely that either would be forthcoming now that the innkeeper had seen Sunrise's wings.

"*What about our lunch?*" Gywie cried, stamping her foot. Next to her, True stood quietly with his lips quivering and tears in his eyes. Despite her anger, Gywie looked like she was on the verge of tears too.

"In a minute," Viggo promised, desperately trying to ignore them as he fixed his gaze on Sunrise's face. She was struggling to draw shallow, erratic breaths, gasping with each effort almost as if she were being strangled.

What could he do? His mind raced for some remedy and came up empty. He couldn't think. He was too tired. She wasn't terribly heavy, but it had been such a long way to walk and every part of him still ached from his fall into the swamp.

Abruptly, Viggo threw aside Sunrise's cloak, watching as every breath she took swelled in her chest and strained against the tightly-laced stays of her bodice. Of course. He'd been so focused on her torn wings and fever that he never once stopped to wonder if she'd been hurt in the fall. Hoping she would forgive him, he began at once to loosen the ties. He did his best to avert his eyes and maintain her modesty, though if he was being honest, he was far too frightened to care what he saw. Relief consumed him as her rapid breaths finally began to slow. To be absolutely safe he loosened the garment further, heaving a weary sigh as he watched her chest rising and falling in peaceful rhythm once more.

"Viggy!" There was a sharp tug on his coat. "*I! Want! Lunch!*"

He briefly closed his eyes, letting out another sigh. He hadn't forgotten. He knew the children needed to eat, and if Gywie shouted it any louder the whole town would know it too.

"Alright," he agreed, knowing he could not put her off any longer. "I'll go find you something." It seemed wiser not to point out that it was well past lunchtime; judging by the darkness falling outside the window, it was probably past their usual suppertime.

"If you stay here with your mother, I'll go-"

A timid knock at the door cut him off mid-sentence. Realizing she was about to lose his attention yet again, Gywie gave his coat an enormous tug and screamed. True sat down in the middle of the floor where he'd been standing, his tears erupting into sobs.

Swallowing hard against the helpless agitation which threatened to get the better of him, Viggo mustered enough good sense to reach for the blanket at the foot of the bed and pull it over Sunrise. He checked this time, as he tucked her in, to be sure her wings were completely hidden. He glanced at Gywie too, making sure the girl still wore her yellow cloak.

The knock sounded again, a little louder this time. Viggo stepped around the sobbing children and opened the door. It was the barmaid. He'd briefly noticed her cleaning tables in the empty tavern when they first arrived. Now she stood on her tiptoes in the doorway, doing her very best to see past him into the room. Viggo leaned against the doorframe, intentionally blocking her view.

"Yes?"

She stared at him curiously, as though she'd only just noticed he was there. "Pardon the interruption, Sir. I don't mean to seem out of line. But when you came in, I couldn't help but to see... That is to say, it was hard not to notice..." The short, ample woman paused a moment to gather her thoughts. "Do you travel with the Lady Demeray?"

Lady Demeray. The name startled Viggo, for it was the first time he'd heard Sunrise called such. He crossed his arms and shifted his weight to be doubly sure he stood between this woman and her view of the bed. He'd been so worried someone might recognize him by his description and report him to the soldiers, it had never even occurred to him that people would be far more likely to recognize the healer from nearby Dairefast.

Though the woman's expression grew ever more puzzled the longer he lingered in silence, Viggo could not quite decide how he should answer. His first instinct was to deny it. But Sunrise's unusual colouring was distinctive and hard to miss. If she had been recognized and he denied it, he would get caught in his own lie, doubtless leading to more uncomfortable questions.

"Yes," he agreed finally, not at all happy with the admission.

But the woman was happy to hear it. Her entire manner relaxed and she pulled a basket from behind her back, thrusting it cheerfully into his arms.

"I thought as much! Lovely woman. I don't care what others say about her – she was such a good help to me last year when I had trouble with my baby. I should like very much to do something in return. You asked about food for the children, did you not? I hope this will do."

Viggo felt an eager tug on his coat. All the wailing impatience had morphed miraculously into sweetness as Gywie leaned up against him, her little fingers grasping for the basket in his hands.

"Lunch?" she asked, eyes wide with hope.

He relinquished the basket to her at once. The moment it was in her possession she vanished further into the room, True's little footsteps pounding after her when he realized what she had. Viggo very much doubted there would be anything left for him.

"Thank you."

"A pleasure," the woman replied, and Viggo could see in her face that it was. "Pert won't be happy if he finds out though. I don't know what he's in such a tizzy about, but you'll have to forgive him. He does get rather excited about things sometimes. Is there anything else I can get you?" She made one final, curious attempt to see past him. "Was the Lady hurt on the road?"

"No, nothing," Viggo muttered quickly, choosing to ignore her second question. But as she turned to leave, he was struck with a bout of indecision. He was afraid to let her in lest she discover Sunrise's secret. But the innkeeper had already seen; and besides, he did not know what to do about Sunrise's rising fever.

"Wait!" he called after her. "There is something. Could you send for a healer?"

The barmaid looked back sympathetically. "Whenever we need one of those, we send for Lady Demeray. It's not a popular art, you know. Doesn't tend to pay well – or at all – if the results aren't as hoped for." She paused, her eyes sweeping down to his boots before jumping back to his face. "Are you family, then?"

Viggo was too tired to think of a good lie. "Yes," he agreed, "family...visiting."

The barmaid beamed, her cheeks round with the force of her smile. "How lovely! She spoke to me once of being homesick. Poor dear. Such a very long way from home, and under such dreadful circumstances. I'm glad she's got family to visit her. Well now, I suppose I could take a look if you like. Twisted an ankle, did she?"

"Please," Viggo agreed, stepping aside to allow her into the room.

"I've completely forgotten myself. My name is Em, and I...oh..."

Em trailed off as she caught sight of Sunrise and approached the bed. It was a real one, stuffed with new wool and mounted on a solid wood frame. None of that mattered, of course, to the unconscious fairy who shivered in her sleep upon it. The barmaid lowered herself onto the edge of the bed.

"This is no little mishap," she muttered, stating the obvious. She touched Sunrise's flushed cheek and made a ritual gesture Viggo did not recognize. "I've heard soldiers talk of this. They say it is not the wounds in battle that kill men, but the fever which follows."

Viggo had heard that too. "Do you know what can be done for it?"

"After my son was born, Violet stayed with me many hours and kept at me with cool water to stave off the fever. Perhaps we should try the same. Wait now and I'll be back."

Viggo took her place on the edge of the bed as soon as she left the room. His fingers stole beneath the blanket and found Sunrise's hand, giving it a gentle squeeze.

"It's going to be fine," he heard himself whisper aloud. "The Dryad said so. They wanted me to promise I would stay until you got better...so they must have known that you would." He wasn't sure which one of them he was trying to convince.

He pulled his hand away when he heard footsteps rushing up the stairs. Em burst into the room with a bucket of water in one hand and a clean cloth in the other.

"Pert is talking about sending for the owner!" she exclaimed, half-breathless from haste. "I don't think he's taken very kindly to you. Best if you keep to yourself and don't draw any more attention. I'll try to get his head on straight. I do wish I could stay but the men are starting to come in for the evening and there's work to be done. You'll be alright on your own?"

"Yes," Viggo agreed thankfully, accepting the cloth and bucket from her hands, "thank you."

The maid whirled to leave but paused in the doorway, smiling kindly toward the foot of the bed. "Poor little dears. They'll sleep soundly tonight, that's certain. Do you want me to light the candles before I go?"

He nodded and watched appreciatively as she bustled about, lighting the various candles scattered across the room. When she had gone, Viggo looked down to see Gywie and True slumped against one another at the foot of the bed, both of them fast asleep. Neither had gotten very far into their meal; both still clutched barely nibbled biscuits in their little hands. Beside them, the basket lay forgotten. He briefly considered trying to lift them onto the bed where they would be comfortable and immediately dismissed the notion. Figuring out how to put them back to sleep if they woke was too daunting a prospect to risk facing. Besides, he had something more important to worry about.

For what felt like hours, Viggo worked to bring Sunrise's temperature down, following the same steady procedure over and over. He dipped his cloth in the bucket of cold water, wrung it out, and dabbed it gently over Sunrise's forehead and down her face. Then again, dabbing the cloth over her neck and shoulders. Again for her arms. Again and again and again until his hands were clammy and he could no longer tell if the water was cold or warm.

At some point, when his mind began to feel as numb as his hands, Viggo switched to washing the last traces of blood from her silver feathers. Then it was back to trying to cool her. Dip, wring, dab. Dip, wring, dab. *Dip...wring...dab. . .*

Viggo jerked his head upright, shocked to realize he had nodded off. A tired sigh passed over his lips. He wanted to stay with Sunrise – to stay up with her all night if need be – but his body was demanding sleep; even just a little.

He reached out blearily to touch her cheek, finding it warm instead of hot. At least she no longer shivered. That would have to be good enough for now, he decided, and slid from the edge of the bed onto the floor. He didn't bother getting comfortable; he was too tired to care. All he had to do was close his eyes and lean back against the bedframe and sleep was upon him, taking him instantly. He was just beginning to dream when Sunrise's shout startled him back to wakefulness.

"Aeron!"

One frantic glance over his shoulder and Viggo's alarm faded. Her eyes were still closed; she was only dreaming. It took him longer to realize she was not calling out for her dead husband, but crying his name in fright.

"Aeron!"

He might have minded her nightmares less, had he not been able to hear voices wafting up dimly from the tavern below. They made him nervous that someone might just as easily hear the fairy's shouts and come to investigate. The return of the suspicious innkeeper was the last thing they needed.

When he saw her lips pull open again, Viggo did the only thing he could think of and scrambled back onto the edge of the bed, cupping a hand over Sunrise's mouth before she could cry out a third time.

The moment Viggo's hand touched the fairy's face he was no longer in the little room on the top floor of the inn. He stumbled as he tried to orient himself, his legs tripping awkwardly over the notion that he was standing – when just a moment earlier he had not been. It was not until his feet were solidly under him that he turned slowly around to look.

Somehow, he had come to be in a marketplace. It was bustling with the chatter of voices and the pleasant sound of water gurgling out of a nearby fountain. Established shops welcomed regular patrons while the flamboyant tents of travelling merchants lured in the more adventuresome clientele. A steady stream of people meandered through the market, not one of them in the leastways concerned with his sudden appearance in their midst.

The scenery was not all that had changed. In Dionne it was night-time, and well into the season of early snow. But here – wherever here was – cool breezes worked tirelessly in the afternoon sun to blow the last few golden leaves from the trees.

As Viggo looked around, struggling to understand what he was seeing, he recognized one of the people milling about. Not that Aeron was milling. The Druid made purposefully for one of the larger merchant tents, his forest-green cloak billowing behind him like the trailing end of a storm cloud. Viggo couldn't tell if the sheen in his eyes was from anger or drink.

He moved to block Aeron's way, knowing he needed to speak with the Druid without knowing what it was he meant to say. How did one ask a dead man why he was alive and well?

Aeron didn't see him; he didn't even slow down. When Viggo realized the other man wouldn't stop, he gave up searching for words and tried to step aside. He wasn't fast enough. Like a cold wind, Aeron passed through him; vanishing away into the merchant tent. Viggo stiffened, a chill shivering up his spine. Was this some place of the dead?

He shook his head, forcing his shoulders to relax as a way of dismissing the gruesome thought. He was not at all convinced the dead went anywhere, and even if they did, he felt certain they weren't coming here. This had to be some sort of dream, though it was unlike any from previous experience. Never in his life had a dream been so vivid that he could feel the unevenness of the cobblestones beneath his boots and smell the autumn crispness in the air. Whatever or wherever this was, he felt instinctively that it was important somehow.

A yelp jerked his attention back to the tent where Aeron had gone. He followed the sound into the spacious structure. The size of the tent along with the sheer volume of goods it held told Viggo these were very successful merchants. At a glance, he would have said they dealt in curiosities. There was everything from decorative Macedonian carvings to bolts of cloth bearing ornate, Gaulish patterns

The traders themselves – of whom he saw six – seemed to be finished with the day's business. They lounged about in various places, perched upon their wares, curiously watching the Druid who had intruded upon them. In the far corner some local boys laughed and jeered as they threw handfuls of stones through the bars of a covered wagon.

Nobody seemed to notice Viggo.

Aeron walked directly up to one of the laughing boys and kicked him in his behind. "Git on home to your mothers!"

The boy shouted in surprise and his companions promptly scattered, racing each other to the exit. Viggo was quicker to move aside this time, not wishing to feel another body pass through his own. Cautiously, after the boys were gone, he crept up behind Aeron and peered over his shoulder to see what the children had been poking fun at. His stomach leapt into his throat when he saw.

It was a sturdy cart, covered and locked, similar to the kind he'd seen in Camelot, used there for transporting prisoners of war. It seemed an overly zealous way to imprison two women. Then again, Viggo knew at least one of them was much more than she appeared. He did not recognize the woman slumped against the back of the cart, her skin so thin and gray she looked halfway dead already; but there was no mistaking the silver-haired woman standing protectively in front of her.

The traders rose to their feet, suddenly wary of the newcomer. Aeron turned on them and Viggo slipped away, sidling nearer to the cart. He did not expect Sunrise to hear him but he whispered her name anyway, wishing she would tell him what was going on. It almost spooked him when she looked his way, the first one to notice his presence. She looked deeply apologetic as she touched a finger to her lips in a gesture of silence, turning her attention back to Aeron.

"I've just now heard it said you keep women for sale," Aeron began, his lips drawn tight.

Judging by the way a muscle kept jumping beneath his left eye, Viggo guessed the practice of trading in human life was not something the Druid approved of, which meant they had at least one thing in common.

"How much?"

"I'm afraid you've heard wrongly, friend," one of the traders said pleasantly, stepping forward with an amiable smile. "We're not traders of *that* sort. These two merely serve to spark curiosity, and those who come to see them inevitably purchase something. It's good business."

"Maybe you don't know where you've ended up, *friend*," Aeron retorted sternly, "but we don't look fondly on slavery here."

The head trader clucked his tongue at the gravity of the charge, but Viggo could see the scorn in his fair blue eyes. "I can assure you, Sir," he said, his voice laden with mock sincerity, "that they are not slaves. We've never once imposed upon them for anything they didn't want, have we, boys?"

There was laughter. The trader stepped closer, inclining his head as though he were letting Aeron in on a great secret. "You can trust me when I say they're both better off here than where we found them."

Sunrise's eyes flashed in hot dispute.

"I doubt that one will be better off staying in there until her baby comes," Aeron shot back, not so far gone with drink that he could not sense when he was being taken for a fool. Viggo peered around Sunrise to get a better look at the other woman and immediately noticed the enormous swelling beneath her dress. From the colour of her languid blue eyes he knew this was Gywie's mother.

"How much?" Aeron asked again.

The man in charge laughed, his eyes twinkling with some secret knowledge. Regretfully, Viggo studied each of the men in turn, his heart sinking with realization. All six of them shared the same pale complexion and fair colouring that he himself possessed. These were Saxon traders. Despite how much he wanted to believe this was all a bad dream, he knew deep down it was not. This was a memory. More than ever, he could not imagine why Sunrise had helped him.

The trader clapped Aeron warmly upon the shoulder, shaking his head with vague amusement. "I see what you're after, and this is a mighty noble thing you're trying to do; but I'm afraid you just don't understand. You wouldn't want these two, I can guarantee you that. This is as safe as they could hope to be in your country or mine." Aeron didn't look at all convinced and the trader could see it also. "Normally I charge a coin or two for this, but for you I make an exception."

Old hinges filled the tent with a sharp burst of anguished creaking as the trader produced a key and unlocked the cart door, pulling it open.

Go now – Viggo whispered silently – *fly!*

But she wouldn't. He already knew Sunrise wouldn't leave the other fairy behind.

"Now take a look at Violet here," the trader suggested, eager for an opportunity to show off that which he had somehow acquired. He reached in and caught Sunrise by her arm, barely acknowledging her attempts to resist as he hauled her out onto the dirt floor. The fairy's face burned red with shame as he pulled aside her dirty cloak to reveal bright, silvery wings.

"Now do you see what I've been saying is true? Nobody in their right mind would want to buy themselves a couple of filthy fey."

If Aeron was at all surprised or intimidated by the sight of fairy wings, it didn't show in his face; there was only pure contempt for the Saxon trader who had just gone too far. In one swift motion Aeron decked the man, dropping him unconscious to the floor. His five companions jumped to attention, brandishing whatever was in reach. But Aeron wasn't looking for a fight.

"How much?"

Without their leader they were less certain, unable to match the Druid's iron will. A price was quickly agreed upon; the money exchanged for a key. While the men dragged their stupefied companion across the tent to revive him, Aeron turned his attention to Sunrise for the first time. She eyed him suspiciously from where she blocked the door of the cart, trying to decide, it seemed, if he was a new threat to her friend.

"Whatever it is you think you've bought yourself," she began immediately, "you're going to be disappointed. I could have gotten away from them, you know. And I'll get away from you just as soon as my friend is-"

Aeron had no patience for the fairy's rambling bravery. "I didn't buy your services; I bought your freedom. Where are you from?"

Sunrise was taken aback by his frank assurance, some of the suspicion easing from her features. Still, she was evasive with him. "Nowhere close." When Aeron remained silent, making no unwelcome moves toward her, she began to glance nervously toward the traders.

"And you?" she tried at last, forcing herself to return his conversation. "You live here, in Camelot?"

"No. I'm from Dairefast, a small town near the mountains. There hasn't been a healer in our village for some years and I've come here to change that."

The brief interest which flickered across Sunrise's face was gone as soon as it had come, replaced by wide-eyed alarm as Aeron knelt at her feet. She shied away from him, her back pressed to the wagon. For one absurd moment, Viggo wondered if the Druid meant to propose marriage right then? But his intentions were more practical than that. He held out the key he'd purchased, making obvious to the fairy what he intended to do.

"Your friend needs help. The sooner I set you loose, the sooner we can get her out of here."

For the first time, Viggo noticed the long, slender chain bolted to the floor of the wagon at one end and shackled to Sunrise's left ankle at the other. The sight of it made him sick. A part of him could not help but wonder how she had come to be in such a situation; the rest of him was glad not to know.

The fairy still wasn't comfortable letting Aeron near her, but she managed to hold still long enough for him to set her free. Her unease was quickly forgotten as they climbed into the cart together and she babbled about all the things she had tried to help her friend, but how the other fairy still wasn't getting any better...

The scenery around Viggo flashed brightly, forcing him to lift a hand and close his eyes.

When he opened them again, he was no longer in the merchant tent. Lowering his hand, he gazed around in confusion at Aeron's house. A soft sound drew his attention to the front door, where Sunrise was just stepping into the house, her movements cautious and deliberate. From the look of curiosity on her face, he could guess this was her first time daring to enter the home of Aeron's first wife.

Another flash – less blinding, but still brilliant.

When it cleared Sunrise stood frozen just outside the door to the bedroom. Her hands were pressed rigidly over her mouth in an attempt to contain her emotions. But Viggo could see the horror and betrayal in her eyes.

Another flash.

Aeron stood in the bedroom doorway, embarrassed but mostly outraged. Sunrise backed away from him, shaking her head as she fought off tears of disbelief.

Flash.

Aeron followed his wife across the floor, his expression livid as he grabbed her arm to stop her retreat. It must have been the first time he'd raised a hand to her in anger, for Sunrise looked genuinely shocked as she cried out his name in fright: *"Aeron!"*

Flash.

Viggo woke with one of the worst headaches he could ever remember having. For a while he lay still and simply tried to block out the orange splotch dancing around under his eyelids. Eventually he reached for his throbbing temples, massaging gentle circles until the pain finally eased.

Sunrise's face was the first thing he saw when he finally opened his eyes. She was curled up beside him, sleeping peacefully, the bright flush of fever gone from her cheeks. Viggo let out a heavy sigh, and in his relief he heard echoes of her little rhymes dancing drowsily through his thoughts. They carried him back to her home, reminding him how easy it had been to sit on her doodled floor and laugh as she teased him.

She didn't know it yet, but it wasn't likely she would ever be going back. Reaching out, Viggo brushed a stray strand of silver hair from her face, smoothing it back into place. If Donovan hadn't liked her before, his opinion wasn't likely to have improved over the past few days. Going back now would be dangerous for her and the children, especially with Aeron's abrupt disappearance. Maybe she could go home when the war ended and the soldiers left, but without her husband he doubted there would be much for her to return to.

Mixed feelings gripped him, bringing a small, unexpected smile to his face. If what he'd seen in the dream was real – and he felt certain it was – then this wouldn't be the first time she'd started over with nothing. She would find a way.

Genuine respect swelled in him as he allowed his hand to linger on her face, his thumb briefly caressing her cheek where it was still bruised. Chain or no chain, she could have escaped that cart sooner or later. She'd stayed with her sick friend for the same reason she stayed with her unfaithful husband. It was the same reason she'd followed him into the Nyth and been willing to see him all the way to the coast. She didn't abandon the people she chose.

He knew suddenly that she was going to be fine. It was hard to believe he'd ever doubted it.

Pulling his hand back to himself, Viggo rolled over and sat up to check on the children, wondering how close it was to morning. To his surprise, Gywie and True were still exactly where he'd left them. They hadn't so much as shifted in their sleep. Frowning, he looked around and listened. Voices, dim though they were, still rose from below, and the candles had only burned down a little way.

A groan escaped him. He must not have slept very long after all.

Though he would have liked nothing better than to close his eyes and go back to sleep, there was no point. His brief doze might not have been enough for his body, but his mind was already running off in other directions and Viggo knew he would never succeed at silencing his thoughts here. Instead, he allowed them to lead him quietly from the room, following them all the way down into the tavern below.

Chapter 13

C OMPARED TO THE DIM candlelight of the room upstairs, the tavern seemed blinding at first. Viggo hesitated on the last step, letting his eyes adjust to the light and his ears to the noisy clamor, trying to sort out what he was after.

No sooner had he made up his mind and stepped forward than hands grabbed his arm and yanked him under the shadow of the staircase. The unexpected tug brought back the pain in his shoulder and he cringed, prying the hands off his coat. Em's brown eyes gleamed sternly up at him.

"What are you doing?" she hissed.

"Getting a drink," he answered flatly, wondering why it was any of her business.

Pride was a thing that existed equally among all peoples, regardless of social standing or occupation. Hers came across audibly in her sniff. "Not looking like that, you aren't."

She glanced him up and down, her lip curling with the same disgust Gywie had displayed for the swamp trees. "I told you not to draw attention," she warned. "If you go out among decent folk looking like that, you're sure to cause a stir. This is one of the more reputable places in town, you know."

Viggo reached up sheepishly and stroked the prickles coming in on his chin. His midnight swim across the river from Dairefast was the closest he'd come to bathing in weeks, and considering all he'd been through since Donovan and Ellaway got their hands on him, he could only imagine what a fright he must look. Em pointed sternly at a small, sloping door next to him.

"I warmed some water for my evening wash but it seems nobody is in a hurry to get along tonight. Not that I mind. I'm as grateful as anyone to hear the news. As far as I'm concerned, all this wretched war did was scare off the Saxon traders; and between you and me, they always had the best quality goods." What began as a friendly eyeroll turned into a curious stare as the barmaid studied him anew, some thought slowly working its way to the front of her mind.

"Thank you," Viggo muttered, pushing open the little door under the stairs and ducking away before she could contemplate his fair colouring any further.

The washing room he entered was tiny, but it was private and the door had a lock. For just a moment after he bolted it, Viggo was suspicious, wondering if when he opened it there would be soldiers fetched and waiting. But if Em had anything like that in mind, she could just as easily have sent soldiers up to the room already.

A single lantern hung from the ceiling, presiding over a full-sized washbasin of gently steaming water. Viggo glanced into a tarnished mirror on the wall; it painted a grim picture. No wonder Em didn't want him in her tavern. He set his suspicions aside, hanging them over the back of a nearby chair along with his clothes. The water wasn't as warm as he would have liked, but there was a sliver of real soap and he used it to scrub every last trace of Britannia from his skin.

For the first time, he removed the bandage from his shoulder and inspected the wound underneath for himself. The purplish bruises would be there for a while, but the split in the skin was healing nicely; or at least it had been until Em wrenched upon it. Fresh red droplets trickled down his arm, staining the bathwater. He found a clean cloth and held it over the cut until the bleeding stopped. It probably needed stitching, but he hadn't the time or patience for that.

It was hard to climb back into his clothes when he was clean and they were not. His own nose was numb to it but just by looking at them he knew they must smell. The cold of the little room forced him to dress anyway, swearing to himself all the while that he would take the time to wash them just as soon as he no longer had the threat of imminent capture hanging over his head.

Looking once more into the mirror, Viggo noted the improvement and decided he might as well make himself look respectable. Removing his little iron blade from its leather pouch, he used it to shave the stubble from his face. When he was finished, he took a minute to run his hands through his clean hair, carefully parting his long bangs to hide some of the cuts healing on his face.

Not so bad now, he thought, the corner of his mouth pulling sideways into a small smile. Not so bad at all.

He tidied up after himself and left the little washing room as he'd found it. Em was nowhere in sight. The tavern was full, blazing with light from too many lanterns and crowded with more people than Viggo might have expected for how late it had become. Nobody sat alone.

An earnest excitement buzzed around the tables, borne along by an unceasing stream of chatter.

He'd noticed this same sort of excitement earlier in the evening, along the main road leading into Dionne. As he was coming into town he saw locals and travellers alike standing in clusters, their carts and animals left unattended as they discussed some urgent matter. He'd been in too much of a hurry to find out what they were talking about, but it seemed to be good news, for there had been a sense of festivity in their faces. Not that anyone was celebrating. He'd seen a lot of quick, excited gestures, but they were coupled with furtive, muted tones; as if giving in to rejoicing too early might jinx whatever the good news was. And while people had certainly noticed him walking into town with a sleeping woman in his arms and two weary children struggling along behind, they'd been so preoccupied with their own affair that nobody so much as looked twice.

It was the same here in the tavern as it had been on the road. Nobody paid him any attention beyond the occasional disinterested glance as he threaded between tables. The only person who really noticed him as he approached the long counter was the man standing behind it.

The innkeeper – Pert, Em had called him – hesitated to serve Viggo anything; seeming even more suspicious of his cleanliness than he had been of the dirt and scruff. But when the assurance of payment came clattering across the counter in the form of gold ingots, he poured a drink readily enough.

"What's all the excitement?" Viggo asked, dipping one finger into the lukewarm mead and tasting it to be sure it wasn't laced with anything stronger.

Pert was too busy scrubbing miserably at his countertop to notice the subtle test, and for a moment he seemed to put his nervous distrust aside, needing someone to confide in. "The King has launched an unexpected campaign north to reclaim the lost territories. His armies are taking back one city after another – so we hear – and they say the whole war could be over in a matter of days."

Viggo took a casual sip of his drink. "Surely the Saxon scum won't make it that easy?"

"Oh, I'm sure they would not have – had they been facing an army of men! But an army of dragons?" Viggo choked on his drink and nearly spat it back into the wooden cup from which it had come. Pert was shaking his head with wistful sorrow. "Who could stand before that?"

"Army of...dragons?" Viggo asked hoarsely, swallowing hard to clear his throat. "I thought the King only had *one* dragon ally?"

"Well, apparently he's found many more allies." The man sighed, refusing to be swept along with the general air of excitement. "They say all these fine men come to guard our city could soon be heading home."

By the heartbroken look on his face, Viggo could guess that "fine men" was another way of saying 'paying customers'. Nodding his thanks, Viggo slipped discreetly away and sat down at the one empty table. It was far enough from the other patrons that he could go unnoticed by staring doggedly into his mug, but close enough that he could hear pieces of their conversation.

"...they're sayin' just the sight of the green dragon is enough to make a Saxon soil himself, for he knows what is comin' to him, he does."

"I thought the King's dragon was black?"

"Who can know? I hear he's got nearly a *dozen* of them."

"I heard it was *two* dozen!"

And so the speculation continued. As it did, their conversation painted a portrait of King Arthur that was ever more fearless and splendid until it bordered on the fantastical.

Viggo had not seen any dragons in Camelot but he had seen the King. As conversation continued and people debated exactly which towns had already been freed, and which ones they expected might be freed in the next day or two, Viggo's mind drifted back to the day he found his way into Camelot.

Had that really been a week ago? It seemed almost like another lifetime.

It had taken many careful hours to do it. His feeling of pride when he finally made his way, not only into the walled city but into the very castle where the famed King resided, made it all worthwhile. For being impossible, it had all turned out to be rather simple. As he thought back on it, he remembered how swept up he'd been in imagining his triumphant return; there would be no more laughter or jokes at his expense!

It had not even entered his naïve mind that he might uncover something of significance. His only real purpose had been to steal a trinket, some bit of proof to show he'd made it all the way into the citadel.

It was sheer chance that a passing servant caused him to duck behind a tapestry and into a small alcove. Luck favored him further when – still hidden away – he'd overheard a knight denying someone entrance to a certain passageway, claiming that the King would not be seeing anyone that day either.

That was when it struck him. What better proof could he take back than an item belonging to King Arthur?

He had waited for a clear moment and slipped up the forbidden passage, climbing the stone steps to an upper chamber with his heart pounding in his ears. He completely expected, as he pushed tentatively upon the enormous wooden door, to find the King inside. But the bedchamber was completely empty.

It was embarrassing really, how long he spent searching through the King's possessions before he finally realized the immense opportunity open to him. His interest in completing the dare and silencing the mockery of his peers was overshadowed then by a far more serious interest in finding something to help his people; something to give them an edge over this dangerous alliance between the Britons and Celts.

Footsteps coming suddenly up the stairs had frightened him. There was no time for finding a better place; he simply dove onto the bed and pulled the heavy fur covers over himself, peeking out from beneath them to see who entered.

It was the King alright, dressed in full armor with the black dragon crest emblazoned boldly upon the breastplate. And then, all of a sudden, there was a woman. Viggo knew he would never forget the sight of her, predominantly because her appearance had shocked him into a state of complete bewilderment.

There was no denying that she was beautiful, even surpassing Aeron's sunshiny hourglass. The striking shade of her green eyes could be outdone only by the fiery hue of her red hair. Her cheekbones were high, her jaw strong, and her figure – as she'd undressed – both sturdy and feminine. Viggo still wished he could have learned the name of the woman who was to be the undoing of Camelot and all who fought in the name of her King.

Briefly, Viggo considered this new information about a dragon army and wondered how it fit with what he already knew. Was it possible he'd misread the situation after all? But no, he had interpreted correctly. The subsequent arrival of the Queen convinced him of that.

What he'd seen in that chamber far exceeded anything he might have hoped for or imagined. The Elders would pay anything at all to learn King Arthur's secret. And once they learned of it, they would find a way of exposing it to everyone. All of Saxony would laugh. They would laugh and fight with new zeal. It would mean the end of the war.

There would be further battles of course – for dignity and honor would demand them. But Viggo knew from experience that the outcome of nearly every battle was determined long before it was fought. Wars were waged primarily in the hearts of men. Those most convinced they could win often did; those who felt betrayed or defeated often were.

King Arthur had become something of a legend among these people. Viggo could hear it in their voices whenever they offered up reverent praise. Their King was famed to stand for all that was just and honest in the world. Once the people learned just how incredibly they'd been lied to, the spell of King Arthur would be broken.

All this had seemed so exciting to Viggo when he fled Camelot. It had driven him to crawl through sharp gorse and sleep in ditches without really minding; it had moved him to play along with a strange woman and stand before the soldiers who sought him, taking smug pleasure in every moment he hid right beneath their noses. But where, he wondered wearily, did all of this leave him now?

The other patrons were getting ready to leave. As Viggo lifted his head to catch the last of their conversation, he gathered most of them were eager to get home, hoping that sleep might hurry them along to morning and with any luck, fresh news from the front.

Viggo tugged on his ear. If these reports were to be believed the war could be over in a matter of days. Would his secret retain any value at that point? Who would really care? The soldiers weren't going to return to the battlefields once treaties had been signed and they were finally home again with their families. By then, any devastating secrets about Arthur might make them whistle in amazement and shake their heads, but it wouldn't change anything.

He reached out and caught Em's arm as she passed. She and Pert were the only ones left in the tavern and the maid was busy setting the place straight. The moment she recognized him, she laughed.

"I almost didn't know you! Who knew there was such a handsome man hiding beneath all that dirt? Luckily for you, I already have a husband." She winked cheerfully to let him know she didn't mean a word of it. "What do you need?"

"How far is it from here to Lin Harbour?"

"Not far," she mused, tucking a stray wisp of dark hair back into the tightly coiled knot from which it had fallen. "I'd say it can be done in a couple of hours if you stick to the main road. I go on my off days to get the freshest goods coming off the boats."

"There are always boats? Boats going north?"

"North, south, every which way. So many traders pass through, you can always find a boat heading one direction or other." She studied him peculiarly. "Why the interest?"

"Just interest."

"Is Violet doing any better?"

"Yes," he muttered distractedly. "Better."

Long after she and Pert had retired for the night, Viggo continued to sit at his table, staring into his untouched mug until the one remaining candle finally burnt itself out

Em snuck into the room at first light to lay out breakfast, tidy up, and check briefly on Sunrise. She wasn't nearly so quiet as she thought she was – Viggo woke at the sound of her hand upon the door. He kept perfectly still and breathed softly in the chair where he'd caught a couple hours sleep, figuring that was easier than listening to her apologize.

When she lingered a long time next to him before leaving, he began to worry he'd made a mistake. Was she becoming suspicious? Or perhaps there was fresh news from the front. Either way, he probably should have spoken to her. These concerns fell quickly into irrelevance as he tucked into the generous breakfast, finally satiating the prevailing hunger which had followed him since Camelot.

Morning sunlight spilled through the single window and crawled across the floor, eventually shining over the bed where the children lay, having woken sometime during the night and crawled up next to their mother. Viggo found himself staring at them while he ate, his eyes focused while his mind wandered elsewhere entirely.

The way he figured it, everything hinged upon one simple question – one decision he had to make. But the longer he thought it over, the more complicated that one decision became.

True stirred first, rubbing the sleep out of one eye while he looked blearily about with the other. His gaze fell upon the food and he dropped his hand to stare, gripping the blanket beneath him and chewing his lip like he was mustering the courage to ask. Viggo smiled at the hesitance and patted his knee, tilting his head invitingly. The boy's soft features lit up and he slid feet-first off the bed, his soft feet padding the floor as he ran over.

Viggo lifted the boy onto his lap and stroked one hand through the tussled hair, straightening it as best he could. A melody rose unexpectedly into his throat. He hummed it out as the boy ate, one knee bouncing gently in time. He hardly remembered his own parents; much less if either of them had ever held him upon their knee and hummed songs to him. And yet there was something deeply familiar about this, something surprisingly easy and content.

The small head tilted backward to reveal brown eyes peeking hopefully up into his own.

"Story?"

Viggo tried to decide if this was a statement or a question. "You want me to tell you a story?" he guessed.

True nodded.

Still bouncing one knee, Viggo leaned back in the chair and reached up to tug on his ear. Although he knew many stories, he was not at all sure which ones would be interesting – or appropriate – for such a young listener. In the end he was spared the decision.

Gywie woke with the abruptness of a swimmer coming up for air. She bolted upright, her alert blue eyes already scanning the room for what she wanted. Seeing it, she leapt off the bed and came pounding over, tugging on his pants as she pointed to the breakfast tray.

"Mine?" she asked, all rosy cheeked and hopeful.

Viggo nodded. He continued to bounce True on his knee as Gywie ate her way through every available bite, polishing off everything on the tray along with whatever remained in the basket from the night before.

"Better?" he asked when she stood sucking crumbs off her fingertips.

"Uh-huh," she mumbled distractedly. Now that her stomach was full, she remembered what else she wanted. Bouncing back onto the bed, she looked into her mother's face and called out loudly.

"Wake up! Come on, Mommy, wake up!" Gywie's blonde curls slid to one side as she looked back toward Viggo, her tiny brows pulling together. "Why don't she wake up?"

Viggo wished he knew. He scooped True into his arms and stood, wandering over to the bed where he looked down into Sunrise's sleeping face. The fever had finally broken and she looked restful, but she still would not wake, not even when Gywie tried shouting in her ear. True whimpered.

"She's just really tired," he explained vaguely, reaching out with one hand to pull Gywie back before she could scream in Sunrise's ear again. "How about we let her rest for a little while lon-"

Gywie exploded, cutting him off with a scream of dynamic volume. Closing her eyes, she bounced up and down as wildly as she could, sucking in a breath each time she went up and screaming it out on the way down. Viggo barely managed to set True aside and catch her before she flopped down on one of Sunrise's wings.

"Lemme go, Viggy!" she screeched, determined to continue the tantrum. "Lemme go, I want mommy!" She wrestled her way out of his grasp with more strength than he was expecting and leapt across the bed. Before he could stop her, she tripped over the edge, falling flat on the floor. There was a brief moment of silence, shattered almost immediately by a shrieking wail of pain.

True threw his hands over his ears and screwed his eyes shut.

Viggo walked slowly around to the other side of the bed, feeling sorry for both of them. He was sorry their mother was hurt; sorry he could not make it all better; sorry he could not find a way to explain it. He sat down on the floor and though Gywie tried to fight him at first, he eventually managed to pull her into his arms, rocking gently from side to side. She buried her face in her hands and sobbed. No matter how hard Viggo tried to pry her fingers away to see where she'd hurt herself, she refused to let him.

"Now how am I supposed to kiss it better if I can't see where it hurts?" he asked.

The fingers parted and watery blue eyes peeked out at him. "Kiss it better?" she asked skeptically.

"Of course," he agreed, and why not? Now that he had experienced the worst this child could throw at him, he wanted to bring back her sweeter side; the side he'd seen when she lay cuddled next to him on the mountain.

Gywie brightened and removed her hands, beaming up at him with such undisguised affection that he felt a swell of identical feeling rising in his chest. Then she stuck out her tongue and pointed to the place where she'd accidentally bit it.

"Eess ett?"

Viggo stared. Now what?

What would Sunrise have done? No – that was the wrong question. He didn't like that question because he was afraid Sunrise might actually go ahead and kiss Gywie's tongue, which he had no intention of doing. He had, in his lifetime, gone up against all sorts of shady and under-handed types, and he'd always been reasonably confident in his ability to outwit them; but young children, he was discovering, were something else altogether.

"I think..." He stared at the long pink tongue and tossed out the first words that popped into his mind. "I think the butterfly already kissed it."

The tongue disappeared and Gywie's round blue eyes doubled in size. "What butterfly?"

"The invisible one. It just kissed your tongue and flew off" – he pointed – "that way."

Gywie bounced off his lap and darted after it, following the direction of his finger. It led her to a nearby wardrobe. She opened the doors and began a thorough search, throwing everything she found within it over her shoulder and onto the floor as she pursued the imaginary butterfly. Viggo watched her with relief until he caught True's gaze, finding it reproachful.

"Don't look at me like that," he grumbled playfully, reaching out to ruffle the disheveled hair further. "I can't fool you, can I?"

There was more to this tiny person than his quiet demeanor let on. The Dryad were right – the boy *knew* things. Viggo couldn't exactly put his finger on it, but True seemed to sense what he needed and try in his own small way to accommodate those needs. Perhaps this knowing of things had something to do with why True was so cautious of strangers and guarded about speaking in general.

"Viggo?"

A smile caught on the corner of Viggo's mouth. He liked hearing True's voice. It was the sound of trust. "Yes?"

True kicked his legs against the edge of the bed, his eyes suddenly averted to the ground. "Are you go?"

"Are I go?" Viggo asked, startled. "Do you mean, am I going?"

"You want to go," True accused, quiet but sure.

Viggo studied the boy's face. He looked just like his mother when he was sad. Climbing to his feet, Viggo sat down on the edge of the bed

"Don't look at me like that."

and put his arm around True, struggling not to feel guilty. He could not deny that he had been weighing his options carefully.

"I don't want to leave you," he said honestly. "I don't want to leave any of you."

True seemed to believe him. He wrapped his skinny arms around Viggo's waist and Viggo stroked his fingers once more through the boy's soft hair, smiling sadly as he watched the boy nuzzle into his side.

It was such a simple little question, but there was no answer that made everything work out the way he wanted.

For the remainder of the day Viggo did his best to keep the children distracted while they waited for Sunrise to wake. It wasn't easy. Her inert presence in the room was disheartening to all of them, and no matter what they did to keep busy, they eventually found themselves staring at her, waiting for something to happen.

Em came twice more, bringing lunch and then supper. The first time she came, Viggo asked for news from the front. She only shrugged and said it would take time for messengers to bring the latest information. In the evening, when she laid out their supper, he asked her again. There was no news, but she lingered and stared at him as though she wanted to speak further.

"Yes?" he prompted.

"I don't know that I ought to tell you, but perhaps you should know..."

"Know what?" he asked, wary of her nervous undertones.

She shifted from foot to foot and clasped her hands behind her back. "Some soldiers came early this morning."

He stiffened, wondering why she hadn't mentioned this sooner. Or maybe she had tried to.

"They said they were searching for a spy and the woman who ran off with him; that they had taken two children from Dairefast." Her laugh failed to sound as unconcerned as she meant it to be. "I don't mean to imply this has anything to do with you, of course. I know you're visiting family, and these two don't look stolen to me..."

True was clinging to his leg and peeking out curiously at Em, while Gywie reached up and stuffed handfuls of whatever she could pull off the dinner tray into her mouth.

"I guess you could say I didn't think much of it at the time, but Pert...he just won't stop talking about it." She propped her hands upon the wide edge of her hips and shook her head. "He didn't say anything to the soldiers, but he did send away for the owner, Lord Perrywood. I don't know what to make of it exactly, but I thought you ought to be warned."

"Thank you, Em."

She smiled apologetically and left. Viggo ran his hands through his hair, staring at the children as they ate their supper, his own appetite gone. The soldiers were not just looking for him anymore. If there had been any lingering doubt it was gone now: Sunrise and her children were not going home.

Crossing the room, he took up a restless pace beside the bed, watching Sunrise sleep. He dared not try to rouse her lest he accidentally intrude upon another memory, which left him with nothing to do but wait until she woke. He wanted a chance to slip off into Ellaway's camp, where he hoped to find what he needed to make his decision, but he could not leave the children unattended any more than he could drag them along.

His impatience was contagious. When the children began to whine of boredom, Viggo produced the bottle of ink he'd taken from Aeron's loft, hoping it would keep them entertained until bedtime.

Gywie got down on the floor with it at once. The moment he handed her a stylus she was scribbling wildly all over the hardwood. True didn't need one. He dipped one finger into the bottle and began solemnly working to make a long trail of perfect round dots. Viggo smirked as he watched them, imagining Pert's reaction when the drawings were discovered. If the innkeeper didn't like it, he could spread a rug overtop.

Eventually both children began to yawn, smearing their faces with ink when they rubbed their eyes to keep the fatigue at bay.

"Alright, time for bed!" He imagined getting them to sleep would be difficult; it did not take him long to realize what a gross underestimation that was.

Gywie fought him all the way to the outhouse. She fought him when he tried to clean her hands and face. She fought him when he tried to cuddle her, covered her ears when he tried to tell her a story, and in the end made it all very simple by refusing to leave her mother's side until she cried herself to sleep.

That wasn't how Viggo wanted her day to end, but his relief mitigated any guilt. True didn't make any fuss, but getting him to sleep wasn't any easier. His eyes drooped with fatigue and he was quite content to let Viggo scoop him up and cuddle him close, but no matter how long

Viggo hummed and rocked, the boy continued to force his eyes open, staring at his mother.

"Do you want that story now?" Viggo asked, exhausted for other ideas.

"Mommy sings."

Viggo remembered hearing Sunrise sing to them in the mountain cave and felt foolish. Of course, he should have thought to try singing earlier. "I can sing you a song, if you like."

"Mommy sings," True repeated, uninterested.

"What if...what if I sing one of mommy's songs?"

The boy cocked his head. Viggo made a frantic dash through his own mind, searching desperately for a helpful memory. He knew he couldn't possibly repeat any of the songs Sunrise sang on the mountain, the words of which had been foreign to him. But he remembered a couple verses from that day he walked in on her while she was singing.

"When blossoms bloom upon the trees,
When the fields are full of flowers...
Lay yourself down next to me,
And pass the moonlit hours."

True yawned hard and finally allowed his eyes to flutter shut. Viggo pulled him closer, grateful when the boy turned into him, his cheek resting comfortably in the crook of his arm. He continued to sing, dropping his volume with each line until his voice was barely more than a whisper.

"Summer grass is quite the tease,
But eventually the storm blows...

Stay by me in frosty breeze,
And hold me as the fire glows."

True was very nearly asleep. Viggo could feel the weight of him change as he drifted off. He was just about to scoop True up and lay him on the bed next to his mother when something startled the boy. Viggo had no explanation for why True jumped suddenly out of his lap and ran away, at least not until he heard the ascending footsteps. It might just as easily have been Em, but True vanished from sight under the bed and Viggo knew better. He rose as the steps neared, opening the door before the stranger's knock could wake Gywie.

In the hall there stood a slender, diminutive man who declared himself promptly. "I am Lord Perrywood, owner of this establishment." His voice, Viggo thought without amusement, was unevenly grand for his stature. "I understand something strange has been going on here?"

"Yes, yes it has," Viggo agreed, folding his arms over his chest and peering downward. "It's very strange to me that a young woman in your establishment needed help and got it only from your barmaid."

The Lord stiffened with obvious offence. "People are talking."

"They tend to do that, don't they?"

Lord Perrywood stared, trying to discern, it seemed, if he was stupid or purposefully insolent. "They are talking about *you*."

Viggo raised one indifferent eyebrow and waited for the other man to get to the point.

"There is talk of a spy chased out of Dairefast. They say another man's wife ran off with him." Lord Perrywood squared his shoulders, lifting his nose and narrowing his eyes with contempt. "I'll have you know this is an establishment of *fine* repute, and I'll not tolerate..."

Viggo stopped listening when he realized what the man was getting at. "I'm paying you good money," he interrupted hotly, "so that my sick cousin has somewhere to rest. If you have no help to offer then you can kindly leave us alone!"

For good measure he slammed the door in the little man's face. He instantly regretted the burst of temper, knowing he'd made a mistake. Cousin was a stupid lie. It had come out, he supposed, because Em believed he was family. Lord Perrywood, on the other hand, had all but accused him of being the sought-after spy, and he might as well have outright agreed to it. Sooner or later, they were going to get it all figured out...if they hadn't already.

As a regretful afterthought, Viggo glanced back over his shoulder, worried his outburst might have woken Gywie. He was nearly as afraid of having to get her back to sleep as he was of having Lord Perrywood report him.

Fortunately, the little girl had not stirred. It was Sunrise who sat upright in bed, her expression wild with panic as she clutched the blanket self-consciously to her chest. All other worries lost their importance as Viggo crossed the room to her side, studying her face anxiously. "How do you feel?"

Large violet eyes followed his movements, brimming with tears. "Where is he?"

Viggo hesitated, wondering how much she remembered. He didn't really want to be the one to tell her.

"Maybe I should leave you alone for a while," he suggested softly, not wanting to upset her with his presence. A Saxon face was probably the last thing she wanted to see right now. But she wouldn't let him go. As soon as he tried, she caught hold of his sleeve and pulled him down beside her.

"True," she rasped, a sob catching between her parched lips. "Where is True?"

Viggo felt stupid for not realizing sooner what she was talking about. She didn't know what had happened since she'd entrusted her children to him in the swamp; all she knew was that she'd woken in a strange place with only one child lying next to her. She wasn't asking about Aeron – she wanted her son.

"True is here," he assured her hastily, resting his hand soothingly over-top hers. "You're all safe in Dionne. True is hiding under the bed."

Saying they were safe might have been something of an exaggeration, but this was not the time to go filling her in. Viggo did the only thing he could and put his arms around her as she began to cry, tightening his hold when Sunrise collapsed into him. She clutched the front of his tunic, soaking a damp spot through the fabric with her tears. He rocked as her shoulders heaved, gently swaying back and forth with his eyes closed and his face resting in her hair. Eventually the emotions spent themselves and her quaking began to settle, her sobs slowly but surely subsiding into silence. Viggo carried on with the gentle back and forth motion until her breathing was soft and he knew she'd fallen back to sleep.

Not confident in his ability to disentangle himself without waking her, Viggo slowly shifted the both of them until he was leaning more comfortably against the headboard with Sunrise settled over his chest.

True never did re-emerge from under the bed. Viggo eventually concluded the little boy had fallen asleep down there and was jealous, wishing he could quiet his thoughts long enough to do the same. He knew Lord Perrywood was going to speak to Ellaway. It was late now, and etiquette would prevent him from imposing upon the Captain until morning... but he would go.

One way or another, Viggo knew he had to leave Dionne tomorrow. There was only one last, simple decision to make before he went. He passed the long night deep in thought, with his eyes closed and his fingers absentmindedly smoothing their way through silvery strands.

Chapter 14

THE SNOW RETURNED DURING the night and the drop in temperature told Viggo it had come to stay. Winter was here at last. He stood in the doorway of the inn, staring out across the untouched whiteness blanketing the open market. It was early, too early for anyone else to have strayed from the comfort and warmth of their homes. Only the smell of rising bread, coming from somewhere across the square, indicated that anyone else was even awake.

There was little he could do about footprints, except not to worry about them. Reminding himself that he was going to be leaving Dionne today, one way or another, Viggo put aside all but the most reasonable caution and left the doorway. He made it only a few steps before he slowed to a standstill, lingering once more in indecision.

The town square marked a turning point in the road. His gaze slid past all the shops and houses, following it as far as he could see. He knew from looking at Sunrise's map that it curved sharply southwest, skimming around the outermost edges of the Sinking Swamps until it reached Lin Harbour.

One decision.

He went the opposite way, back toward the neat cluster of red tents that made up Captain Ellaway's outpost.

It was only one decision, but it had so many factors. Did he still want to take his secret back to Saxony?

Obviously, he *should* want to. And he did. Mostly. But could he get back in time for his secret to accomplish anything? That was the question he had to answer first. He wouldn't know, not for sure, until he found out how far north Arthur's armies had really progressed. He couldn't risk taking that kind of information on rumor; it had to come from a more knowledgeable source, preferably from Captain Ellaway himself.

Viggo knew Ellaway was back in Dionne. He'd known it when he first walked into town, passing the camp on the way. The men were purposeful and eager as they went about their tasks, betraying the presence of their Captain, who might be found watching at any moment. Fortunately, the same excitement gripping the townsfolk had also taken hold of the soldiers and not one of them had been watching the road as he'd passed by.

Nobody seemed to be watching it now, either. All was still as Viggo walked. Everything, even his own footfalls, were muffled and soundless. The snow fell in big, puffy clumps that clung to him and melted into damp spots when he tried to brush them away. They obscured his view and made it easy to imagine he was all alone in this world of silent white.

Passing the last of the houses, Viggo ducked aside into a stand of slender aspen where he waited and watched. There was no good approach to the camp. It had been set up in an empty field, just past the edge of town. There were no trees, no shrubs, no gorse or boulders; nothing at all that he could use as cover to sneak in close. Ellaway was a smart man, he reminded himself. He'd probably had the field cleared for just such a reason.

Though the camp was quiet, it was very much awake. Smoke drifted skyward from numerous fires placed strategically around the tents. Now and again he saw the silhouettes of soldiers against their light, moving about in silence. Viggo paid careful attention to the tents they entered and was able, by process of elimination, to deduce which tent belonged to the Captain. It was the only tent which nobody entered and from which no one emerged.

It was odd to Viggo that everyone was awake so early when they seemed not to be doing anything in particular. Were they waiting for something? That was his guess.

Stamping back and forth to ward off the cold, he blew upon his fingers and weighed out the chances of going unnoticed if he made a mad dash toward the tents. Even with the snow, his odds weren't good. He was about to try it anyway when he heard the soft footfalls. The sound was muffled but it was there, coming steadily up the road. Viggo stood perfectly still among the aspen, peering through the snow to see who was walking his way.

It was Lord Perrywood, Viggo would have made a wager on it. He couldn't actually see the man's face beneath the heavy furs he wore but the height was right and it seemed unlikely that anyone else of equal stature was making for Ellaway's camp at first light. The moment Ellaway caught wind of the strangers at Perrywood's inn, he would be there. Viggo wasn't ready for that. He was still undecided what to do about Sunrise and the children; taking them along would only slow him down when he needed speed more than ever. But whatever he did, he had no intention of leaving them in danger. He just needed more time.

Viggo stayed motionless until Lord Perrywood passed. It would have to be silent, he told himself as he leapt forward and wrapped his arm around the neck of the other man. Silent and quick. The furs made it take longer, preventing him from pulling his arm as tightly against the throat as he would have preferred. Even so, in less than a minute Lord Perrywood's flailing struggles gave way to limpness.

Viggo released him at once, catching him beneath the arms and dragging him back into the stand of aspen. Propping him against one of the narrow trees, Viggo pushed a hand past the furs and touched the man's throat, counting the heartbeats until he was satisfied he had not permanently injured him. Lord Perrywood would wake, eventually, but not until after Viggo had done what he needed to do.

Another sound, coming along the road from the other direction, drew his attention. The snow was coming down too heavily to see anything of the camp other than the brightly coloured tents, and even those were dulled by the billowing whiteness. But he could hear horses. There were at least five of them, if he had to estimate, and he could just as easily guess who rode in the lead. Soon he would know if he was right.

There was an audible commotion as the soldiers left their tents to greet the anticipated arrivals. Viggo could hear them gathering on the far side of the camp. It was now or never. He made the mad dash.

Nobody saw as he darted openly across the field or crept right up against the scarlet fabric of Ellaway's tent. It was almost too easy. But that was the way of a hunter. Inevitably, people expected their prey to run and hide. The fact that they did not expect their quarry to come brazenly to their doorstep was their greatest mistake. Viggo found a flap where one layer of heavy material overlapped another and slipped between them.

Ellaway was there, framed in the tent entrance, watching patiently for his guest to come. Viggo dropped silently to the ground and lay himself out flat. The tent was lit by the soft, blurring tones of candlelight and he hoped that if he kept still, the brown of his coat would blend in well enough with the crimson tent cloth. There wasn't anything to hide behind. The nearest thing was a wooden chest, hardly big enough to provide cover. Unlike Donovan, Ellaway was simple in his tastes and did not look to possess anything more than he strictly needed. The only real piece of furniture in the tent was a large, round table – smack center. Viggo wondered if it was homage to King Arthur's renowned knights.

Just as Viggo expected, the eagerly awaited guest turned out to be Captain Donovan. The greeting between him and Ellaway was warm and familiar, and though it was petty, Viggo couldn't help but feel a little disappointed they were not still at odds with one another.

"What news?"

The stockier of the two men nearly tripped over himself in his haste to roll out a map upon the table. "Here," he said, pointing, "and here...all the way up to here."

Ellaway stood next to him and leaned over the map, studying every place where the other man's finger touched. Viggo glanced up at them as often as he dared and wished he could have somehow watched from above. If only he had wings. A smile touched his mouth. Oh how much easier spying would be if he had wings of his own.

"All of that?" Ellaway questioned, clearly astounded. "In so little time?"

"With one blast of a dragon's breath, ten men fall scorched! Are you surprised?"

Donovan might not have been surprised, but Viggo still was. A dragon army – he could hardly fathom such a thing. For as long as anyone could remember dragons had been the enemies of men. They were as dangerous as they were rare; a scourge upon any land unlucky enough to have one. News of King Arthur making formal peace with a dragon had spread through Saxony like wildfire. It was shocking, unheard of, and utterly vile to the Saxon way of thinking. Only in the privacy of his own thoughts had Viggo been able to nurse a spark of admiration. But a whole army of dragons? Where did one even *find* an army worth of dragons? He suddenly realized how ignorant he was, not only of dragons and faeries, but of all other kinds. It was a shortcoming he was determined to remedy.

"I suppose... Yes, I suppose I am surprised. What about this?" Ellaway pointed to some spot on the map.

"No, not that. At least, not that I know of. But that wasn't our territory to begin with."

"Maybe not, but they are so close. Why not take it all?"

Donovan was not one to question the decisions of their beloved ruler. "Perhaps the King will only take back what is rightfully his? This campaign of his might be swift and harsh, but it is fair."

As a nobleman, Ellaway was open to questioning the will of the King. But he could not dispute the fairness of their benevolent leader. "You speak well."

"There is more news!"

"Out with it then!"

Viggo listened with closed eyes, his forehead pressed to the frozen dirt as Donovan described a large envoy making its way from Saxony to

Camelot, bearing a peace treaty issued by the Saxon Elders. The King, he said, had already returned to Camelot to await their arrival.

It was over. Even if no one stood in his way, even if he caught the first boat and traveled afterward upon the fastest horses, Viggo knew he could never make it back to Saxony in time to beat the treaty.

His one decision was irrelevant, and strangely he was relieved. His head hurt from making and unmaking decisions. Now he didn't have to choose. Though, if he was being really honest with himself, he knew in his heart he had already made his decision, and had been making it further with every moment he stayed in Dionne rather than leaving.

"They're suing for peace!" Donovan concluded breathlessly.

"No," Ellaway countered, and Viggo glanced up in time to see smug pleasure smeared across his narrow face, "they're begging for surrender."

Donovan clapped Ellaway on the shoulder. "I suppose I shall soon be returned to my home, and you to yours. And to think how quietly the war has gone by for us out here. The Saxons never did come down the coast, though who is to say – perhaps we shall get to be heroes of the next war!"

Ellaway's face did not lose one smidgen of its smoldering delight. "We can still be heroes of this war."

"What do you mean?"

"Saxon *armies* may not have come this way, but a single spy *did*. A single spy the King himself wants caught and returned. You and I, my friend, will be the ones to catch him. We can still do that much."

Like hell you will.

"But you've lost him! He never came through the valley like we expected. He must have turned back and gone east."

"If he'd gone east, then you'd have been the one who lost him," Ellaway corrected. Viggo didn't like the cunning gleam in the man's eye. "But he didn't go east. He's come this way; I'd bet my life on it. I don't know how he did it, since as you say, he was not sighted in the valley." His fingers tapped sternly against the wooden tabletop. "Are we certain the Druid's wife ran off with him?"

"It certainly seems so. Why?"

"I see."

The silence stretched on so long Viggo eventually closed his eyes again, pressing his lips firmly together to keep from sighing loudly as one does to hurry along a digressing conversation.

"Well?" Donovan demanded, finally becoming impatient enough for them both.

Like hell you will.

"The Druids are the only ones who can navigate the Sinking Swamp, isn't that right?"

"That's right."

"Then perhaps the man taught his wife. She must have known her way through the Swamps and played guide for our spy. Likely, he seduced her for that very reason."

"Bloody bastard," Donovan growled. "Do you think he's made it all the way to Lin Harbour by now?"

Viggo held his breath hopefully.

"No, Captain Olliver sent messengers to me last night. He's letting no boats out of the harbour until the spy is caught. So far there has been no sign of the man."

Viggo felt his shoulders sag and had to resist the urge to slam his fist down in frustration. Above all else, he had been counting on those boats. Now what was he to do? What other way was there to escape? His mind, racing swiftly, produced one grim answer: there was no other way, at least not by land or sea. Unless Sunrise could fly, they were trapped. He needed to see her. He'd left early, while she and the children still slept, because he wasn't ready to talk or explain things before he had all the facts. Now it was going to be even more difficult, for he had no good news to share.

"What of the Druid?" Ellaway asked casually, still deep in thought. "Has he returned yet to Dairefast?"

"No. Half the people feel he must have gone after his family, while the other half say he's likely gone away to one of his mistresses."

Viggo remembered Sunrise saying the night he met her, that nobody would find it strange if her husband returned home and disappeared again within short order. Aeron had not done himself any favours. It would probably be a long time before anyone figured out what really happened to him – if they ever did.

Ellaway nodded slowly and seemed pleased. "Good. He's either gone away, or he went after them and they did him in. Had he managed to retrieve his property, he should have returned by now. I think it more likely he's out of our way… one way or another."

Donovan shook his head, seeming to feel Ellaway was straying from the matter of real importance. "But the spy? How do you intend to find him?"

"We know he has not returned to Dairefast, and he's not yet made it to Lin Harbour. Today, at first light, we search Dionne – every house, every shop – until he's found."

"And then?" Donovan pressed.

"Then? Then he goes back to Camelot. I intend to take him personally."

"I will, of course, accompany you." Donovan hardly wanted to miss out on the glory now. "And the woman?"

"We can't have women tainting themselves with our enemies," Ellaway said casually, as though the answer should have been obvious. "No sense hauling her all the way to Camelot when she could hardly be of any significance to the King. We'll do our duty and be rid of her ourselves."

Viggo had already known Sunrise wasn't going home, but hearing Ellaway say it with such cool indifference was enough to make his breath feel tight in his chest, his heart tripping with new urgency.

"But if her husband does return?" Donovan asked, less concerned with the idea of killing Sunrise than the possibility of awkward consequences.

Captain Ellaway waved his hand in a dismissive manner. "As I understand it, they were not fond of one another anyway. If he makes trouble, we can tell him the spy did it." Another map was produced and their talk became less speculative as they studied Dionne and decided which soldiers should be sent to search where in the city.

It was time to go. Only, when Viggo began to roll carefully aside, intending to shimmy under the heavy tent cloth and slip away, he discovered a problem. A pair of boots blocked his way.

Had someone found him out?

Glancing tentatively upward, Viggo saw a face – or rather, part of a face – peeking through the tent folds. It was Donovan's niece. He knew her by the lock of strawberry blonde hair he could see hanging over her eye. Her attention was wholly focused upon the two Captains and she did not seem to have noticed him where he lay on the ground below her. She must have accompanied her uncle to Dionne – or else followed secretly behind him. Either way, she was obviously eavesdropping on his plans.

While Viggo respected this and had no problem with her doing so, he wished she would have chosen a vantage point different from his own. With her one boot tucked neatly behind his knee, there was no easy way to move without alerting her to his presence and spooking her into giving them both away.

Viggo held still and waited for as long as his patience would allow, hoping the girl would satisfy her curiosity and leave. She did not. When a young soldier arrived, distracting the two Captains with the delivery of their morning meal, Viggo seized his chance. Pulling his legs cautiously from around the boot, he sat up and crawled onto his knees, moving ever so slowly, hoping to avoid catching the eye of either Captain. Both were well within sight but the tent was poorly lit and they were focused on their meal, neither one expecting company. He went upward by inches, carefully shifting his weight until he stood upright with his back to the tent wall – just out of sight of the girl.

Unfortunately, she was still in his way.

Viggo braced himself, mentally playing through every move he wanted to make so there would be no hesitation once he began making them. Turning on his heel, he reached both hands through the fabric and grabbed the girl. One hand found her arm and held tight as he slipped between the tent cloths, pushing her forcibly back; the other clamped down over her mouth right before she yelped in surprise. Outside, in the snow, he twisted her arm around and caught her close, keeping his hand over her mouth as he listened for any alarm within the tent.

Silence.

Relieved, Viggo glanced around. They were generally out of sight of the other tents, but he could see soldiers standing near one of the fires. He was going to have to find a better place than this if he wanted to talk to the girl.

Helena had overcome her initial shock enough to begin squirming. Before she could twist her arm free, Viggo dragged her behind a nearby wagon where he dropped into the snow, pulling her down beside him. Leaning back around one of the large wheels, he swept the area once more with his gaze. So far, no one had seen them.

"I'm going to let you go now," he whispered finally, pressing his mouth directly into the frightened girl's ear. "If you're trying to find out what happened to Violet, you'll stay quiet."

Helena stopped fighting him. He released her mouth first, slowly, and then her arm; carefully holding up his hands to show he meant no harm. To her credit she did not scream, despite the enormous distrust in her dark eyes.

"She went across the river, looking for Gywie, but she never came back!" Her tone, though she spoke in whispers, bordered dangerously on hysteria. "My uncle thinks she ran off with you but I know she wouldn't have done that! What did you do to her? If you hurt those childre-"

Viggo spoke soft but quick, trying to sooth her agitation before he had to clamp his hand back over her mouth. "Nothing, I swear I did nothing. Gywie followed me. I had no idea until it was too late. By the time Gywie caught up to me and Violet caught up to her, it wasn't safe for any of them to go back."

The distrust eased somewhat and Helena sat back, stunned and confused but willing to believe. "They're going to kill her if they find her," she whispered miserably, not realizing he already knew.

"They're not going to find her."

"But I just heard them talking about-"

Viggo put his hand over her mouth again. He didn't want to frighten her further but there wasn't time for being polite.

"They're going to start searching the town this morning, did you hear that?" he asked. She nodded. "Violet has got to get to Lin Harbour. The snow will make her easier to follow and the children will slow her down. I need you to stop that search from happening right away. Just delay them, I don't care how. Any time you buy will help."

She pushed his hand away. "But none of the boats are being allowed to leave!"

"I know. I can take care of that. Can you buy me time or not?"

Helena nodded solemnly. All the fright evaporated out of her face, replaced with stalwart determination. They were allies now. "I'll buy you time. How long do you want?"

"Whatever you can get me." It was too late to get his secret home but Viggo knew he could still help Sunrise and her children get away safely. All he needed was time; enough time, hopefully, to figure out how Sunrise was doing and when she could travel.

"I'll get you lots."

"Good."

There was some commotion stirring within the camp. Helena got partway to her feet before hesitating, chewing her upper lip as she studied him.

"What?"

"It's just... I didn't know when she went across the river, she wouldn't be coming back. If I'd known I would have said goodbye or...or something. Now I'll never see her again..."

Viggo smiled wistfully. He understood more than she knew.

Helena swallowed her regrets, assured him once more she would buy time, and scampered off. Viggo leaned his head back, resting a moment as his eyes drifted lazily up to the cart. It was a prisoner's cart, like the ones in Camelot, like the one in the dream. It was probably how Ellaway envisioned transporting him back to the King.

Shaking his head to oust that unwelcome image, Viggo waited for the first clear moment and made a second mad dash across the snowy field. If anyone saw, they made no noise about it. He detoured long enough to check on Lord Perrywood, found him still sleeping, and made swift time back to the inn.

The tavern was not yet occupied with customers and Viggo hoped to slip up to the room unnoticed. But Em was lingering near the bottom of the steps, twisting a rag anxiously through her hands. She knew. From the look on her face when she saw him there could be no doubt of it.

"It's you, isn't it?" she asked him slowly. "You're him? The Saxon spy?"

Viggo saw no reason to deny it. There were no lies convincing enough once someone made up their own mind on a matter.

"Yes," he agreed, "but that doesn't change a thing."

"Doesn't it?"

"Not as long as you care what happens to Violet."

The maid hesitated. She did care.

"They're going to kill her," he said plainly, not above shocking her into silence. "If you turn me in now, she pays the price. I promise, one way or another, we'll all be gone from here soon.

He noted the dismay in her eyes, realizing he had just stumbled upon another ally. With Lord Perrywood out of the picture there was no reason for the soldiers to start their search here. But Pert was suspicious, and that made him a problem...

"Soldiers will be coming soon to search the town. All I ask is that you keep Pert busy when they come. Don't let him speak with them, whatever you have to do. Can you do that much? Will you do it? For her?"

The woman's mouth wavered uncomfortably over a lack of words. Even so, her head bobbed slowly up and down like she didn't want it to, but couldn't stop it either. Viggo smiled. It was too bad Sunrise thought she was disliked and mistrusted; if only she could see how easily she was turning one person after another away from their expected loyalties.

"Good. One more thing. Is there a key for the room?"

He saw the barmaid's hand slip unconsciously into her apron pocket, automatically protecting the object in question. Viggo held his palm out flat until Em, still in a daze, handed the key over obediently.

"Why do you need that?"

"Just in case." He pocketed it, thanked her, and darted up the stairs before she could come to her senses and change her mind.

Viggo was expecting to hear the children before he even reached the door. When he didn't, he thought they might still be sleeping, or devouring breakfast, or drawing on the floor with the last of their ink. But they weren't. He pushed the door open to an empty room. Sunrise and her children were gone.

Chapter 15

A QUICK SEARCH OF the room only confirmed what Viggo already knew. True was not hiding under the furniture, Gywie was not searching for butterflies in the wardrobe, and Sunrise was not asleep on the bed. Only the doodles across the floor proved the children and their mother had ever been.

Viggo was whirling in the first throws of panic when he heard small footsteps running up the stairs. They were not gone after all. Sighing with relief, he turned back through the doorway and looked down to see Sunrise walking up toward him, the children racing ahead of her. Peering over the banister, he caught sight of Em at the bottom of the stairs, smiling sheepishly up at him. She had been so flustered by their exchange she'd neglected to mention that Sunrise and the children were in her little washing room. All three of them were wrapped up in their cloaks, their hair still damp from bathing.

True made it to the top of the stairs first. He paused in front of Viggo and stuck out one boot, pointing smugly to the bit of snow around the edges. Viggo knelt, smothering his anxious thoughts behind a genuine smile. "You walked in the snow by yourself," he observed, guessing they had been to the outhouse. "That was very brave!" True beamed at the compliment and marched past him into the room.

Gywie ran after her brother, tossing a brief "Hi Viggy!" over her shoulder. How quickly she had come to accept his presence, taking it entirely for granted that he would still be here.

Viggo rose when Sunrise neared, his smile melting into worry as he watched the careful, guarded way in which she moved. She had somehow come into possession of a new dress, as highly buttoned and smothering as her old one. He was sorry she had hidden away her wings, even if he understood her reasons for doing so.

"Viggo?" She paused upon the top step, trying to hide the surprise in her voice with a laugh as she studied him head to toe. "You look much better!"

The moment the words were off her tongue her cheeks coloured and she clamped a hand over her mouth with embarrassment. "Oh no," she mumbled from behind her fingers, "no, that's not what I meant. That is, I didn't mean to say you looked bad before. I-I just mean that you're so much – cleaner!" Her eyes widened and her other hand came up to join the first. "That was worse, wasn't it?"

He nodded, causing the red on her cheeks to spread throughout her face. He felt he should say something to save her from herself, but it was too amusing to wait and see what else might fall out of her mouth.

"You look different," she mumbled finally, lowering her gaze sheepishly when she saw his widening grin. "That's all. I just meant to say you look different."

"Uh-huh."

He stepped aside to let her into the room, closing the door firmly behind them. "How are you feeling?" he asked slowly, in no rush to tell her what was happening just yet. If they left now, they would succeed only at leaving an obvious trail through the snow. No, they had time. Not a lot, but some. Leaving would happen after the soldiers had come and gone.

"I've been better," Sunrise admitted, lingering nearby, staring at him like he was a puzzle she could not find the solution for. "Probably won't be able to fly for at least a fortnight, but things will heal. What are you doing here?"

No flying. That settled it then. He knew what he had to do. But in the meantime, her question took him aback. Where did she expect him to be? Sunrise noted his silence and clarified.

"Em told me how long I was out. I would have thought, I mean...shouldn't you have been well on a boat by now?"

Viggo shrugged and tugged self-consciously on his ear. "After you saved me?" he teased, using her own words. "First in Dairefast, then on the mountain, and again in the swamp...how could I possibly do any less?"

He was trying to make her smile. Instead her expression was struck with guilt.

"None of that was because I expected anything from you!"

"I know," he said seriously, and it amused him that she seemed more concerned with his lack of progress than he was. "And that's exactly why I stayed."

"Thank you," she whispered, the guilt on her face easing into a soft smile. Her eyes brimmed with questions. "I can't imagine how you did it. How did you manage to get all of us out of the swamp?"

"I had help," he responded vaguely, watching her face, wondering whether or not she knew about the Dryad. Her eyes pulled wide, suggesting she did.

"You saw them," she breathed, her fingers rising to cover her mouth. "You saw them and they helped you?"

"I'm guessing that's not common?"

She shook her head vigorously, still stunned. "They help the Druid – no one else. Never anyone else."

"But they aren't what the Druid believe, are they?"

Sunrise's hand strayed from her mouth, finding a damp lock of hair and twisting it between her fingers like a little girl who wasn't allowed to say. Eventually she shook her head. "No, they're not. They live in the oak trees but they're not spirits. The Dryad are another kind."

"Then why the deception? Why fool the Druid with nonsense about the future?"

"I don't really know," she admitted honestly, her puzzled gaze resting on his face. "Why did they help you?"

"I don't really know. They didn't seem to like me very much. They said they wanted me to make things right." Viggo looked over toward the children, watching them play. They had found a few pebbles outside and Gywie was tossing them across the floor while True fetched them back. "They seemed to like True though. They called him one of theirs."

"Maybe that's why they helped you. They must have known his father was a Druid."

"Maybe," he agreed, distracted by her reference to Aeron in the past tense. She remembered. "How are they?" he asked gently, deciding to change the subject.

Sunrise came to stand alongside him, her shoulder brushing his as she stared at the children. "I haven't told them what happened yet."

"And you?"

Her answer was slow in coming and Viggo kept his eyes focused elsewhere. He could only imagine how difficult this was for her. She might not have loved her husband, but she hadn't wanted him to die either.

"I'll be fine," she said at last. "You can't lose something you don't have, and Aeron was never mine to lose. That doesn't mean he deserved to...to..." There was a catch in her voice as she trailed off, taking a deep breath to steady herself. "I guess maybe I just haven't had time to let it all sink in yet."

Viggo nodded slowly. There was less time than she knew.

"I know you saw the dream." This brought his eyes snapping back to hers. "And I'm sorry. That wasn't supposed to happen. If I'd been well, I never would have-"

"It's alright," he interrupted, cutting off what he could foresee becoming another embarrassed ramble. He tugged his ear again. "I guess your husband had a good reason for hating Saxons."

Sunrise stared at him oddly. "He didn't hate Saxons because of me. His first wife was killed bartering with a Saxon trader. It was an accident. People in Dairefast told me she could be very aggressive when she was driving a bargain. She grabbed the man's wife, they argued, she fell and hit her head upon a stone...Aeron never got over it."

"You never mention her by name."

"I don't know her name. Aeron never told me. And I never asked anyone else because I wanted to hear it from him. I guess I thought fair was fair; unless he trusted me with her name, I wouldn't trust him with mine." She tugged sheepishly on that bit of silver hair still twisted about her finger, the blush returning to her cheeks. "It was my little way of being angry back, I suppose."

Viggo couldn't help but chuckle softly. Never before had he admired someone so much for such a childish way of thinking.

Sunrise sighed. "I feel like you know absolutely everything about me while I hardly know anything about you. But then, I suppose that's what makes you a good spy."

There was a growing strain in her voice that Viggo could not ignore and he gestured her toward the bed where she could sit. He sat down beside her, angling himself so he could look over her shoulder and see out the window. It offered him a full view of the market. Still clear. There was still time. Time enough to share his secret with at least one person, since he would likely never get the chance to speak of it again.

"I'm not a spy," he admitted, watching to see what she'd think.

Curiosity sparked in her eyes. "But you are a soldier?"

"Sort of."

"How is one 'sort of' a soldier?"

A sheepish smile forced itself onto his face. "I wasn't a very good soldier." Sunrise's head tilted with interest and he continued, surprised by how freely the words came. "I never made it further than the training camp I was recruited to. I'm not very good at taking orders. Never could quite seem to be wherever I was supposed to."

She saw through his self-deprecation to the real heart of the matter as easily as if he'd outright told her. "But Viggo, if you didn't want to be there, why did you go?"

"It was a draft." He shrugged. "Deserters aren't looked on too fondly during wartime. So I went. Strangest thing happened though; I kept getting lost in the nearby woods." His little grin betrayed this had not been wholly accidental.

"You might've gotten in trouble for that," she suggested, returning his grin.

"I suppose I might've."

"Then I think you were very brave to avoid the fighting."

Viggo shied away from her gaze, shaking his head to fend off her compliments. It was a nice sentiment, one his Commander would dismiss as silly and misguided. "Back home they call it cowardice."

"I don't-"

A knock sounded at the door and Viggo jumped to answer it, letting Em in. She breezed by him without hesitance, already accustomed to having a spy under the same roof.

"Breakfast!" she announced cheerfully and set down the tray, fussing over the children when they ran over. She sat them down and put out their food, glancing over her shoulder at Sunrise. "Biscuits?"

Sunrise didn't want biscuits. Briefly they argued, with Em insisting upon food while Sunrise maintained she was not well enough to eat. Eventually, they compromised on tea.

"And for you?" Em questioned, glancing at him while she handed Sunrise a cup.

"Nothing."

She didn't bother trying to fight with him. As soon as she was gone, Sunrise set aside her cup and turned back to him with questions. He couldn't help but wonder if her disinterest in food was really about how unwell she felt or whether it was merely symptomatic of her pressing curiosity.

"So how is it you wound up in Camelot, if you were neither a spy nor a trained soldier?"

That was a long story. Viggo tried to make it brief. "It started out as a joke, really. I was listening by the fire one night as my Commander spoke with a company of men getting ready to head for the front. They were complaining about the slow progress of the invasion. My Commander said everything would be different if we had a spy in Camelot. But it wasn't possible, he said, because the Britons are too in love with their King. And even if someone could be coaxed or bribed into turning over information it wouldn't matter, because no one would ever be able to sneak in or out of the citadel to retrieve it. They all said it was impossible..."

Viggo smiled wistfully, remembering the cold of that night. He remembered the leaf he'd been fiddling with as he sat with his back to a dead stump. It was an oak leaf, broad and golden red; he had twirled it back and forth to watch as it caught the shadows of the dancing fire.

"I could do it."

The words had come out so quietly, Viggo hadn't really expected anyone to hear them. But someone had heard, and they had laughed.

"You all hear that? Vig here can't make it to breakfast on time, but he could get into the citadel!"

They had all laughed. Someone had rested an elbow on Viggo's shoulder and jeered loudly into his ear. "You could sooner make it to the front than into that fortress!"

The laughter intensified, because that was their favourite joke. Three groups of recruits had come and gone since he'd been here; three times he'd failed basic training and been held back from going along with them. *By the time Viggo makes it to the front*, they liked to tease, *the war will be long over!*

Viggo had pushed the heckler away. "I could do it!" he insisted, defiant and loud. That was when his Commander had become serious. He came over and knelt, bringing his blue eyes even with Viggo's frustrated grey ones.

"You think you can get into Camelot?"

"Yes."

"You really believe you can make it into the citadel and back out alive?"

"I don't have to believe. I know I can."

The older man's smirk had been daring, but his eyes were deadly serious. "Prove it."

Viggo came back to the little room above the tavern, back to Sunrise and her wide eyes, back to the story he had just shared in far more detail than he'd meant to. "So I did," he finished lamely.

"And you found something important?" she guessed.

He nodded.

Sunrise's gaze dropped to his coat, her eyes flickering back and forth between his pockets. "To think something so small could cause so much trouble. Was...was it worth it?"

That, he thought, was an enormous question. One he had no easy answer for. But he smiled sheepishly, realizing she still thought – as he had allowed her to think – that his secret was hidden away somewhere in his coat. "It's not small. It's not even a thing. I saw something."

She leaned forward with interest. "What?"

Viggo almost laughed at how eagerly she asked. Sunrise was so caught up in his story that she took for granted he would tell her all the rest of it. And he would. He wanted her to know now that the secret could not put her in any more danger than she was already in. He told her about finding the stairway up to the King's chamber. He told her about the footsteps and hiding in the bed. He told her about the arrival of the King and described for her the woman he'd seen.

Sunrise lifted one silvery eyebrow, exceedingly unimpressed. "I don't see how it would really be such a big deal, the King being with a woman he shouldn't. Not right, certainly, but not so very uncommon either."

Viggo smiled, both at her tone but also at himself, realizing how he had misled her by his turn of phrase. "You don't understand. I didn't mean to imply that King Arthur was *with* a woman..." Unable to help himself, he paused for dramatic effect. "What I'm trying to say is that King Arthur *is* a woman."

Sunrise stared at him, stunned momentarily into silence. Viggo glanced around to see what the children were up to and found True sitting at his feet, staring up at him.

"What do you think?" Viggo asked, realizing the boy had been listening all along. "Would that have made a good story?"

True nodded and held out his arms. Pleased, Viggo reached down and pulled the boy onto his knees. There was so much he wished he could say to this clever little person, but True smiled at him through soft brown eyes and Viggo felt the boy knew all of it anyway. He settled for running his fingers through the child's brown hair – already mostly dry – while he watched Gywie decorating the inside of the wardrobe with inky

Viggo's Secret

handprints. True noticed what she was doing too and slid away to join her, bringing their little moment to an end. Viggo wanted, more than anything, to call Gywie over and get one little hug from her. But he didn't know how to do it without alerting all three of them to his plan.

Sunrise finally found her voice again. "Are you sure?"

"Pretty sure," he agreed, tearing his eyes from the children to grin at her.

"But you said...I thought you said the King came in first?"

"No..." he clarified slowly. "I said the King came in. For all intents and purposes, she is the King – whoever she is. I don't know what else to call her other than Arthur. She wore the armour of the King, but when the helmet came off...well, I already told you that."

"But King Arthur couldn't have been a woman, not all along!"

"I agree. I don't know what happened to the real King but there's been a woman in his place, probably for some time."

"How do you know?"

"The Queen came up to help her out of the chainmail. They were talking about how they couldn't keep it up much longer; that more and more people were demanding personal audiences with the King and questioning the vague refusals."

"The Queen knows?"

"Whatever the scheme is, she's in on it completely. And I have to imagine others are too. Otherwise it would be an awfully hard secret to keep all the time. But from the way they spoke, I don't think even the knights know...at least, not most of them."

Sunrise's face filled with new comprehension. "If everyone found out their King wasn't who they thought at all...that he was...that *she was*..."

The fairy trailed off, knowing she did not need to explain all the implications to him. "Viggo," she whispered seriously, "if news like this made it back to Saxony, it would end the war."

Viggo couldn't help but chuckle at the irony. "The war is already over."

"Over? What do you mean over?"

"Em didn't tell you?"

"Tell me what?"

"Arthur, or whoever she is, somehow gathered a whole dragon army to help her take back the annexed Briton territories. A peace treaty is on its way to Camelot. It's all over."

"Oh." She dropped her eyes away. "I'm sorry."

He stared, surprised. "Are you?"

"I never meant...I mean, I wasn't trying to...I never wanted to interfere with-with whatever you had to do. I was only trying...I wanted...I guess I thought..."

Viggo smiled at her inability to find words and touched a finger to her lips, sparing her the trouble. "You managed to do what neither Donovan nor Ellaway nor all of Arthur's armies could – you stopped the Saxon spy from getting home. You should be proud of yourself."

Her cheeks flushed red, making her look guiltier than she had before. "I didn't do it for that."

"I know."

"You don't know!" The fairy shifted uncomfortably, winding another bit of silver hair around her finger and tugging upon it. "I didn't do it for you either. I did it for me."

"How so?" he asked, his interest piqued.

"Do you remember I told you I had a dream where you got away?"

He nodded. If she pulled any harder on that bit of hair she was liable to break it.

"I wasn't...I wasn't talking about you getting away from Dairefast. I was talking about here, now, in this room. I dreamt of this room and I saw you. I saw you getting away from me. I didn't know where this was or how it would happen or why...I didn't even know who you were. All I knew for sure was how unhappy I felt when you left." Tears brimmed in her eyes, threatening to overflow. Viggo struggled to hide how nervous her words were making him. He was suddenly afraid she knew what he was planning, and even more afraid she would find some way of stopping him. "I saw you get away and I knew it was going to hurt. So I did it for me."

"I don't understand." Or maybe he did.

She wiped the wetness from her eyes with the back of her hand and took a deep breath. "Some things hurt so badly that afterward nothing else seems worth hurting over. At some point I stopped hurting...I think I stopped knowing how. Aeron took that from me. And then there was this dream telling me I could still find something worth hurting over." The morning light was catching on her tears, forming rainbows in her eyes. "Everyone, my whole life, has talked about Saxons like they're all the same – Aeron worse than most. People talk about fairies like that too. I wanted Aeron to be wrong. I wanted everyone to be wrong. I saw you in my dream and I wanted to know that not everyone is the same."

Viggo nodded slowly, struggling against the emotions threatening to spill from his own eyes. "They aren't," he assured her, reaching out without thinking to catch a single teardrop as it slipped down her cheek. "People aren't all the same."

"I knew that." She smiled and caught his hand before he could pull it away, giving it a little squeeze. "But now I believe it. I didn't know everything else that would happen. I didn't see any of that. I only saw this room, and you getting away, and me hating it. I didn't open my door that night knowing it would be you. But then, there you were. I should have told you to run. I should never have pulled you inside, but I...I wanted to know..."

Viggo cut her off, pulling her into a hug. He did it carefully, not wanting to hurt her, but wanting her to know without a doubt that he did not blame her. Nothing had been her fault. Her attempts to help had been sincere and neither of them could change what was already done.

If Sunrise knew or guessed what he intended to do, she didn't let on. She simply hugged him back, her face resting comfortably on his shoulder. Leaning his chin down into her hair he breathed in the smell of soap, detecting beneath it the lingering scent of her garden – those hints of sweat peas and rosemary.

"I've decided to leave," she mumbled into his neck.

"Have you?" he inquired, watching the stirrings in the market below. He held her tighter so she would not see the soldiers, listening half-heartedly as she described islands to the north that made up the heart of the Irish Kingdoms – her homeland. She was going home.

And his time was running out.

"What if I didn't get away?" he blurted out stupidly. "Would you travel with me?"

It was an unfair question and he regretted it instantly. Her answer would not change a thing. But it would matter. The knot in his stomach told him it mattered far more than it should have.

Sunrise pulled back to study his face, checking to see if he was serious. "With you?" Her gaze slipped sideways to the children. "I could never risk taking them to Saxony. If anyone figured out what we are..."

"I know."

"And I'm not sure it would be any safer for you where we're going." A rueful smile touched her lips as she reached up to run her fingers through a bit of his blond hair. "The clans hate Saxons too."

Viggo coiled a little bit of her wet hair around one finger, admiring its shine. He wasn't sure when the silver strands had become so fascinating. "It's a shame I couldn't go along," he muttered, "just far enough to see that you find your way to wherever it is you're going..."

The way her eyes lit up told him everything he needed to know. Whether this would make it easier never to see her again – as he'd hoped – or a great deal harder, Viggo would have plenty of time to debate later. For now, it was all he could do to take one last look at her lovely face, committing every detail to memory.

A smile curved across her mouth, hopeful and maybe just a little coy. "And what if I never find my way to where I'm going?"

Viggo pulled her into one last hug so she would not see the regret on his face. "Then I guess it could have been a very long trip." Releasing her, he stood abruptly, unbelting Aeron's sword and laying it firmly across her lap. "Take this with you."

Sunrise stared first at the sword, then at him. "But I don't know how to-"

"It doesn't matter," he interrupted seriously. "Most people will be intimidated enough if they think you do. Besides," he added gently, "it isn't soup, so I'm sure you could get the hang of it."

The fairy laughed. "You talk as if you're not coming with us!" The smile dropped off her face as she realized what she'd said.

There was no other way. She needed time to travel with the children, time she would not have as long as the soldiers were looking for her. But they'd stop looking soon enough once they had him. And more importantly, they'd release the boats. From outside, Viggo heard the barking of orders. He glanced toward the wardrobe where the children played and wished Helena had bought him just a little more time.

"Promise me you'll get them out of here," he whispered, his voice breaking.

"Viggo, what are you-"

He cleared his throat and cut her off, speaking rapidly. "If Ellaway finds you, he'll kill you. As soon as the soldiers leave, you go. I'll keep them plenty busy. Get to Lin Harbour. The boats will be allowed to leave as soon as the Captain there hears of my capture." Viggo pulled the little money bag from his pocket and pressed it into Sunrise's hands, smiling into her dumbstruck expression. "Be on the first boat that leaves. Find your islands. Plant another garden. Let them draw on your floors and keep singing to them. Just be safe."

"Viggo, please..."

She reached for his sleeve and he drew back, casting one final glance at the children. Gywie had paused her play to stare at them, confused by the note of alarm in her mother's voice, while True merely looked on knowingly. "I'm so honoured to have met all of you."

"Viggo!"

He turned and darted for the door. He heard the sword clatter to the floor; heard Sunrise's steps as she followed him across the room; heard her hands hit the door a second after he pulled it closed behind him. Viggo turned the key in the lock and smiled wistfully as he let his hand rest on the door across from hers. Then he left, taking the stairs two at a time.

Em stood in the kitchen doorway when he passed, her eyes wide as she clutched a hefty soup ladle to her chest. He could guess, judging by the limp heap which lay crumpled behind her, that she had used the implement to keep Pert quiet. Counting on her reflexes, he tossed the key. She caught it, snapping out of her daze to look at him.

"You can let them out, but only after the soldiers have gone."

"Let them out?" She paused, listening to the pounding upon the door upstairs. "Oh."

"Back exit?" he asked.

She pointed. He nodded his thanks and went off in the direction of her finger.

The back door let out into a little alley which he followed around, slipping back into the marketplace from the other direction. Donovan and Ellaway were busy in the middle of the large square, tossing out orders while their men rushed to obey. The soldiers were in such a great hurry to get where they were going and search for him that they did not notice him lingering in a shop doorway, waiting to be seen.

For just a moment he wondered if he'd overestimated Ellaway; if there was yet some other means of escape. Then he saw the soldiers headed for the front door of the inn.

"You're almost making this too easy!" he called, catching their attention. A bemused smirk found his lips as every person in the market slowed into stillness, their eyes fixed upon him with disbelief. "Well?" he prompted at last. "What are you waiting for?"

Chapter 16

*T*HE *DRYAD DON'T SEE* the future; they decide what the future
should be and make it happen.

This was the conclusion Viggo came to in the confines of a jolting cart,
where he had an abundance of time to think as two horses and a company
of ten soldiers rattled him back to Camelot. In retrospect, he saw that the
Dryad's demand – for him to accompany Sunrise and keep watch over
her until she was well – had only been a means to their end. They had
prophesied through the Druid priests that Arthur would win the war,
so naturally they could not have some Saxon spy getting away with his
secret and foiling their foretold outcome.

He didn't know why they did what they did, but he was beginning to
understand how clever they were about doing it. There was a sly element
of justice in it too, for they had told him a life lost demanded a life given.
Staying with Sunrise like they asked had cost him little; while letting her
go, on the other hand, cost everything – something he had given willingly
to make sure she got away.

Cunning little kind.

The cart bounced over a bump in the road, spilling him across the
wooden floor. Donovan laughed. Regaining his balance and blowing on
his hands to warm them, Viggo glared sideways at the Captain. It was not

the discomfort and humiliation of the cart nor the cold and snow which had become unbearable to him; it was the unceasing smug pleasure of Captains Ellaway and Donovan.

Never had Viggo seen two men more enamored with themselves. No opportunity was too insignificant to be seized upon and used to congratulate one another further. Their pension for self-adulation was driving him insane. Under different circumstances, Viggo might have been flattered they considered his capture such a profound achievement. But as it was his thoughts were elsewhere, traveling through wind-swept waves and winter storms with all the ships sailing north, desperately hoping they made their destinations safely. The constant gloating of the Captains served only as an intrusion.

He was relieved to finally lay eyes on Camelot, towering square and mighty atop a great rise in the land. Sheer vertical cliffs marked the city's southern edge while three successive walls blocked the citadel from all other approach. It was an impressive sight, this fortress which had withstood the failing might of Roman armies and, more recently, the full wrath of Morgan Le Fey when she sieged the city to claim its crown. It was a stark reminder that the Britons were both defiant and resourceful, though not quite so defiant and resourceful as they thought they were. They hadn't managed to keep him out. It was a mistake to put so much faith in the natural barrier created by those three hundred feet of southern cliffs.

"You've got one last chance to let me go," he suggested suddenly, turning his face so it rested against the bars of the cart.

"Quiet," Donovan hissed. His eyes were focussed eagerly on the squad of soldiers riding out to meet them, led by one of the King's knights.

"You're going to be sorry."

"*Shut your mouth!*"

The Captain drew his horse near, kicking out against the bars with his boot. Angrily, he tossed a glance forward, his eyes narrowing with envy as Ellaway spoke quietly with the knight. Whatever he said was persuasive. Without further question, the knight turned about and escorted them through the heavily guarded gates of the first wall and into the Lower City.

Ironically, Viggo thought, he had now found *two* ways into the citadel.

People paused to stare as they passed. Even though they must have seen plenty of prisoners they were still curious about them, bobbing their heads to catch glimpses of him through the bars. At first this irritated Viggo and he met their gazes, staring fiercely back until he unsettled them into looking away. But after a while, when he tired of seeing women pull nervously upon their children at the sight of him, he settled for resting his arms upon his knees, his face turned down between them. He did not need to see as they trundled up to the second wall, passing through another set of gates into Mid-City.

At some point Viggo felt a prod in his side and glanced up to see Ellaway looking in at him. "Look and see, boy. You won't be leaving this place alive."

Viggo took a casual look at the immense wooden gates of the third wall. "That's not for you to decide," he retorted, and dropped his face once more. Ellaway would get no further satisfaction out of him.

He could feel the heat of Ellaway's annoyance but there was nothing further the Captain could do about him now. They were trundling along, making their way through the Upper City toward the citadel proper. Viggo knew they'd entered the palace courtyard when he heard the clop of hooves upon smooth flagstone. The cart rolled to a stop and the knight who had led them through the city snapped out orders, dismissing the palace guards. A moment later, a key rattled in the lock and the cart door swung open.

Viggo lifted his head slowly, gazing into the curious face of a young man hardly older than himself, his brown hair tied back in a neat queue. Sharp eyes glittered with interest. A second knight appeared beside him, twice his age and half as impressed.

"You're quite sure this is him?"

"Yes Sir," Ellaway assured the older knight. "There can be no doubt."

"Quickly then."

Two of Ellaway's soldiers jumped into the cart to grab Viggo and force him out. He went willingly enough, stumbling over cramped legs he was glad to stretch. They did not give him much time. Taking him firmly by the arms, the two knights marched him up the stone steps and through the great palace doors, with the two Captains and their men in hot pursuit.

Viggo wasn't sure what to make of the surreptitious route they took through the palace, marching along in swift silence through back hallways and long-forgotten stairwells. They knew, he decided eventually. The knights knew what he'd seen and were concealing his presence from anyone not privy to the King's secret.

Everything began to look familiar to Viggo as they neared the southernmost wing of the citadel where the King resided. He recognized the knight who stood guarding the entrance to the King's chambers; it was the very same man whose nose Viggo had slipped under the last time he'd been here. The younger knight broke away to confer with him in low tones. After a moment, he waved Viggo forward.

"Sir Kay will take you from here."

Sir Kay was a big man, towering a good foot over the rest of them, and Viggo had to tilt his chin up a little to look into the man's eyes. They stared back without feeling, the blank and brooding eyes of an unpredictable man capable of anything. Unsettled, Viggo dropped his gaze and stepped forward. Somehow, despite all the days of travel, he had neglected – until just now – to be nervous.

"Send these men back to their posts," Sir Kay instructed shortly, stepping aside to grant Viggo access to the spiralling steps.

"Just a minute!" Donovan protested, shoving his way between the other knights to confront Sir Kay. "He's *our* prisoner."

"You do realize who this is, don't you, Sir?" Ellaway chimed in.

"I do," the knight returned coldly. Viggo risked another glance upward and took pleasure in the sight of those dark eyes regarding the two Captains with undisguised contempt.

Ellaway spoke slowly and carefully, like he was explaining himself to a daft child. "Then you well know, Sir, that the King wants him returned personally. Surely, he will wish an audience with us to hear how the spy was caught."

Viggo smirked, pleased with where this was going.

"I am well aware of the King's wishes. He will see no one but the prisoner. Good day to you."

With that curt dismissal, all of Ellaway and Donovan's hopes for glory and reward shattered around their stunned expressions. This did not make everything okay, not by a long shot, but it did make it a little easier to swallow.

"Shame you came all this way for nothing," Viggo muttered smugly. They scowled, and Viggo could see by the tensing of their arms how sorely they would have liked to ram his words back down his throat. But with the tall knight standing imposingly at his shoulder, there was nothing either of them could do. Donovan tried anyway.

"There must be some reward!"

"You are paid from the King's coffers to be loyal guardians of the realm. You ought to need no further reward for doing your duty." With a single backhanded gesture from Sir Kay, the other two knights began urging Donovan and Ellaway, along with their soldiers, back down the hallway.

"And to think I let *you* drag me all the way to Camelot for this!" Donovan huffed.

"Drag?" Ellaway challenged. "*You* forced *your* presence on me, and I had to endure four days of *your...*"

Viggo enjoyed their descent into enmity, gratified to know they would not part ways as friends after all. When Sir Kay inclined his head toward the stairs, Viggo went without hesitation. In truth, he was rather looking forward to meeting the King properly; he had a lot of questions for her.

It was the Queen who answered Sir Kay's sharp knock at the chamber door. Guinevere was a lovely, dainty woman, the perfect picture of regal bearing and grace. Her eyes flickered over Viggo with only the briefest disinterest.

"What is this?"

"The Saxon spy, Milady."

She did a doubletake and there was the eventual dawning of recognition. Viggo couldn't blame her for not knowing him at first. Her opportunity to see his face had been, admittedly, rather brief.

"Of course, bring him in."

"Just the spy, Kay!" shouted another female voice from within the room, one Viggo recognized. "You go back down and keep a look out. I'll need plenty of warning when that envoy arrives."

"As you wish."

Sir Kay retreated down the steps.

The Queen stepped back, opening the door wide for him. Viggo passed her with a strange sense of apprehension. Sir Kay had not hesitated to leave him – a notorious enemy spy – alone with the two women in this room. The knight obviously thought at least one of them was more dangerous than he was. Guinevere, with her deeply coloured skin and soft eyes, did not look threatening to him. Neither did the other woman, though looks could be deceiving.

It was hard to imagine how she had fooled so many people. All the heavy leather and wool she wore beneath the King's armor when he saw her last had been put away, replaced by an expensive dress of emerald green finely embroidered with golden thread. She wore her long red curls back from her face, her entire bearing adorned by the circlet of gold resting on her brow. Whoever she was, there was no doubt she viewed herself as King. She looked perfectly at home on a throne of solid copper, gesturing him with one outstretched hand into the small wooden chair before her.

Though he couldn't imagine how, she seemed to have been expecting him. Viggo obliged her and sat.

"You jumped out my window."

Admittedly, it wasn't the first thing Viggo expected her to say. "You ordered your soldiers to hunt me down," he countered.

One red eyebrow arched upward with vague amusement. She seemed pleased he was here. "I guess we both had our reasons."

Viggo leaned forward. "I'm very interested in yours. How long have you been doing this?"

That eyebrow went higher, further amused by his audacity. "I'm more interested in knowing why you made it as far as Dionne and then turned yourself in?"

That silenced him, at least momentarily. Viggo wasn't sure how she knew about that, but he had no intention of sharing his reasons with her or anyone else. He turned the questioning back around. "Where did you get the dragons?"

He hadn't even noticed the sword. It must have been resting against the side of her throne, hidden in the swaths of her dress. With one smooth motion it was resting forcefully against his neck. The redhead caught a fistful of his coat and held on with an iron grip, preventing him from pulling away. This was definitely the dangerous one, he thought, not daring to move much less breathe.

"You left me no choice," she growled, her green eyes flashing with fury. "I thought you'd gotten away and I had to act fast. I have never, in my life, asked the dragons for anything...not until now. If any one of them had been hurt..."

She didn't finish her sentence but it was implied she would have held him to blame. Viggo had misjudged her. He had assumed the King wanted him back alive, therefore reasoning she didn't intend to kill him.

He'd been wrong. Viggo could see she was perfectly capable of killing him or anyone else if they threatened what she cared about. And by mentioning dragons it seemed he had, quite by accident, touched upon her weakness. He carefully set aside his flippancy.

"I'm glad none of them were."

She frowned, her expression dimming from one of anger into one of suspicion. Viggo took a breath, sighing it out when her grip on his coat relaxed, the sword dropping away. It made a clink as the tip hit the stone floor. She leaned forward on the hilt, appraising him thoughtfully.

"Since your information is no longer of any use, I may as well spare your life. And I would appreciate some answers in return. Why did you stop in Dionne?" The redhead tilted her shoulders back as she spoke, allowing him more of a view than he was interested in. If she was hoping for his attention or a little flattery, she would have to find it elsewhere. He wasn't in the mood.

He leaned forward to match her posture, staring evenly into her green gaze. "To sort out my truest self."

That red eyebrow kinked upward again. "Excuse me?"

He smiled at her confusion. "A friend of mine once told me bad things happen so we can discover our truest selves."

The woman leaned back, relaxing into the throne as a knowing smile curved her lips. Viggo realized quite suddenly that by withholding the attention she fished for, he had given her the answer she wanted. "Smart friend."

Viggo changed the subject. "You can't be the real King Arthur."

"Can't I?"

"Who are you really?"

"No one important."

She played this game of ambiguous answers as well as he did. "How long have you been impersonating the King?" he tried again.

It was the Queen who answered, coming to stand next to the red-head with her hands clasped demurely before her. "My husband's death was...poorly timed. Had we announced it, the repercussions would have been disastrous. Saxon armies were taking one city after another and we would have lost the war when it was barely begun. I wasn't going to let his legacy end like that – not when he was promised to be the Once and Future King."

"This was your idea?" Viggo asked curiously, his tone softening as he addressed the woman. She was a widow still grieved; mourning a loss that choked her up when she tried to speak of it.

She nodded. "No one else can fight like Arthur; it had to be her."

This was more of an answer than Viggo had been expecting, and the ease with which they were both sharing their secrets caused him to wonder with sudden reserve if they intended to lock him up permanently or do away with him altogether?

"You won't be able to keep me from escaping," he asserted abruptly. "You might as well let me go."

"I imagine that's true," the redhead said, unsuccessfully hiding a smile. She stood, stepping up to the large window and resting one hand mean-ingfully upon the sill from which he had jumped when she caught him hiding in her bed. "It's an awfully long fall into the moat."

It was – he remembered.

"Exhilarating, isn't it?" Something in the amused set of her eyes sug-gested he was not the first to take that particular leap. "Still, I'd hate to force you to do it again. I am going to let you go – soon. The war, as you must know by now, is almost over. Of course, even after Arthur signs this treaty there will be skirmishes. King Arthur will, quite tragically, die in a final battle, securing the borders and completing his victory. Once he is dead you are free to leave, on the condition that you never return to any place you are known."

Viggo said nothing. There was nothing to say. These women had worked a long time to turn Arthur into a martyr for his people and they would not consider letting him go unless they felt he could no longer ruin their plans. They asked only that he disappear permanently from public consciousness, a request which, surprisingly, did not bother him. There was nothing to look forward to if he returned home a failure. And if anyone back home guessed he had not failed... every which way his mind went with that scenario was far too complicated and did not end well.

"Tell us what you want," the Queen added, filling the void of his silence. "Tell us what you want as compensation and you shall have it."

The Queen had misinterpreted his silence as hesitance and made him an unexpected offer that did him no good – everything he wanted was too far gone. But it was too good an offer to pass up, and so he decided to spend his compensation elsewhere. "You are aware of the pact protecting the Nyth?"

The two women exchanged a look of confusion. "We are aware of it."

"Does it apply to dragons?"

Green eyes narrowed. "Why would you ask that?"

"A griffin was killed recently, outside the Nyth. She had three kits nesting in a cave. I want someone to check and see that they're cared for.

I understand no human can go, but I thought maybe, since you seem to be friends with dragons, one of them might be able."

Both women stared at him strangely.

"That's all you want?" the redhead inquired.

"That's all," he agreed.

"I'll see to it personally."

"Thank you."

"Then I have your word of silence on this matter?"

Viggo had already shared his secret. He would be content enough knowing with whom he shared it. There was only one thing he wasn't content to leave without. "I cannot give my word to someone without knowing who they are."

A slow grin spread over the redhead's mouth, revealing the dimple in her left cheek. "You're determined to know something about me, aren't you? Very well, would you give your word to Xarabeth?"

"Is that your name?"

"It is." Her eyes searched his face with hawk-like interest, waiting to catch even the faintest hint of a reaction, as though she expected him to recognize her name from somewhere. But he didn't. The name meant nothing to him except that he now knew to whom he was making promises.

"In that case, you have my word."

Sir Kay returned just then. He knocked out of respect but opened the door without waiting for an invitation. "The Saxon envoy has arrived and is waiting at the lower gate for the King to greet them."

"The King will not greet them," Xarabeth chided, striding past Viggo, his presence already a small and forgotten thing in her mind. "Take them into the courtyard and let them wait in the dragon's shadow until the King is ready to receive them."

"And take him," Guinevere added as Viggo rose to his feet. "He's to be made comfortable as my personal guest."

Viggo was halfway out the door when Xarabeth called suddenly after them. "Not too comfortable. I may yet have use for a Saxon..."

And so it happened that Viggo found himself at the end of all that might have been, with nothing to show for it and no one but himself knowing the whole truth of the matter. He would not be returning home to any celebration or reward, and deep down he was okay with that. He had gained something of far more value than whatever the Saxon Elders might have offered him. While he still did not believe in the impossible, he did believe in a great many more things than when he had started. And of course, the end of all that might have been was also just the beginning of all that could yet be. . .

Epilogue

I T HAPPENED ONE MORNING near the end of February, when all the snow had melted but cold still gripped the land. An enormous ash tree stood alone, its barren branches making spindly silhouettes against the brightening sky. Viggo was fast asleep on the sturdiest bough, entirely unaware that he was dreaming.

It did not seem at all strange to him when he was suddenly walking down an unknown street in an unknown village. The sun was sinking low in the sky, kissing the roofs of the westernmost homes. His docile, dreaming mind required no reason for why he wandered out past the houses, veering from the road and setting off through large fields of some yellow-flowered crop. He followed little trails between the heady plants, making his way steadily toward the trees that fenced in the farmland.

A group of young people came into view, gathered outside a modest cottage. Nobody seemed to notice as Viggo walked right into their midst, watching as they lifted their bows and aimed at targets that had been hung for them from the prickly branches of a yew tree.

An unused bow and arrow lay neglected upon the grass and Viggo picked them up as naturally as if they had been left there for him. His waking mind knew a thing or two about archery, but as is often the case with most things, his subconscious mind knew more. While the teacher moved along behind the students, adjusting posture and dispensing quiet correction, his dreaming thoughts picked out a single, dangling target. Nocking the arrow, he raised the bow and took steady aim.

It was the powerful pull of a familiar scent which snapped Viggo into sudden awareness. All at once he knew he was dreaming, but even so that familiar, peculiar blend of sweet pea flowers and rosemary sprigs made his heart leap. It had been a long time, but not so long that he'd forgotten. He felt the steadying touch of her right hand against his elbow while her other hand reached around to tap his left wrist upward ever so slightly.

"And...release!"

His arrow shot wild.

Viggo glanced over his shoulder and stared into eyes as surprised as his own. None of the young students around them seemed to find it odd that their teacher was frozen, having forgotten entirely about her lesson.

"Viggo?" Her expression was as disbelieving as it was hopeful. "Is it really you?"

He couldn't bring himself to dash her hopes by telling her it was all just a dream; something wishful conjured by his resting mind. And yet...would his mind have fashioned all the convincing little details, like the distant roar of ocean waves and the shrieking cry of seabirds? Had his mind produced the cold breeze which blew around them, already bearing subtle promises of spring?

"I think so," he whispered, afraid to speak loudly lest he somehow break the spell that had brought them together after so much time. How he wished it were true.

Sunrise did not wait for him to be sure. With a little squeak of unrestrained joy she threw her arms around him, her long frame pressed up against his. His breath caught. She was real. He did not know how and suddenly he did not care. He embraced her, holding so tight he felt her feet lift away from the ground.

"Are you safe?" he begged, needing to know.

"Yes!" she gasped, laughing breathlessly through her smile. That single word lifted a weight from his heart and widened his smile to match hers as he set her back down on her toes. "We all are. Look, this is home now!" She pointed to the little cottage, beaming with pride. The sight of it, rundown though it was, made him proud also. He'd been right about her – she had found a way.

The students were leaving, waving their goodbyes as they set off across the fields to their own homes. They'd left their bows leaning neatly against the trunk of the yew tree in anticipation of further lessons.

"How I earn my keep," she said, by way of explanation. "And you?" Her beautiful eyes studied him with as much concern as ever. Some things, he thought with amusement, would never change. And that was okay with him. "Tell me you got away."

He wished he could tell her that, if only because he knew she would like to hear it. But he could not lie to her. "Not exactly, but that's alright. I've been just fine and it seems you have too. The children? How are Gywie and True?"

Her eyes shifted left and he followed her gaze, his smile faltering when he saw the little girl sitting in the dry grass, ripping early wild flowers out of the ground while her brother anxiously gathered up each one, attempting unsuccessfully to put them all back. How long had it been? A whole year, more than that actually, and already they looked so different.

They were exactly as he remembered and yet nothing was the same. They were bigger, older, growing.

Neither seemed aware of his presence.

"She was awfully mad at you."

"Was she?"

"You never said goodbye."

Viggo winced. He'd had his reasons but that didn't mean he couldn't suffer regrets. True had known exactly what he meant to do, and because of her dream Sunrise must have known it too on some level. But Gywie could not have anticipated what was going to happen or why, and for that he was sorry. He was sorry there hadn't been another way.

"I wish I could talk to them."

Sunrise pulled away from him and Viggo felt a sudden lump in his throat when she knelt beside Gywie, whispering in the little girl's ear. Just because he wanted to talk to them didn't mean he knew what to say. Blue eyes shot up, drinking him in with awareness.

"Viggy?"

He knelt, fighting a surge of emotion as he reached out for the girl. For a moment she wore a bright smile as she jumped to her feet and ran towards him. Then she remembered and stopped short, standing just out of reach with a frown quivering upon her little mouth.

"You didn't come back!"

Before he could say anything, she kicked him hard in the knee.

"Gywie!" Sunrise cried, horrified.

Viggo grimaced, both from the sudden pain in his knee – not at all dull or dream-like – and from the newfound ringing in his ears. But he shook his head to tell Sunrise it was alright. Leaning gingerly forward upon his good knee, he took Gywie by the hand. She sulked and tried without really meaning it to tug her hand away.

"I would have come back," he promised, pulling her close so he could whisper into her yellow curls, *"if I'd known how to find you."*

She chewed the inside of her cheek, eyeing him suspiciously. Viggo opened his arms to her again. She shuffled forward, shifting one foot moodily after the other until she flopped against him. Releasing the breath he'd been holding, Viggo hugged her tight. After a very long moment, she hugged him back.

A pair of skinny arms slid around his waist and Viggo smiled, knowing even without looking that it was True. Getting one arm loose, he wrapped it tightly around the boy.

"Did you go home?"

Viggo looked over to see Sunrise kneeling beside him, her eyes full of all those unending questions. If he'd had a free hand, he would have pulled her into the hug too. Missing them had been so much harder than he'd expected. "No," he replied vaguely. "I've been...busy."

Gywie pulled away to stare at him. "You don't have a home?" she demanded incredulously, forgetting her anger. Her face brightened and she bounced up on her tiptoes. "You can home here! I'll make you a map!"

It fascinated Viggo to see a piece of parchment simply appear in front of the little fairy. When she grabbed a pen out of thin air and began to scribble something across the page, he nearly laughed at himself. How easy it had been to forget this was all a dream.

The completed doodles were thrust his way so abruptly Viggo had to jerk his head back to keep from being hit in the face with them.

"There," Gywie announced, "now you can find us!"

Viggo took her 'map' and studied it with a barely suppressed twitch at the corner of his mouth. Maybe she had not grown so much after all; her doodles looked exactly as he remembered them. Sunrise did not manage to contain her laugh as well as he was containing his.

"One of the ship captains showed her all his maps and she's been fascinated with them since. She's got the drawing part down – it's the map bit she hasn't quite mastered."

Viggo finally gave in and chuckled. He was half afraid Gywie would kick him again for it but she was yawning and rubbing sleepily at her eyes. Anxious that the dream was ending, Viggo tried to pull her into one last hug. He could not. His arm swept right through her and she was gone. There was just enough time to look down and see brown eyes and a sleepy smile before True vanished away also.

His time was running out – again. Rising to his feet, he caught Sunrise's hand and helped her up, pulling her close as if this could keep her from vanishing away next.

"Has anything changed?" He needed to know, before he let himself fall victim to this fluttering in his chest again, that she was not already spoken for by someone else.

She smiled softly, the look in her eyes suggesting he need not have asked. "Nothing has changed."

"Tell me where to find you."

She tried but the words were lost to the rushing wind, which stole her voice as easily as it was stealing the scenery from around them. Everything was blowing away, the fields swirling up into the sky as the sunset folded into the ground; all of it blurring out of sight in a flurry of fading colours.

Sunrise gleamed before him, glowing like the sun was rising at her back. Viggo knew it was the gleam of wakefulness. He was about to lose her.

Sunrise knew it too. She reached out and caught his other hand, drawing his attention back to the map Gywie had drawn him. The last thing he saw were the indistinct squiggles rearranging themselves with purpose.

Viggo opened his eyes, blinking slowly into the soft sky of morning. For just a second he could have sworn there was a passing hint of sweet peas in the wind. It vanished quickly; a trick of the imagination. Unconsciously, he reached down to rub his knee where it ached. He froze. His knee ached.

Suddenly very much awake, Viggo thrust a hand into his pocket, pulling forth the map he had been carrying around these many months. On it were drawn all the lands under the rule of Camelot and its allies. His finger found Lin Harbour and traced the trade routes north into the Irish Kingdoms. There were islands, many dozens of them, but his finger found just one and lingered over it. A smile turned his mouth upward as he leaned back and admired the spot where his finger had left a small smudge.

He knew.

He knew.

About The Author

J.J. Sutherland is a restless adventurer trapped in the body of an introverted, tea-drinking homebody.

The solution?

She writes. Over the years, she has worked as a model, ghost writer, and language interventionist; but writing has always been the one true passion.

Sharing her imagination with a host of unique characters allows her to tell their stories in immersive, compelling ways, bringing their personalities to life. By weaving history with legend, J.J. crafts fast-paced stories to transport herself – and her readers – into worlds of surprise and suspense, where nothing is as it seems.

At home on the stunning shores of Vancouver island, J.J. often walks its many wind-swept beaches with a teacup in hand, heeding the call of inspiration. The Island boasts crashing waves, mist-shrouded mountainsides, and vast cedar forests; the perfect playground for an author's fantasies to run wild. As she chases them down, her characters reveal new stories, new adventures, and new secrets...

The Once and Forgotten Thing is her debut novel.

Preview From The Once and Fractured Thing

Outside the estate all was quiet, holding its breath, waiting for the inevitable. The only sound came from a black flag erected on the main roadway between the gates. It snapped in the deepening twilight, kept aloft by the insistent bluster of a winter that refused to yield. Within the estate there was a man, his heels scraping over stone as he crawled backwards across the floor, very much abandoned to his fate. He had been hunted into a corner; hopelessly trapped in the deepest recesses of his own home.

"Please!" the man cried, addressing the approaching figure. "I'll give you anything!"

Lord Wheatley was under no illusions. He had heard rumors of the mysterious villain haunting Britannia this past year, executing noblemen upon a whim and without mercy. Now it had come for him. Orange light from nearby torches gleamed off the full suit of black armour, drawing a silhouette of fire in the gloom. He did not imagine, as the silent figure drew its sword, that he would escape with his life. Still, he tried.

"More money than you could ever dream of!" he promised. It was not an empty offer. Lord Wheatley was in possession of all the farmland from

Amesbury in the south to Amurich in the East, and for the past two seasons he had not paid one coin for all the labour that worked it.

The trailing end of a long, black cape swept across the floor as the knight approached, raising the sword without sympathy. It was only then that Lord Wheatley realized there was another figure lurking beyond the knight, his features shrouded in shadow.

"You!" he cried, pointing, completely aghast. While the knight remained poised with the sword ready to strike, the fair-haired man came forward into the torchlight. He was attractive as far as young men went, with fine straight features and a perpetual quirk in the corner of his mouth that made him appear of good humor. But there was nothing amused in the hard set of his grey eyes, and that quirk had become knowing and ominous. Lord Wheatley wagged his finger, disbelieving. "You're working with the Black Knight?"

Viggo shrugged; he could not deny it. "You have one chance to live," he replied evenly.

"I trusted you!" the Lord cried, outraged to think he had ever taken the Saxon into his company.

"That was your third mistake," Viggo retorted, kneeling so he could be even with the Lord. There was something pathetic about seeing a man cower on the floor, as if some secret method of escape could be found at lesser elevations. "Your first mistake was inviting me in when I said I could smuggle Saxon children over the border cheaply."

Viggo was never sure what he would find when he began his missions. This particular Lord, he'd been told, served under King Arthur during the war, openly defying direct orders when he slaughtered a Saxon Commander who was bound for Camelot as a prisoner of war. In the wake of the war it had become apparent to Viggo that the men who commit atrocities on the battlefield are the same ones who commit them at home. Still, Viggo had been unprepared to step onto Lord Wheatley's estate and see a man's body hanging from a wooden stake where he had been left to die beneath the frozen February sun. When he inquired, the estate servants told him the man's only crime was refusing to surrender his young child into the Lord's service.

"Your second mistake," Viggo continued, feeling no pity for this particular Lord, "was telling me how you planned to cut off the supply of winter grain to Amesbury unless they sent their children to labor in your fields." He feigned a thoughtful look and tilted his head, his bangs sliding out of his eyes so that the Lord could not possibly miss the loathing within. "I wonder how the Queen would feel if she knew what you had in mind for her hometown?"

Briefly, Lord Wheatley spared another glance toward the knight. If the Queen ever found out what he'd been doing he was as good as dead, though it seemed unlikely he would live long enough to die by her order. Then again, there was a glimmer of hope in this threat. Men did not make threats unless there was something they hoped to gain. "What do you want from me?" he asked, thinking he might yet be able to buy his way out from under the Black Knight's sword.

Viggo leaned forward, enjoying the shock on Lord Wheatley's face as he thrust a bundle of dirty farm clothes into the Lord's lap. "You're going to leave," Viggo told him plainly, as he had told so many others before him. "You're going to walk away from your home, your lands, and your title. I don't care where you go or what you do, but know that we will be watching. And if you ever try to return – if anyone in Britannia so much as hears your name again – the Queen will know the truth."

Viggo took a moment to pause, glancing up at the long sword which hung over them with unwavering strength. "But don't let the Queen scare you," he finished lightly. "I promise the Black Knight can find you before she does."

Keep up with Tempest & Jay for updates on the upcoming sequel:
"The Once and Fractured Thing."
Follow us on Facebook,
or go to
www.tempestandjay.ca

Printed in the USA
CPSIA information can be obtained
at www.ICGtesting.com
JSHW080027230724
66593JS00004B/16

9 781738 935901